THE HUNTING OF MR. GLOVES

Adam Spencer Holden is a most unusual man. He is a respectable citizen, a family man, a member of the golf club, and well thought of by his employers. He is also a successful petty criminal. Holden meets no serious resistance until his activities come to the attention of Frank Gardener, a brave and intelligent police officer transferred to light duties after a severe battering. An intriguing battle of wits between the two men leads up to a highly unorthodox conclusion.

PHILIP DANIELS

THE HUNTING OF OF MR. GLOVES

Complete and Unabridged

LINFORD
Leicester

First published in Great Britain in 1986

First Linford Edition
published 2004

British Library CIP Data

Daniels, Philip, *1924* –
    The hunting of Mr. Gloves.—
    Large print ed.—
    Linford mystery library
    1. Detective and mystery stories
    2. Large type books
    I. Title
    823.9′14 [F]

    ISBN 1–84395–320–X

Published by
F. A. Thorpe (Publishing)
Anstey, Leicestershire

Set by Words & Graphics Ltd.
Anstey, Leicestershire
Printed and bound in Great Britain by
T. J. International Ltd., Padstow, Cornwall

This book is printed on acid-free paper

1

He walked quickly up the steps from the taxi, the chill evening air slicing at him in that brief passage. Then he was pushing thankfully at the revolving door, and the scented warmth of the hotel lobby enveloped him.

The blonde girl at the reception counter looked up as he approached. Not bad, she decided. Thirty-five or so, nice overcoat, one night only by the size of that bag, two at the most. Oh, what nice teeth when he smiled.

'Good evening, sir. Have you a reservation?'

'Yes. I phoned yesterday. Name is Holden.'

She consulted the reservation list by her right hand.

'Ah yes, here we are Mr. Holden. Single, with bath. Dinner and breakfast, one night. Will you fill in this card please?'

1

He took a pen from his inside pocket, and filled in the vacant spaces rapidly. Nice pen, she reflected, none of your ball-points. Like his hands, too. Strong and sort of capable, but well cared-for. Wonder what he does? On business, of course, with the firm paying. Must be a good position though, to book him in at a three-star like the Metropolitan.

She took the completed card, scanning it swiftly. Adam. She hadn't come across an Adam before. Adam Holden. Had an impressive kind of ring to it. The first man. Her first man had been Sidney something or other, she never did find out the rest.

'You're in 205, Mr. Holden.'

She took the key from the numbered slots under the counter, and handed it to him, with a brief smile.

'Thank you.' He took it with his free hand. 'Would you ask the operator to give me a call at seven o'clock in the morning, please?'

'Certainly. The dining room is along —'

'It's all right, thanks. I know the hotel quite well.'

Regular then. She watched him as he headed for the lift, then remembered the morning call, and made a quick entry on the duty list, 205, 7 a.m.

Upstairs, Holden emerged from the lift and followed the printed arrows until he located 205. Unlocking the door, he pressed at the light-switch and went inside, leaning against the door until it clicked. Hotel rooms were no new experience to him, and he wasted no time in studying the layout. He'd been in a thousand rooms like it, varying only as to points of detail. The important thing was to check at once that everything worked. It was only six o'clock in the evening, and he would have a fair chance of getting some results if he had any complaints. Early experience had taught him that it was no use waiting until bedtime before learning that the television didn't work, or that he had a leaking kettle. All he would get then would be a lot of apologies and excuses, but not much action. Walking around the room, he switched on everything that was supposed to work, filled the kettle, and put it to boil. The news was on, and he watched briefly, as gunfire rattled in the rubbled streets of some city in the Middle East, then swapped the channels quickly. There was news everywhere, except for B.B.C. 2, which was showing an art appreciation programme on the Open University. He left it there for a few moments, while he looked at the various leaflets and folders on the dressing table. Oh, good. The in-house movie today was a John Ford western, and it had only just started. He pushed at the fifth button, and there was more gunfire, but this time from marauding Indians as they encircled a group of covered waggons on some remote prairie. Pushing the portable trolley so that he could keep half an eye on the picture, he snapped open the locks on his small suitcase. Unpacking was a brief affair. Pyjamas, bathroom kit, clean shirt for the morning. These were quickly disposed of. Also inside the case was a roll-top thick sweater, and a pair of jeans wrapped around a pair of crepe-soled running shoes. Leaving these articles inside, he locked the case, and pushed it away at the top of the wardrobe. The kettle began to boil, and he made coffee, took off his jacket, and sat down to watch the film. To anyone watching, the picture presented by the new arrival was easy to understand. He was a visitor to the city, no doubt with some important business meetings scheduled for the following day. Tonight, he was alone, and accustomed to the experience. He would watch the film, possibly have a bath, more out of boredom than necessity, and then proceed downstairs to a solitary dinner. After that, he might sit in the bar for an hour, then find his way back upstairs at about ten o'clock, where he would run quickly through his business papers, watch television, and finally switch off the lights. Anyone could tell at a glance, there was nothing unusual about the occupant of Room 205.

Anyone would be wrong.

Adam Spencer Holden was a most unusual man, but the chance of anyone but himself realising that fact was very small. Indeed, he went to a great deal of trouble to minimise the possibility. On

5

the surface, he was a moderately successful salesman, pushing a good product,
and well thought of by his employers. In
the previous year, his salary plus commission had earned him in excess of
seventeen thousand pounds, and he was
improving on that in the current year. His
life was an open book. Four bedroomed
house in a good area, company car for
himself, small runabout for his attractive
wife Sheila. Two children, one of each
kind, both doing well at their respective
schools, a fourteen handicap at the golf
club, and a regular attender at school
functions. Holden had no debts, outside
of the huge mortgage on his house, and
that scarcely counted, because it was in
the nature of things, that everyone was in
that position. He was in good health,
financially sound, and there was never
even a whisper of scandal about his
marriage, on either side. If anything,
Holden, with his small empire, was a
model to be studied and copied by the
world at large. He had every reason to be
satisfied with his situation and his
progress.

No-one knew about his inner desperation, his utter boredom with the routine of his life, and the horror with which he regarded the future. Even Sheila, who knew him better than anyone, could never understand the fits of blank despair which had overtaken him occasionally in their early years. He would try to explain to her, because he wanted very much for her to understand, but he could never find the words, and Sheila would always be at a loss to comprehend. The conversation inevitably went wrong.

'I don't understand it at all Adam, I really don't. You're doing so well, the company thinks highly of you, we have a nice home. I am trying, I really am, darling, but I don't see what it is that you say is missing.'

That would set him off again, in a torrent of words, pointing out the futility of it all. He was getting on for thirty, and life was already ended. Mapped out, all of it. Every bloody step of the way. Nothing would change, ever. They would get older, the children would grow up. Gradually, they would acquire more and more material things, and then what? One day, they would turn around, and find that they were old. Well off, probably, with little fat grandchildren, and old. And what would they have done? What would they have accomplished? Nothing.

Sheila would become frustrated, then eventually tearful.

'But that's the same for everybody,' she would protest. 'Why should we be different from everybody else?'

'It's not the same for everybody,' he would counter, trying to hold on to his temper. 'Some people are sailing around the world in bath tubs. Some people are climbing Everest, others are playing for England. They'll have something to look back on. Look at your actors, your writers. They can say, 'I was in that film, nearly got an Academy Award,' 'I wrote that book, sold a million copies.''

'Yes dear, but you're talking about unusual people,' she would point out, 'people with special gifts, special talents. They're not the ordinary kind, they've got this extra something. How would it be if the whole world suddenly decided to cross the ocean in a bath tub? Or do all those things you're always on about? There wouldn't be any ordinary life, no ordinary people. There'd be nothing at all. I'll tell you this much, ninety per cent of the people in this world would be jolly glad to change places with us, to have what we've got. More, probably.'

'That's not what I'm driving at,' he would answer, 'that isn't the point.'

'Well, what is the point, then? What is it you're so dissatisfied about? Is it the job, the house, the kids? Or is it me? Perhaps that's it. Perhaps it's me.'

It always came to that in the end, and once Sheila contrived to convince herself that his problem derived somehow from a lack in herself, future discussion was pointless. There would be dramatics, protestations, sometimes a row, but always a reconciliation. Once that was achieved, Sheila would be satisfied, and drop it, no nearer understanding what he was saying than she had been at the outset. Holden had never been able to decide how much of Sheila's putting the blame on herself was genuine, or whether it was a final desperate gambit to get away from her own lack of understanding. Either way, the end product was the same. From his initial position of trying to explain what was happening inside himself, he invariably ended by comforting his distressed wife, assuring her that there was absolutely no lack of anything on her part, and realising, with quiet despair, that once again the moment of recognition had passed.

The hell of it was, and in a way he'd always recognised this, what she said was substantially true. He was never going to portray a memorable King Lear, and neither was he going to keep goal for England. Whatever it was, that drove people to their achievements, and other head-line-making activities, he did not possess it. Nor did most of the people in the world, and yet they didn't feel the same way as he did. He'd spent enough time talking to friends and colleagues to realise how narrow their vision was. They really believed in the whole miserable process. For them, the important things in life were to get that next promotion, to buy a better car, to go further on their holidays than the chap next door. At first Holden had thought they were keeping something back, that in the deepest recesses of their hearts they felt as he did. But gradually, and it had been a very gradual process, it had been borne in on him that they meant it. Achievement, for them, equated with material progress, and that was all there was to it.

Quod Erat Demonstrandum.

Rubbish. Not for them, perhaps, but for him. It might suit them, to go through life, or their particular concept of life, under this enormous self-deception that their existence mattered. For Adam Spencer Holden it was not enough, and it never would be. Somehow, he had to break out of this ghastly mould, distinguish himself from that grey, uniform mass of humanity. There had to be a way. If he concentrated all his thinking, really set out to find the path, it would be there. Somehow, somewhere in this world, was an answer which would lead him out of the wilderness, and what he had to do was to find it.

That was how he finally became a crook.

* * *

George Thomas looked at the clock, sighed and carried on with his paperback novel. Twenty past nine was right in the middle of his dead period in the little corner shop. Nothing much happened between nine and ten. Then, the early leavers from the nearby public houses would begin to trickle in for their small purchases on the way home. Little things they'd overlooked during the day, but always knew they could rely on getting from the little man on the corner, who never seemed to close. Open always until midnight, except for Saturday when the late revellers had made life too difficult. Open again in the morning, seven sharp, winter and summer. Of course you paid a little bit more over the odds at the corner shop, but you didn't object to that, what with it being so handy and everything. Besides, look at the hours the old man put in. There wasn't a trade union in the world would stand for those hours. And it wasn't as if he was making a fortune or anything. Just about holding his own, most likely. Not much of a life, with his sick wife upstairs and everything.

George knew what went on in the minds of the locals. They were his customers after all, and it was kind of like a big family in a way. What they didn't know, and George would be the last man in the world to tell them, was that the little shop was more of a sound financial proposition, taken all round, than many of the High Street chain stores. No massive rates and rents for George. No overheads, worth speaking of, no advertising or staff problems. Goods In, mark up, Goods Out. That was the simple system operated by the George Thomases of this world, that plus a lot of personal hard work and sacrifice. In another three years, perhaps less, George and his wife would leave the district forever. Nice bungalow in the country, cash down, and a peaceful future to look forward to.

Deep in his adventure story, he was distracted by the jangling of the bell on the shop-door. He was still getting to his feet when he realised the customer had already crossed the floor and was beside him behind the counter.

'Here — ' he began.

'Shut up,' growled a hoarse voice.

The newcomer was dressed in a rough seaman's jersey with dark blue jeans, but it was the stocking over the face that struck fear into the old man.

'The till,' came the guttural order.

George didn't hesitate. The hand on his shoulder was like a vice. He wasn't going to get himself hurt for forty or fifty quid. He touched No — Sale, and the till sprang open. The masked man scooped out the notes and shoved them into his pocket.

'Where's the rest?'

'That's all there is,' George began, then winced as the iron fingers gripped tighter.

'Shall I ask the missus? Sharp now.'

George shook his head miserably. Couldn't let this animal anywhere near Ivy. No telling where it would end. Reaching down, he unlocked a drawer marked 'Tea'. The entire day's takings

14

were in there, close on two hundred pounds. There was a grunt of satisfaction from behind, and the hand forced him down until he was on his knees.

'Lie down.'

He hastened to obey, sweating now in the confined space, and listening as the money was removed from the drawer. The thief spoke for the last time.

'Stay there.'

George Thomas was afraid, but he was no coward. He had no wish to provoke his visitor and was willing to do as he was told, so long as the man left the shop. But if he didn't, if he opened the door that led upstairs to the helpless Ivy, George would attack him, hopeless though it would be. It was with considerable relief on all counts that he heard the front doorbell for the second time. Slowly, and fearfully, he raised his head. Then, seeing that the man was gone, he scrambled to his feet and hurried to the telephone, dialling 999 before he spotted the dangling, newly-cut wire.

Outside, the tall man in the dark clothes walked swiftly through the narrow cutting that led to the main road into town. The bus was due at 9.23, and he could just make it in time to the bus-stop. The yellow single-decker pulled to a halt, and there was a hissing sound as the doors swung back. The man in the heavy sweater waited while an elderly woman clambered aboard, then followed her up on to the step, tending his fare. He was already in his seat halfway down the bus as the blue flashing light of a police car appeared from the opposite direction. No-one paid him any attention throughout the ten minute journey, which ended when he alighted in the town square and crossed the road to the back entrance of the Metropolitan Hotel.

Inside, he walked quickly up the rear stairs to the second floor, pulling a key from his pocket outside Room 205. With the door shut safely behind him, Holden gave a great whoosh of relief and threw the key on the bed. No time for self-congratulation. Not yet. Quickly, he pulled down his suitcase, and opened the lid. Then he reached under the tight elastic of the sweater, pulling out handfuls of money and dropping them into the case. Then it was off with the sweater, jeans and shoes, all of which joined the money in the case. A quick wash, and he dressed again in his business clothes. Locking the case, he replaced it in the wardrobe, took a careful look around the room, retrieved his key, and went down to the bar. There he struck up a conversation with another man. Holden had two drinks only, then looked at the clock.

'Good Lord, ten o'clock already. Well I must go up. Got some work to do before I go to bed. I find ten o'clock at night just about my best time.'

The other man was only politely interested, but he would remember. Not that there was very much chance that anyone would ever ask him, but Holden was not the man to leave anything to chance. Anything at all. Having established that he'd been at the bar for what he would later claim as being about half an hour, which no-one would seriously dispute, he now made his casual way through the main lobby and to the bank of lifts.

To the bored blonde behind the desk he said an elaborate 'Good night,' and made certain that she noticed him. Then he was back in his room again, and able to relax.

It had gone very well.

They all had, so far. Mainly, this was due to careful planning and forethought, but he was also well aware that he had been lucky. No matter how much attention he paid to detail, the day would inevitably come when he found himself faced with the unforeseen, indeed the unforeseeable. Some quirk of fate, which would throw the whole operation out of gear, leaving him to improvise. He feared that day, because he was uncertain of his own reaction. Would he really shrug, give a resigned grin, and let himself be taken, the way he had rehearsed so often in hotel mirrors? The gentleman thief unmasked, the Cary Grant touch? That was fine in theory, in the romantic light-hearted world inhabited by the suave gentlemen of the screen. The people who wrote those things didn't bother to delve into what happened next. Little matters, such

18

as disgrace, public dénouement, broken homes, prison cells, slopping out, the exercise yard. These were the realities, the harsh facts behind the moment of apprehension. Would he be willing to accept all that, in exchange for a moment of gentlemanly surrender? Or would he, as he feared, become transformed at once into a snarling animal, grabbing at any weapon that came to hand, and battering his senseless way to freedom, any freedom, if only for another precious ten minutes? He didn't know, and that was the plain truth. Certainly, he carried no offensive weapon, his only tool being the little pocket knife he used if there was a telephone to deal with. Technically, that could be described as a concealed weapon, and the police would not miss the point, but it was always his intention to discard the penknife at the slightest whiff of danger. A strong man, he always selected targets where the victim would be no match for him in open combat. That was not cowardice, Holden was no-one's coward, it was a matter of simple prudence and no more. By removing the possibility of violence, he removed the need for it, and his crimes were automatically less drastic in the eyes of a judge and jury. Threatening behaviour was one thing, but the use of physical force was quite another, particularly if accompanied by a weapon. Oh yes, he'd thought it all out, not once, but a hundred times, even before that first job.

Adam Spencer Holden had come to realise, in his late twenties, that he was in the throes of some kind of identity crisis. All the pointless discussion with associates, the fruitless arguments with Sheila, had brought him slowly to the realisation that he was going to be unhappy for the rest of his life, and the solution lay in his own hands. Either he must conform, or take some positive step of his own. The first of these alternatives received little more than a cursory inspection. Any pretence at conformity would be exactly that and no more. All the while, beneath the surface, there would be this festering discontent, which would only worsen, and which would inevitably erupt one day, probably in some futile outburst. He would lose control, tell the managing director's wife what he really thought of her, or something equally stupid and puny.

No. The answer must lie in the taking of that positive step, and in order to decide what that should be, he would have to analyse his own need. To do it with honesty, answerable to no one but himself. What was it that he really craved? Fame, women, money, what? Many long hours were spent in dissecting his own feelings and inclinations. At different times, he would feel he had finally found the answer, only to find a flaw in it during his next session of self-counselling. When eventually, and after many false starts, he arrived at the truth, he found it was a solution in two parts. Basically, he wanted to be outside the system, to beat it. At the same time, he wanted to feel the element of risk in whatever he did. With only himself to consider, there would have been no lack of opportunities to meet both requirements. But he had to consider Sheila, and their two infant children, as they then were. Holden had little time for people who abdicated responsibility for their dependants, and it would never do for him to create a new life for himself at their expense.

Neither could he embark with them on some gypsy existence, as he recognised only too well. Sheila was devoted to him, and would probably make some real attempt at adjustment to a new kind of life-style, if she had only herself to consider. The children were the key factors. Their futures were already mapped out, as part of a natural evolution from the circumstances into which they had been born. She would fight tooth and nail against any lowering in their standards or prospects, and, in his innermost self, Holden could only agree with her.

It was a Catch 22 situation, the ultimate dichotomy.

He had to break out of his way of life, on the one hand, and it was quite impossible to achieve it, on the other. It took long months of self-interrogation before the answer came. He would lead a life within a life. A secret life, to be shared by no-one, not even Sheila. Especially Sheila.

Because the answer was crime. He would turn to crime, he decided. The decision came to him one warm May afternoon. He was sitting in the garden, keeping an eye on the children. Four year old Graham was trying to persuade Patricia to kick a large soft ball back to him, but the little one preferred to sit on it and roll about. Sooner or later there would be an uproar, and he would be required to intervene as adjudicator, and, if necessary, punishment officer.

In the midst of this peaceful domestic scene, the solution thrust itself unheralded into his mind. At that moment, he had not, for once, been thinking about his problem at all, and this somehow gave the decision added authority.

But what kind of crime?

Later that evening, with the children tucked away, and Sheila glued to the television screen, he locked himself up with his famous paperwork, and settled down to some serious thinking.

Murder never entered his head. There was no-one he wanted dead, for one thing. He could never bring himself to the act, for another, not in cold blood. Holden could imagine himself lashing out in uncontrollable fury, given the necessary provocation, but then, so could practically everyone.

Theft was an entirely different matter. Theft was already deeply ingrained in most people, and practised by an enormous number, who would have been horrified if accused. Every man who claimed extra hours on a time-sheet was a thief. Every salesman who rode on buses and claimed taxi-fare was a thief. The housewife who automatically overcharged her husband for the children's clothes was a thief. Overclaiming on income tax returns was theft. The butcher, with his fifteen ounces to the pound, was a thief. The list was virtually endless, and embraced vast numbers of the population. All thieves, and yet, challenged with the fact, all would have been outraged.

Who, me? How dare you. A thief is

someone who steals a woman's handbag, breaks into a man's house. You can't compare that with a little bit of fiddling. Everyone does that. Yes, they do, reflected Holden. And they are all thieves, including me. I'm not above a bit of padding on the expense-account, for one thing. And, having thus rationalised the position in general, and his own in particular, it was no more than a logical extension of an existing situation when he turned his attention to the more recognisable categories of theft. It did not take him very long to dismiss a number of the more obvious areas. His own lack of criminal knowledge was lamentable, he quickly realised. The disposal of stolen property was a closed book to him. Even if he brought off some classic manoeuvre, and managed to acquire a Renoir or a Picasso, he wouldn't know what to do with it. There were crooked dealers in the world, no question of it, but how did one get in touch with them? It was scarcely a matter for the small-ads in The Times. No. Stolen property of whatever kind was a non-starter.

Cash, then. It would have to be cash. At first, he thought in terms of large sums of money. Say fifty thousand upwards, if the job was to be worthwhile. But the more he went into the practicalities, the more he realised that this, too, was a non-starter. People didn't walk about with sums of that size on their persons. They used steel-grilled vans, armed security guards. Holden had no illusions about his chances against two or three grim faced men with truncheons or, worse, revolvers. Even if one were to overcome all these practical problems, and managed to get hold of a large sum, what then. Building Society? He could visualise the conversation.

'A deposit sir? Certainly. How much did you wish to leave with us?'

'Fifty thousand pounds.'

'Quite so, sir. Would you excuse me for just one moment?'

It would be the same everywhere. Having the money was one thing. Getting rid of it was something quite different. In the meantime, where would he keep it? Holden had never actually seen that much money, but it must take up a lot of room. Trying to hide a large cardboard box full of cash, in a house with a busy housewife and two prying children, would be a near impossibility.

The more he thought about it, the more the problem worsened. Strangely enough, it had been Sheila who unwittingly supplied the answer. A little after nine o'clock she poked her head tentatively round the door.

'I know you're busy dear, and I'm sorry to interrupt, but the fact is, I've run out of eggs.'

'Eggs?' he repeated mechanically.

'Yes, you know, those oval things that chickens lay. People eat them for breakfast.'

He grinned.

'Sorry, I was miles away. All right, I know what's coming. Would I mind walking down to the little grocer's, right? You'd go yourself, but you know I won't let you go walking in the street in the dark. Do I have an alternative?'

'Of course,' she replied primly. 'You can have an egg-less breakfast for one

27

thing. And you can go off to work knowing your poor children are sitting here in tears, because their miserable tyrant of a father — '

'I'm going, I'm going.'

It was to be a fateful experience for him, all the more so because everything came together so unexpectedly. Certainly, there was nothing portentous about his gentle amble along the pleasant avenue he lived in. It was interesting to see the various front gardens he passed, and to note the extent to which each had blossomed in this particularly fine May weather. Not all of course, he noted with grim disapproval, as he passed Number 23, with its weed-infested concrete, and a dilapidated motorcycle lying on its side in front of the house. It was people like that who affected house-prices in an otherwise immaculate little community.

His walk took him into the more densely populated area, with its rows of semis and the occasional small block of flats. This was the poorer part of the village, and here was where he would find his objective. No matter where you lived there was always a place called 'the little shop on the corner', even though it wasn't always on a corner. Small places generally, and crammed to the ceiling with the most astonishing variety of foodstuffs and household materials, many of them unfamiliar brands. Wedged to one side, or in a corner, would be the counter itself, cluttered with small items, leaving just sufficient room for the proprietor to stand and take the money. Sometimes, there wasn't even a proper till, just a metal cashbox divided into sections. The most attractive items, from the point of view of a casual thief, were usually kept behind the proprietor. Cigarettes and tobaccos, wines and spirits if the premises were licensed. Prices in such places were always a few more coppers than in the more regular shopping precincts, but the very convenience of the place outweighed that disadvantage. It would be open at all hours, weekends included, and there were very few domestic needs which could not be met from the bulging shelves.

Holden knew this one well, and had often been thankful it was open in the early morning, when he found he hadn't sufficient cigarettes to get him through until lunchtime. He went in, past a group of gangling youths who were wheeling bicycles around aimlessly outside, gathered there because it was the only lighted focal point in the district. The old woman behind the counter watched him as he searched around.

'Can I help you?' she called.

'Eggs,' he explained, 'I was looking for eggs.'

'Behind you,' she instructed, 'third shelf down. We've only got Size 1 and 2 at the moment.'

He smiled to himself. 'At the moment' indeed. They never had any other sizes but the two most expensive, and he knew it. Selecting a box of Size 2, he opened the lid and checked that none were broken. Then he went over to the counter, presenting his purchase. As he did so, his eyes lighted on a small tray of batteries. He'd been intending to get a few in stock for the various battery-operated devices in the house, but it kept slipping his mind. This was his chance to correct that omission, and so he bought four.

'I'm afraid I've only got a five-pound note,' he apologised.

'That's all right, sir. I can manage.'

She opened the lid of a metal box by her side, and inserted the five pound note under a spring clip. Holden watched, fascinated. From a quick glance, it looked as though the tens and fives, plus the thicker stack of ones, would probably amount to about eighty pounds, perhaps more. There was no-one in the shop but himself and the old woman. It would be the simplest thing in the world merely to lean over, clean out the box, and walk away. This old dear couldn't stop him, she must be closer to seventy than sixty. It was just a mind-game, of course. He wouldn't get ten yards up the road before the old girl would be screaming the place down. He was easily recognisable from his clothes, and a patrolling police car would have every chance of catching him before he even reached home. And, even if he evaded capture that evening, he couldn't very well move his house and family. Sooner or later they would have him, as he went about the normal routine of simply living in the locality. Imagine the uproar, all that background thrown away for eighty miserable quid.

'Your change sir.'

He picked up his money, and put it in his pocket.

'Very quiet tonight,' he remarked conversationally.

'Always is at this time,' she confided. 'Not much doing between half past eight and ten o'clock. People have had their dinner and they're watching telly mostly. Picks up again when they start coming out of the pubs.'

'At ten?' he queried. 'That's a bit early, surely?'

'Oh no, not for some. They only pop in for an hour, and ten o'clock suits them. Nice walk home, bit of supper perhaps, bed by eleven o'clock. Lot of early risers round here you see. Factories and that. After turning out time, of course, we're rushed off our feet for half an hour. You'd be amazed at what some people decide they're short of at eleven o'clock at night. Once they're gone, that's when we close.

Used to keep open till midnight, but it doesn't pay these days. Too many funny customers about once it's late. Never used to be like that, more like a family atmosphere once. Still that's the same all over isn't it? Young people running wild everywhere. Cut your throat for a packet of King Size.'

'Ah yes,' he sighed in sympathy. 'I'm afraid you're right. Well, good night to you.'

The eggs wouldn't fit in his jacket pocket, so he walked along with them in his hand, feeling rather self-conscious. He was anxious to get home now, and into the spare bedroom he called his study. There was some very serious thinking to be done.

2

The final plan decided upon by Adam Spencer Holden was not shaped on that May evening. He quickly realised that all he had in his mind was an embryo. This would need to be nurtured, fed and worked on in fine detail before it reached its flawless maturity. It was a subject that called for more than mere headwork. A plan had to be committed to paper, itemised, and studied for flaws. There were a number of factors to be taken into account, and if he missed out on any one of them, he was sunk. His first draft read like this:

Availability of suitable premises
Access and escape
Hotel requirements
Frequency of areas
Reconnaissance
Police involvement
Disposal of profits

As so often happens in the early stages of planning, Holden quickly found there was considerable overlap between his headings, and sometimes two or three would merge together. More than once, he was on the verge of abandoning the project altogether, but the basic soundness of the scheme always stopped him. Things do not complicate themselves, as he could recall one of his old lecturers saying, they are complicated by people. The only people involved in this particular exercise was one man, himself, and so he had better re-shape his thinking and start again.

1. *Availability of Suitable Premises.*
The first need was to define what he meant by suitable premises. He was speaking of small general shops which were open late at night, in side streets of large towns. While there may well be two people working during the bulk of the day, there must only be one on duty at night. That one must be elderly, and female if possible. If there was any

outward sign of a burglar alarm system, then the premises came off the list.

The second requirement was to define availability. The premises should either be within short walking distance of the hotel at which he would be staying, or at most a ten minute bus ride. This, in turn, required that there must be a bus-stop within easy reach, and that the timing of the raid should coincide with the scheduled arrival time of a bus.

It was of the essence of the plan that Holden should operate on foot. Cars were always liable to let people down at the most unlikely moments. Cars were easily identifiable, for another thing, and only second class criminals got involved in such tedious and time consuming devices as false number plates. Besides which, the police were in their element with cars. Fully mobile themselves, monitored by radio, and with almost empty streets at the time he had selected for the raids, they had a smooth and efficient machine which they could bring into play to trap him. Indeed, it was the very mobility of the police which had gone a long way to persuade Holden that travel by foot was the answer. So many forces had abandoned the familiar figure of the beat-bobby on his rounds, complete with walkie-talkie, that the task of getting away by foot had been simplified.

2. *Access and Escape.*

The shop must be at street level. He had no intention of slipping on some unseen object while descending a flight of stairs in a hurry. The door must open onto a street, not into any kind of arcade. It must not lie in a direct line with his hotel, but must necessitate cutting through at least one other street or alleyway before meeting either with the road on which the hotel was situated, or the main road along which ran the bus service.

3. *Hotel Requirements.*

All hotels have a rear entrance, and frequently this leads directly into the car park. The important requirement was that the rear entrance, and the rear stairs, which were normally adjacent, must be out of sight of the main lobby. He could not afford to be seen by reception area staff, coming back into the hotel in his jersey and jeans. It was part of his plan to establish with those people that he had been seen in ordinary clothes at about the time in question.

The hotel must also be close to a bus-stop which would be on the same route as the one near the selected premises. Equally important, it must not be too close. It would never do for him to alight at the front door of the hotel, and then proceed in full view of the rear, before going in.

His room must be no higher than the second floor, and at the rear if possible.

4. *Frequency of Areas.*
This was a thorny one, and Holden spent many unhappy hours scratching his head over it.

His job took him to a very large number of major towns and cities, and to a certain extent the choice was his. His task was to hold meetings with the local area representatives, and make a quick assessment of their performance. His keen analytical mind could shaft through a jumble of figures, and pinpoint unsatisfactory areas in very short order. These sessions were held at nine sharp, and by ten he would have isolated those points which required further explanation, warned people who seemed not to be pulling their weight, and be ready for the next stage, which was new prospects. Everyone worked largely on commission, and in theory if they did not produce new business then they drew no commission, and it was no-one's loss but their own. That was not the way the company saw things, in the shape of Holden, and people with little or nothing to report in that direction could expect an uncomfortable two hours before the thirty minute lunchbreak at twelve. After that, those without appointments of sufficient importance to warrant the presence of the man from Head Office would go about their affairs. The others, the ones with likely-sounding new business in view, would remain with Holden, taking it in turns to escort him to the client's premises. Holden's rule was that he must be free by four o'clock. That was the hour at which he would set out by himself, getting what he called the 'feel' of the place. He had an uncanny knack of spotting opportunities which the local man had either overlooked or failed to grasp, and these would form the basis of a castigating memorandum which he would prepare immediately on his return to London.

This four o'clock solitary excursion now took on a new dimension. It now became the time he could devote to an entirely different purpose, that of seeking 'suitable premises'.

What was giving him pause was the frequency of his visits to any one particular area. A place like Bournemouth for example would not be of much value to him. It was too far, from the type of hotel at which he normally stayed, to the kind of place he was looking for. Birmingham, too, was not very hopeful. He had to go to these towns, and others like them, if he was to do this job properly, but what he wanted was the smaller places, where all the business and high life was concentrated in a narrow area in the town's square or by the harbour, and where a ten-minute walk or bus ride would lead one immediately into very different surroundings.

The timing and frequency of his trips had always been a priority subject in his work planning. It would have to become even more so, he realised.

5. *Reconnaissance.*

His four p.m., 'feel' walks would be utilised for this purpose. He realised early on that it was no use simply locating one shop, and concentrating his whole plan around it. In every case he would attempt to find at least two, with three as the ideal. Having satisfied himself about suitability under Heading One, he would enter the premises, familiarise himself with the layout, and make a few small purchases. If possible, he would engage the proprietor in a little seemingly

41

harmless gossip. People are always notoriously willing to talk about the drawbacks of their occupations, particularly when it comes to the working of long hours. Back in his hotel room, he would make exhaustive notes about each shop he visited, along with careful marking on the local street map, and bus time-table details. There would be a delay of six months before his next visit to the shop, and his purpose then would be to act, having first carried out an extended check to ensure that the notes he had made were still valid. A new burglar alarm, a change of proprietor, any deviation from the original, and the project would be cancelled. He would ensure that he was aware also of any change in the schedule of the bus company. He would then move along to his next selection in that locality, and check again.

His aim was to carry out one operation per week, with targets scattered widely over the United Kingdom. It was going to be well-nigh impossible for anyone to build up a pattern to his movements, and that brought him to his next heading.

6. *Police Involvement.*

Holden was an intelligent man, and he knew at the outset that it would be fatal to underestimate the police. At the same time he would give proper weight to two factors which were very much to his advantage. First, there was the size of each job. He expected to gain somewhere between two and three hundred pounds in cash, without the use of weapons or violence. That made it a small theft, in police terms, and only one of several per week, or even per day in the more congested areas. It would receive proper investigation, in the routine of things, but there would be very little to investigate, and Holden would see to that. His knowledge of police procedures was slight, but he could apply common sense to their difficulties. They were hard-pressed for manpower, he knew that much, and with the quantity of what he would call 'new business' which landed in their laps every single day, the amount of time available to be devoted to one enquiry would be limited. And, in his case, what did it amount to? A small job,

43

by any standards. After a few days, it would find its way into a basket marked 'Outstanding' or something of the kind, only to be buried quickly under other, similar, cases. The local station would no doubt circularise brief details to other units, who already had plenty of work on their hands. The circulation would certainly be limited in extent, and he could not visualise his little crime being featured on any list that might be sent to other police authorities, other counties. That was why he must be at pains to avoid building up any recognisable history in any one location. Paperwork and records can be buried away, but there is no burying a man's recollective process. Holden knew there was a certain type of police officer who could almost work without paper, because of some remarkable gift which enabled him to store masses of information in his own memory. He must do nothing which would be likely to prompt any of these gentlemen to go probing into old 'Outstanding' files. This made the scattering of his activities all the more important.

If anyone, anywhere, once cottoned on to the idea that there was a small-time criminal acting on a national scale, his days would be numbered.

Holden did not propose to worry himself about the possibility, but he most certainly intended to keep it in the forefront of his mind.

7. *Disposal of Profits.*

If everything went according to plan, Holden would find himself with somewhere between two and three hundred pounds in cash, to be disposed of each week. On the surface, it sounded like a problem most people would be glad to have, but, unless it were handled with the utmost care, it could prove to be a serious embarrassment. After a few months, he could find himself with thousands of pounds of unexplained money in his possession, and that must be avoided.

Up until that time, he had operated a

very sensible budget account arrangement with the bank. So much was set aside each month to allow for all bills coming in. Electricity, gas, rates, mortgage, insurance and many more. Indeed the vast bulk of his monthly salary went straight to that account. Holden, like many people in his position, used very little cash. His was a world of Standing Orders, Credit Cards, and cheques where necessary.

What he must do was to isolate those instances where cash could be substituted for the existing arrangement, and thus allow his bank balance to build up from entirely legitimate sources, viz. his salary and expenses. The expenses were an important feature, he quickly realised. He incurred at least one hotel bill per week, plus first class railway travel. In addition there was his car allowance, which was made up of a monthly fixed sum plus so much per mile. It would be a poor month indeed where those expenses, all genuine, would amount to less than six hundred pounds. Until the time of the plan, Holden had used his credit cards for the hotel, and the railway ticket. It was frequently an anxious few days, at the end of each month, between the arrival of bank statements drawing attention to various overdrafts, and the deposit of the expenses cheque which would put things back to normal.

In future, he would pay cash for everything. Hotel, rail fares, petrol, meals, everything that was a rechargeable expense. That would absorb a good percentage of his expected takings, the rest he would learn by experience. He did not wish to draw unwanted attention to his affairs, by the sudden cancellation of too many standing orders. Any major alteration in a customer's affairs was drawn automatically to the attention of management, and the bank manager was a golfing acquaintance. No, he decided, those were best left as they were, at least in the initial stages.

One other detail was essential to the plan. He must not spend money in any town which had been acquired in that town. The chances of cash being traced were not high, but they existed, and he could not take any risk. Therefore, he would always be one week behind, in his disposal of the cash. Money stolen in Lincoln, for example, would remain in his possession until he went to Newcastle on his next journey. It was probably rather a high-flown precaution, but this new Holden, the criminal Holden, was to be a very cautious man in all his dealings.

* * *

The man in Room 205 had come a long way since the foundation of the plan. He had carried out more than a hundred raids, in four years, which worked out at about one per fortnight on average, well short of his one-per-week target. Sometimes, external circumstances had caused a change of plan. Extra meetings in the evening would be called at short notice. An occasional drama at home had meant that he must return at once. Twice, he had himself been unwell, and thankful to climb into bed with a few pills and a hot drink. Mostly, though, his achievement rate had been slowed by his own decision to abort a particular operation. He had never swerved from his original intention. If everything wasn't absolutely right, down to the finest detail, Holden would call it off. There had been three times when he had no obvious justification for cancelling. Those had been times when all he felt was an inner warning that all was not well. He never attempted to explain it, but he always accepted it, and was certain he was doing the right thing.

However, mustn't dwell on that. Tonight had gone well enough, smooth as silk. Checking once again that the safety lock was securely in place on the door, Holden lifted down his suitcase, and opened it, removing the crumpled bills inside, and beginning to count.

It took him almost ten minutes to smooth out the currency notes and assemble them in denominations. The haul was larger than he had anticipated. Two hundred and seventy-one pounds. He made an entry in a small black notebook which always remained in the suitcase. Then he put all the notes neatly together, and placed them, together with the stocking, in a large manilla envelope, which was addressed to himself at home, and ready stamped. There was just one more thing to be done before he settled for the night. Bearing his precious envelope, now well-sealed with adhesive tape, he made his way down to the lobby and slid it into the Post Office collection box. The envelope was now in the custody of Her Majesty's Postal Service, and out of the reach of anyone else until it reached its destination. The job was completed, the follow-through was completed, and all he now needed to do was to go back upstairs and put it out of his mind, although he knew from experience it would not be that simple.

When he got back to the room, the trembling had started, but he had learned how to deal with it. He could recall quite clearly his horror on the first occasion. It had been his very first job, and he had been in a state of high tension for most of the day. At the last moment, changed and ready in his hotel room, he had come within an inch of dropping the whole thing. Several precious minutes had ticked away, while he convinced himself that he must go through with it. All his doubts and fears recurred, and he had to deal with them right there and then, as he was well aware. It was not simply a question of dropping this first job, he realised. If his nerve failed him then, it would be the end of the scheme, and he knew it. It was an act of high resolve on his part, when he finally left the room, and set out. During the actual raid, he found himself transported mentally to some new level of performance. There was no fear, no reserve, merely a feeling of detached resolve, with every detail clicking into place exactly the way he had planned it. It was afterwards that the reaction set in. Afterwards, when he was back, undetected, and safe in the anonymous privacy of his hotel room, that was when the shivers began, and the waves of nausea. It caught him unprepared, and he had not known what to do. Finally, he had asked room service to send up a bottle of scotch, and he had attacked it with unusual vigour, falling eventually into a drunken sleep on the bed. When he awoke, in the small hours, he was disgusted to find himself fully dressed, and with a monumental banging in his head. The level in the bottle announced that he had drunk half of it, in less than half an hour, and he knew it would not do at all. The trembling had gone now, but he still felt uneasy in his stomach, and that, he reasoned, was because of the whisky, and not the robbery. Clearly, he had a problem, and it must be dealt with methodically as part of the plan.

A few days later he went to see his doctor, and told him a yarn about being unable to sleep when away from home. He had been prescribed sleeping tablets, and these became an integral part of his overnight kit. Later, they would play a deeper part in his overall plan. Sheila had been a little surprised when she came across them one day.

'What are these for?' she demanded.

'Sleeping pills,' he replied, annoyed with himself for not having made them secure.

'I can see that,' she assured him. 'What

I'm asking is, what are you doing with them? You never have any trouble getting to sleep.'

It was quite true. As a rule he was asleep within seconds of getting into bed.

'I didn't want to worry you, darling,' he explained. 'The fact is, that I've been having trouble getting off while I'm away. The doctor says he's quite used to people going to him with the same story. Strange town, strange bed, quite a few people can't sleep properly. So he gave me those.'

Sheila rattled the bottle thoughtfully, then kissed him on the cheek.

'Poor old love, why didn't you tell me?'

'Not much point. You'd only have been worried, and there's nothing you could have done about it. I'll be all right now I have these.'

In a way, Sheila had been secretly pleased. Like most young married women, she didn't like Adam to be away from home, and could not help wondering occasionally what he did in those far-off towns. You heard such terrible stories, and the Sunday papers were always full of reports about what she classified as 'goings-on'. It wasn't that she entertained any serious doubts about her own husband, but there was always an area of his life which remained, in a way, unexplained. To learn that the poor lamb had actually resorted to the doctor because he couldn't sleep, did more to put her mind at rest than any dramatic avowals would have done. In fact, it had become Sheila who always checked that final item.

'Now, you've got your tablets?'

'Yes dear,' he would smile. 'Already packed.'

And now, when the trembling began, Holden knew exactly what to do. Unscrewing the safety cap on the little bottle, he tapped out a pill, and set it beside the ashtray. Then he took a miniature of scotch from the little refrigerator in the bedroom, and poured that into the tooth-glass. Stripping off, he went and stood under a hot shower for two minutes, cleansing away the smell of fear. He'd read that somewhere, and the phrase had lodged in his mind. The smell of fear. It was true that his pores exuded something extra along with his normal perspiration, an acrid kind of smell, and perhaps that was due to latent fear. He didn't know for certain, and there was no way he could ask anyone, so he just had to put up with it. After the hot water, he towelled himself off hard, then got ready for bed. One swallow of whisky, to loosen up his throat, then he took the pill, washing it down with the remaining scotch. A quick check to ensure that everything was switched off, and he climbed into bed. Already, the drug was beginning to make him drowsy. Reaching over, he groped for the bedside lamp.

Out went the light.

Out too, went Adam Spencer Holden, husband, father and thief.

3

George Thomas was almost beginning to regret he'd called in the police at all. They'd already been in the place over an hour, different men doing different things, asking different questions. If he'd sat down and thought about it before he telephoned from the upstairs phone, he might have realised he would be wasting his time, and probably theirs, too. After all, what was there to report? A man had come in, with a stocking over his face, pinched all the cash, and run off. He hadn't said a dozen words, he could have been any colour under the sun, or it might even have been the man who lived next door. That was how much George Thomas knew about him, and he'd tried telling that to these people a dozen times already. Really, you'd begin to think they were wondering if you had made up the whole story yourself, the way they kept on.

'Do you think you'd know him again Mr. Thomas? Say he walked in here now, to buy a bar of soap. Would you know him?'

George frowned.

'Well, if he was dressed the same. If he had his face covered up. And if he used that funny voice. Yes. Then I might have a chance. Not otherwise.'

'Funny voice? What way was it funny, Mr. Thomas?'

'Hard to say, really. Not natural, if you follow me. What I mean is, he was speaking very low, and sort of hoarse-like.'

'You mean you think he might have had a cold?'

'No,' he refuted. 'No, I don't think so. I can see what you're getting at, of course, and I think you're right in a way.'

He stopped there, as though he'd answered the question, when all he had done had been to leave it in mid-air. D. C. Devlin looked across at his colleague and raised his eyebrows imploringly.

'Don't quite follow that, Mr. Thomas. Perhaps I misunderstood you. I thought you said he didn't have a cold, but you thought I was right in a way. Which is it?'

He'd spoken plainly enough surely, or were they trying to trap him again? Carefully, he said.

'What I mean is, I don't think he really had a cold, but he was making his voice sound as if he might. Now do you follow me? Sort of disguising it, like.'

'And there was no accent? He didn't sound like a local man?'

Old George shrugged.

'Making his voice funny like that, it's hard to say.'

Devlin sighed.

'But you didn't get the impression he was Irish say, or Scottish?'

'He didn't say begorrah, if that's what you mean, and he never had a kilt on. I've told you. He only said a few words. Not much to go on.'

Too bloody right, agreed Devlin savagely. For all the information he was getting out of this witness, the tea-leaf could have materialised out of one of his sweet jars, then disappeared back inside.

'But he knew about Mrs. Thomas being

ill upstairs?' he queried, changing the subject. 'That makes him sound like a local man surely?'

The shopkeeper screwed up his face, thinking.

'True enough, everybody round here knows about Ivy. But so do a lot of people in the town. People at the hospital, doctors, the W.V.S. They're very good, always popping in. Lots of people ask about her.'

Nonetheless, the detective constable was inclined to favour the idea of a neighbourhood man being responsible. There weren't too many doctors or voluntary workers in his experience, who spent their evenings robbing isolated grocers' shops.

'And you say he knew the money was in two places? How much do you estimate was taken altogether?'

There was the merest hesitation before the answer came, and Devlin knew perfectly well why. It was always the same with these cash robberies in one-man businesses. They were covered by insurance, and the natural tendency was to bump up the loss so as to receive increased compensation from the company. At the same time, they couldn't come it too strong, otherwise the Inland Revenue or the V.A.T. people would wonder whether they were getting correct information about the annual turnover. They usually compromised on a figure greater than the actual amount, but not sufficient to cause eyebrows to be raised in other quarters.

'Must have been close to four hundred pounds,' decided George eventually. 'Eighty to a hundred in the till, and the rest down below.'

'You've been quite busy then,' observed Devlin drily.

'Early closing,' was the immediate reply. 'I always have a good day when it's early closing in the town. People never seem to allow for it, they don't plan you know.'

'No.'

Devlin wrote down 'Four hundred pounds app', in his notebook, and made a mental reservation that it was probably nearer three. He turned his attention to the cut telephone wire.

'And the first you knew about him having a knife was when you found he'd cut this?'

'Yes. I was surprised, I can tell you.'

'You're quite sure about that, Mr. Thomas?'

Alf Richardson had let his colleague do most of the talking thus far, but he was concerned about the knife.

'Course I'm sure, why shouldn't I be sure?' came the belligerent reply.

'Seems odd. Here's a man, carrying a knife, and yet he doesn't threaten you with it, doesn't even show it you? Think very carefully.'

George tried to visualise the scene again, with himself pushed almost to the floor. Tried to remember what had been said and done. When he next spoke he sounded quite triumphant.

'I'm positive, and when you think about it, he couldn't, could he?'

'Why couldn't he?'

'Because his left hand was on my shoulder, gripping it very tight. Very tight indeed, so he couldn't have been holding anything in that one. Except me. And I saw his other hand when he picked up the money. That was empty, too. No. There's no question about it. Not only did he not threaten me with a knife, he couldn't have, because of what he was doing.'

The two detectives looked at each other and nodded. It made sense, much as it went against the grain. Pity. Use of a deadly weapon was always a nice extra, but the best they could hope for here was possession. There was a bleeping sound from Devlin's pocket, and he went to a corner of the shop, speaking softly into a small black box that he carried. Then he went back to his partner.

'We have to be leaving now Mr. Thomas,' he explained. 'Could you come down to the station tomorrow morning, and make a statement? Might have a few photographs for you to look at. Never can tell. Twelve o'clock be all right?'

'Won't take long, will it?' was the anxious enquiry. 'I don't like to leave her for very long.'

'Make it as quick as we can, don't you worry.'

Outside, Richardson said,

'What's up?'

'Off-licence in New Street has been done.'

'Same bloke?'

'No. Three young roustabouts this time. The uniforms think they know one face already. Might have a bit more luck round there.'

They climbed into the car, banging doors.

'Yes,' agreed Richardson. 'I must say I fancy our chances a bit more with three hooligans than this phantom robber geezer. What do you make of him?'

'Well Alf, I'll tell you this. I'm not given to pessimism, but this boyo doesn't sound like one of ours at all. It's my guess, he's either a straight, who just got desperate for a few quid, in which case Gawd help us. Or, he's new, and he'll go through the motions again. If he is new, he'll probably get away with it three or four times, and then we'll have him.'

'All the same, I'll spend half an hour on the Open files, I think. Never pays to rely entirely on your memory, not mine anyway.'

'You're right there,' Devlin nodded. 'Well, let's go and chase some yobbos, eh?'

★ ★ ★

The morning after the robbery dawned bright, but with a sharp east wind cutting at the early pedestrians.

Holden was already awake, and drinking his first cup of tea, when the telephone shrilled.

'Hallo?'

'Your morning call sir. Seven a.m.,' announced a cheerful female voice.

'Yes. Thank you. Would you order a taxi for me please? Eight o'clock. Tell them I want to catch the London express at 8.15. Thank you.'

He finished his tea, took a quick bath, then shaved with the portable electric shaver which had been a last-minute birthday present from his sister a couple of years previously. At seven twenty, he presented himself at the dining room to find the scene much as usual at that hour. There were four other people having breakfast before departing on their various business activities. The staff were mainly part-time middle-aged ladies, each busy with her own section of the room, preparing for the main body of the guests, who would not begin to descend before eight o'clock at least. Holden ordered scrambled eggs, bacon and coffee, then opened up his newspaper to see if there was any reference to his activities of the previous evening. There seldom was, because of the lateness of the hour, but sometimes he had found a blurred two-line entry in the stop-press. To get the full story, he would have to wait for the publication of the local weekly paper on Friday. Long ago, it had been established that when Holden paid a visit to any provincial centre, the local man would send him a copy of that week's paper. Holden claimed that it enabled him to round out his own impressions, and to pick up anything of interest on the local business scene. It was a harmless idiosyncrasy on his part, and the expense to the company was only a matter of a few pence per week, so no-one queried his action.

At seven fifty, having finished breakfast, he was at the reception desk, where another eighteen year old greeted him with an automatic smile.

'My bill, please. 205.'

She turned to the machine which rested on a small table at right angles to the desk, and pressed buttons. Then she pulled the account clear, read it, and turned it round for him to read.

'That's forty seven pounds fifty two, Mr Holden.'

He glanced at it quickly to be certain he hadn't been charged for telephone calls to Hong Kong or something equally bizarre, but could find nothing wrong. Reaching inside his pocket, he lifted out his brown leather wallet, and began to count out money.

The girl was surprised. He didn't strike her as being the cash type. There were quite a few people who paid cash, even these days, but you could usually tell them by their clothes, or their attitude. This man did not come into any of the normal categories, being much more the credit card variety. Still, you never stopped learning in the hotel business, she reminded herself, accepting the notes and counting them again. Forty eight pounds. Turning, she slipped the money into a built-in cash register, and took out coins.

'Your change Mr. Holden. Forty eight pence. And your receipt.'

'Thank you.' He scooped the change into his pocket, picked up his suitcase, and went to sit in one of the deep comfortable chairs in the corner of the lobby.

Soon, the swing doors were pushed, and a small gust of fresh air swept in, on the heels of a tall man with an anxious face.

'Two O Five?' he asked, staring round. 'Taxi for Two O Five?'

'Yes.'

Holden got up, walked towards the driver, and nodded to the girl behind the counter. The driver took his suitcase.

'To the station, was it sir?'

'Please, yes. I want to catch the London train.'

'Plenty of time. It's only five minutes from here.'

Holden settled back in the taxi, and smiled to himself.

★ ★ ★

Just as the hotel telephonist rang Room Two O Five, George Thomas unsnapped the catches on the front door of his little shop. A thin-faced man came in almost at once.

'Twenty Marlborough, George. Morning.'

'Morning,' was the grunted reply. 'Hope you're not going to give me a ten-pound note.'

'What, the day before pay-day?' grinned the customer. 'Where would I get ten pounds? What's up then, short of change?'

'Short of everything,' snapped the old man. 'Got done last night.'

'Done? Burgled, you mean? Go on.'

'True.'

George launched into his story, and the thin man was joined by other early risers

68

as the tale unfolded. Here was a nice juicy yarn to start off the day, and George found himself bombarded with questions.

'Think they'll have him then, Mr. Thomas?' queried a young man.

George tapped mysteriously at the side of his nose.

'I'm not supposed to say much,' he winked, 'keep meself to meself, that's what the police told me. We know what we know, and it wouldn't pay to let him know now, would it?'

'That's right,' agreed several voices.

'So they reckon it's somebody local then?' persisted one man.

'I'm not saying it is, and I'm not saying it isn't. Now then, what was yours, please?'

Old Thomas had not been looking forward to opening up that morning, but, to his surprise, it was one of the most enjoyable days he'd spent for a long time. It was also very profitable, people finding all kinds of excuses to pop in and buy something, in order to get the story at first-hand. He was quite the neighbourhood hero within a few hours, and he became so involved he very nearly forgot about the insurance. It was when he took Ivy up a cup of tea at about eleven o'clock that he was reminded.

'Has he been yet?' she queried, as he punched up her pillows.

'Has who been, love?'

'Him from the insurance. What's his name. Griffiths. Mr. Griffiths.'

Blimey, thought George, I almost forgot about him. Better not tell her that.

'No. His number was engaged,' he invented quickly. 'I'll try him again in a minute.'

'See you do,' she instructed. 'Might look a bit fishy if you don't report it quick. All that money.'

'You're quite right love. Yes, I'll have have another try.'

Mr. Griffiths was quickly on the scene, once he received the call. As local agent for the Trusty Assurance Company, Alun Griffiths welcomed the whiff of real-life drama which the robbery would bring. A conscientious, painstaking individual, he was an ideal man-on-the-spot for the company, always reliable, punctual with his returns. Not in the first flight of new-business seekers, perhaps, but producing just enough to justify his retention on the coveted roll of the company's Top Fifty of the field force.

He knew the Thomases. They were existing clients when he first took over the area fourteen years earlier. He would have no need to spend any great length of time probing into the background of the claim, but simply complete the formal questionnaire as speedily as possible. The police, he knew, would have gone into everything very thoroughly, and he would call later for an appointment with Inspector Dalton, whom he knew slightly. As an old hand, he persuaded George Thomas not to set his loss at four hundred pounds.

'People don't like round figures, Mr. Thomas,' he explained. 'Not in a case like this. It's too neat altogether. Draws attention. If you were to say three hundred and ninety four, nobody will look at it twice. Think about it like buying a shirt. You might think twice about paying eight pounds for a shirt. But somehow, although you know there's no real difference, seven ninety five doesn't sound such a lot. You take my point?'

George Thomas had indeed taken his point, and with some relief. For a moment he had been afraid that Griffiths might be going to query the claim altogether. To reduce the sum by a mere six pounds was a relief.

★ ★ ★

Seven a.m. Inspector Knott took another sip at his lukewarm coffee, and carried on with the summary of the station's activities during the night. It was very much the usual history of road accidents, public house fights, domestic disorders, muggings, burglaries and all the other petty crime which goes to make up the normal experience of an average community. A few people had been taken into custody, for their own protection as much as anything else. Others had also been apprehended, but for very different reasons, and they would not be leaving in a few minutes' time with a friendly warning. Especially those three little thugs who'd done the off-licence. They'd been all full of big talk when they threatened one unarmed man the previous evening, but practically on their knees when faced with determined police officers a few hours later. Scum.

He read the Thomas report for the third time. Strange little case, that was. Very neat, very efficient, and all over in a minute or so. The planning was more the sort of thing you'd expect to find in a big payroll job or that kind of caper. And all for four hundred quid. If he really got four hundred quid, he amended. Inspector Knott knew all about the inflated losses suffered by small shopkeepers when there was insurance money in the offing. Ah well, not his problem. The super could bring his great mind to bear on that while he, Knott, was at home catching up on his sleep. He made one final check that all the copies were in order, especially the blues, for Division, and the pinks, for County.

★　★　★

The alarm clock seemed to be noisier than ever that morning. Sheila Holden stirred, groaned and reached round blindly for the source of the irritation. Then she remembered that she had forestalled herself, by leaving the clock on the dressing table, where she couldn't reach it. The ringing would continue for a full minute before it stopped. Then the clock would tick patiently away for three more blissful minutes, before setting up its racket again, only this time at extra volume. The choice was her own. Either she could get up, and stop the noise now, or she could wait, with mounting anticipation, for the ear-splitting sound which would inevitably result. Unhappily, she swung her feet clear of the bed, stood upright, and tottered across to the offending clock.

'I hate you,' she told it.

Talking to clocks now, she realised. It was coming to something when a thirty-two year old woman started talking to clocks. Outside, in the corridor, there was a rushing of feet, and Patricia came tumbling through the door, clutching her

74

precious donkey, Gizmo.

'Is Daddy home?' she asked, without preliminaries.

Sheila stared down at the shining little face, and smiled.

'And good morning to you, too,' she replied gravely. 'No dear, you know Daddy's away. He'll be home later today.'

'Gizmo said you were talking to somebody.'

Patricia held the chewed woollen toy out, accusing her.

'Well, Gizmo is wrong, and you can tell him I said so. He probably heard me tell the clock to shut up. Go and give Graham a shake for me, there's a good girl.'

'Why?' demanded the newcomer.

'Because it's time he was up,' explained Sheila. 'Besides, we're both up. Why should he lie around in bed? Typical male.'

'Not Graham, mummy. I mean why did you tell the clock to shut up? Did it say something rude?'

Her mother sighed. It was bad enough pretending to be a human being first thing in the morning. To have to get involved in these tortuous discussions with a wide-awake seven year old was really asking rather a lot.

'Not rude, exactly,' she explained. 'But it makes this terrible noise, and my head can't stand it.'

That seemed to satisfy her questioner. It was an accepted part of life's pattern that Mummy's head could not stand certain things. Patricia nodded solemnly, and went down the landing to wake her brother.

'There you are Gizmo,' she chided. 'You were wrong. It wasn't Mr. Hayward at all. It was that silly old clock, and Mummy's head can't stand it.'

In the bedroom, Sheila Holden froze as she listened to the childish explanation. What was she talking about. Why on earth should she suddenly mention Bruce's name? He'd only ever been once to the house. That had been for a few minutes only, and the children had been at school. They had agreed they must be extremely careful about that, or about anything involving the children. As far as she was aware Patricia had only met Bruce

Hayward once, and that had been quite by accident, when they all happened to be in the library at the same time. Knowing that she ought to leave the child alone, she found herself compelled to the doorway, where she forced a bright smile onto her face.

'What's that rascal chattering about now?' she laughed.

The grave round eyes turned towards her.

'He's just being silly,' was the explanation. 'He thought it was Mr Hayward you were talking to. He's got a buzz in his bonnet. I've got a good mind not to let him have any marmalade today.'

'Bee,' corrected her mother, automatically.

'Where's the bee?'

The child looked around for the feared intruder.

'You don't get a buzz in your bonnet, you get a bee.'

'That's not nice,' decided Patricia. 'How does it get in? It would have to crawl in through one of your ears while we're asleep. Gizmo won't like that. I'll have a good look after I get Graham up. I'll get him to help me. Graham's not afraid of bees. He killed one once in the garden.'

The subject of Bruce was now forgotten by the child. Despite her anxiety, Sheila knew it would be most unwise to raise it again. On the way downstairs, her mind was in a turmoil, as she explored every possible avenue of her memory for any connection between Bruce and the children. That time in the library, they had been very circumspect in what they said to each other, and not merely for the sake of the children. There were plenty of other townspeople in there, who knew one or both of them. Any hint of a relationship which was other than casual would have been noted by eyes more experienced than those of the two small children. Later, she would telephone him, and arrange to meet him for a lunchtime drink. Perhaps he would be able to recall something, any tiny thing which had slipped her mind. Something which had impressed itself sufficiently on Patricia for her to mention his name outside her mother's bedroom, in the first light of dawn.

Meantime, there was the morning's activity to get under way. Bathroom supervision, breakfast, clothes check, lunch-money. Already, in the upstairs chatter, she could hear Graham's scornful dismissal of something the unfortunate Gizmo was supposed to have done.

Sheila began automatically to slice bread.

4

Frank Gardener put down his pen, and yawned enormously, looking at his watch. Almost two o'clock, he noted, and still he hadn't started on the night reports. Might have to stay on for a bit this evening, and the thought did not please him. What he was doing was important work, and he fully realised that, but try as he might, he couldn't bring the same kind of spontaneous enthusiasm to bear on it, that he'd been able to summon in his earlier career.

Rising now from his chair, he went to the window, and stood looking out at the well-kept lawns close to the building, and beyond them to the gentle rolling hills which hid the country town. The view was a bit different, too, he thought grimly. A damned sight different.

Frank Gardener had spent ten years as an active police officer in the great city of Liverpool, and loved every minute of it. A resourceful, brave and determined man, he always put his heart and soul into whatever job came his way. There was no doubt in the minds of his superiors that he could have achieved the top flight had he set his mind to it, but he was a man who could not settle behind a desk for any length of time. Making out reports, interviewing people, these things were part of the routine of life, and he did them uncomplainingly and well. But he was always anxious to get back outside into the teeming life of the city, getting on with the proper business of what he considered to be police work. Of course, there had to be people behind desks. Someone had to make the decisions, give orders, and Frank recognised both the need and the importance of the roles played by such people. Indeed, he had no basic objection to being one of them himself, with a major reservation. Having reached a decision as to what line should be pursued in a certain enquiry, Frank could not then sit back and send someone else to follow it up. He wanted to be able to make the administrative decision, then go outside and get on with its execution, and no large organisation runs that way. His dilemma was by no means unique, but had been faced many times by others in his position, who had to decide, sooner or later, to opt for one course or the other. Frank never had any hesitation. His place, as he never doubted, was out there 'where it was at' as he was fond of saying. Eventually, he would achieve the rank of inspector. Perhaps, some day, if he was ever able to curb his instinctive desire to respond to every call personally, he might even make chief inspector, but beyond that he would never rise, and he knew it. Knew it, and didn't mind. It wasn't that he had any in-built reservations about rank, authority or privilege. It was simply that he could not visualise those things as being any real substitute for the hard-pressed life of a station officer, which was all he ever wanted to be.

One strange by-product of his attitude was that it made him into a kind of ground-level spokesman for the top brass. When others complained about an assignment, it would be Gardener who justified it.

'All right for them, sitting around in a nice warm office, issuing bloody orders,' came a typical grumble one cold night. 'They haven't got to lie flat on this bleeding roof at ninety below zero for hours on end. Probably nothing will happen anyway.'

Frank had grinned to himself in the darkness, looking at the disgruntled outline of his companion's face, as they stared down into the warehouse yard, far below.

'You want to think a bit more about your facts, my son,' he counselled. 'It was Chalky Stone gave us this job. He spent fourteen years doing what we're doing. And worse. They didn't give him that job for nothing, you know. If I know Chalky, he'd sooner be out here with us, than sitting in his office. At least we know what's going on. All he can do is to worry about it.'

'H'm,' snorted the other. 'Let him come then. He can have my place. I'll sit and drink his tea, and worry for him.'

It had been another assignment, about a year later, which had brought to a temporary end Frank Gardener's work out in the field. A tip-off had been received about a coming bank-raid, and he was one of a number of officers stationed at strategic points around the area. There was a pitched battle with the bandits, who were armed with clubs and steel bars. Two of the raiders, realising the job was impossible, had headed on foot for an emergency get-away car in a side street, where Gardener and another officer were ready for them. The first blow took Gardener's companion out of the action, leaving him to cope with both assailants for the few precious seconds before help could reach him. He gave a good account of himself, but was badly battered before relief came, and there was considerable internal damage caused by the vicious weapons. Gardener had been hurt before, but this time it was different. There wasn't to be a three-day stay in the hospital, followed by a week on light duties. He was to languish in hospital for several months, and even when he finally emerged, he was far from whole.

'It's going to be some time,' explained

the surgeon-in-charge. 'A year, or perhaps even longer, before you're fully active again. All the repair work has been done, and there's nothing more for us now. It's up to your system to make good those repairs, and it isn't a five-minute job.'

Frank had sought clarification from his superiors about his future. The Chief Constable had even seen him personally, to express his concern about what was to become of him.

'I'm quite ready to hear the worst sir, after all this time,' explained Gardener. 'Does it mean I'll have to spend the rest of my life behind a desk?'

His superiors had given a lot of thought to the future of Sergeant Francis Gardener. The immediate plan had been to find him a quiet post on the force, one where his experience and background could be put to work, but where at the same time he would be removed from the daily rough and tumble of a policeman's normal existence. His own Chief Superintendent had been the man who pointed out the flaw in that scheme.

'It sounds fine, sir, but it's the old story

of the horse and the stream. I know Gardener. We can park him in some quiet corner, but we can't make him accept it. As soon as he starts feeling a little bit fit, he'll be finding excuses to turn up on the patch. He'll keep running into his old mates by accident, in canteens, at football matches. He'll make it his business to find out what's going on, and in my opinion it won't do him any good at all. It'll only make him feel more useless than ever, and we shall finish up with a very discontented officer on our hands. Not only that, he could impede his own recovery simply by fretting.'

The C.C. had listened carefully to this argument.

'I take your point, but it sounds a bit self-defeating. It seems that you're suggesting it doesn't matter what we do with Sergeant Gardener, it isn't going to work. What's our alternative?'

The Chief Super hesitated.

'Well sir, I was wondering whether there might be any chance of getting him off this force altogether. Say for about a year. An exchange posting with another force. Perhaps one of your colleagues could use a bright intelligent officer like Gardener for a spell, and he could loan us somebody who could benefit from a bit of big city experience. Even Gardener would find it hard to keep in touch if he was a couple of hundred miles away.'

'Ah. Very well, I'll see what I can do.'

And now, here was Gardener, waiting to hear his fate. Looking at that questioning face, and knowing the man's history, the C.C. was relieved that he'd taken so much trouble over the case. As to the prospect of a life behind a desk, well, at least he could reassure him on that one.

'Lord no,' he laughed. 'Can't have you wasting all your back-ground on that kind of life. Matter of fact, I have a rather promising offer to make to you Sergeant, and I hope you'll accept it.'

The Midshire County Constabulary was one of the smaller forces, and also one of the last to invest in its own computer. Basically an agricultural county, it boasted only three large towns, all former market towns which had grown to include a few light industries and small manufacturing concerns. The county headquarters, which included the new computer centre, were situated in five acres of rolling parkland, three miles from the county seat. It was to this pleasant oasis that Frank Gardener found himself posted, following his interview with the Chief Constable, and after much personal soul-searching. His new role was in the collation and interpretation of the crime reports which flowed in daily from the various divisions. He had at first been rather suspicious of the work, feeling that its importance was being inflated in order to make it more acceptable to him. He fully expected to find himself shuffling paper from one place to another in the typical office situation where the documentation, classification and final resting place took precedence over the nature of the contents. If File X was missing, it would probably be more important to prove that it wasn't in the possession of a certain officer, than it would to worry about the apprehension of the thief or criminal whose work was outlined inside. Gardener had the outside man's typical suspicion of paperwork, and those who dealt with it. File X could be a snatched handbag outside the supermarket, or the latest in a string of psychopathic rapes. It was all one to the office people. Their main preoccupation lay in avoiding responsibility for its loss.

His computer job proved to be a pleasant surprise. It was true that he was expected to categorise the incoming pinks for the building up of the monthly and quarterly statistics, but any competent clerk could have done that. Frank Gardener was encouraged to do more. Instead of merely scanning the reports to decide on classification, he was expected to spend a couple of minutes studying each case, thinking about it. Freed from the geographical impositions suffered by individual stations and even divisions, he could bring an overall county view, which had two major advantages. The first, and most obvious, was the capability to study trends in criminal activity. The second was the opportunity to watch out for criminals who were inconsiderate enough to cross police boundaries in the course of their activities.

The vast majority of petty crime is carried out by a small criminal fraternity in any given locality. They know their local police, who in turn know them, and whilst it might not always be possible to prove a case in court, the men at the station usually have a fairly close idea of who is responsible for which activity. So much crime requires local knowledge, and this is hard to obtain outside one's own locality, but with improved communications, the criminals are finding themselves less constricted, and this in turn compels more comparing of notes between stations and divisions. Still, there is a limit, and this is quickly reached. The police as a whole are notoriously undermanned, and there is quite sufficient work at any given unit to keep everyone fully occupied. As a result, the amount of time available to consult across borders is very limited, and sometimes the treatment is downright perfunctory.

It had been found necessary, years earlier, to work on the principle of economy of scale. In Midshire, arbitrary figures were applied to the cross-fertilisation arrangements. Crimes involving sums below five hundred pounds were merely listed, with a one line entry for each. Those from five hundred to two thousand five hundred formed a separate list, with a small descriptive paragraph on each case. Above that figure, each case had to be read at least at Chief Inspector level, to give weight to its importance. Most burglaries, thefts and robberies came under the first two headings, with the major exception that any use of violence, weapons, or offences against the person, were always put into a separate category, to receive maximum attention.

In theory then, it was possible for a small-time crook, for whom violence was not a part of his method, to get away with the occasional small robbery, so long as he kept moving from one police district to another. They are, in the main, unimaginative creatures and not blessed with over-much intelligence. Nevertheless, there occurs the odd one who is a notch above the rest, and it was hoped that a by-product of the computer, with its centralised pooling of information, would be to bring to the fore any such cases of boundary crossing, planned or fortuitous.

The advent of Sergeant Frank Gardener, a front-line policeman, with a wealth of first-hand experience, and a highly-developed sense of 'feel' for a crime situation, proved to be a sound investment on the part of the authorities. The existing staff had viewed his coming with mixed feelings. There were those who thought they would be carrying an invalid, a passenger, whose contribution would be minimal. Others, with a background restricted to the gentle Midshire pace, resented the intrusion of a man from a big-city force, an undoubted knowall, with a history of armed confrontations and riot control, who would be condescending in his new surroundings, at the very least. Another, smaller group, took a reverse view, that of the experts. They were computer-trained people, steeped in terminology and the technical aspects of computer work, and they did not wish to have some unknowledgeable new man, particularly at sergeant level, intruding on their jealously guarded preserve.

None of them had reckoned with the man himself. Gardener had spent many thoughtful hours in solitude, before agreeing to accept the transfer, and he had foreseen the various kinds of reception he could expect. If he was to be a part of the Midshire force, he did not intend to report for duty in the same state of preparedness as any raw recruit. His first move had been to obtain a copy of the annual Midshire report for the previous year, with its invaluable statistical summaries, and divisional breakdowns. A visit to W. H. Smiths provided him with a traveller's guide to the county, and he also invested in the relevant Ordnance Survey maps. The result was that he had a good working idea of what to expect on the policing front, well before he was due to make the move. With the willing cooperation of his superiors, he also attended a one week computer-appreciation course at a technical college, where he gathered a secure grounding in the basics of what was to him a new subject.

He knew he would have to gear down his thinking, to adjust to the more leisured approach he was going to find, and this he found easier than he had at first imagined. The reason was not far to seek. All the medical advice he received contained the same basic message. His rate of recovery was in his own hands. The more calmly he approached each day, the more quickly would he fit himself for return to the kind of duty he revelled in. The result was that the man who presented himself at computer headquarters was found to be a quiet, thoughtful individual, with at least a rudimentary knowledge of the force and its work, and quite capable of reading and interpreting a print-out. He settled in quickly, careful to avoid offence to his new colleagues, while at the same time leaving them in no doubt that his rank of sergeant had been thoroughly earned through years of solid police work.

The greatest single advantage of the computer was its speed of recall. If Frank Gardener, in studying one of the pink crime reports, thought he recognised some familiarity of description or method, he could at once put his thinking to the test by searching the memory banks of the computer, and the little visual display unit on his desk would show whether or not his first reaction was worth pursuing. It was a far cry from the days of having to wade through hundreds of files, only to finish up with a dead end.

In the first three months of Gardener's attachment, the rate of apprehension in the Midshire force improved by one per cent, due mainly to his thoroughness and application. One per cent might seem a figure scarcely worthy of consideration by someone like a High Street trader, but in police terms it was a notable upward trend.

The pink report on the robbery at George Thomas's little shop landed on Gardener's desk one sunny afternoon, along with the rest of the previous day's activities. On the face of it, there wasn't much of interest. Under four hundred quid in cash — query? three hundred — no personal violence, no use of weapons — masked intruder wore gloves — cash policy carried with Trusty Assurance, no problem there — telephone cut off. Intruder had got clean away, no sound of a car or motor cycle engine, so the shopkeeper had said, but then, he'd be in a state of nerves. The investigating officers had concluded that it was probably a local man, above the usual run of intelligence, who had been driven to the crime by debt or, more likely, unemployment. On the face of it, Gardener saw no reason to disagree with them. If it had been one of the regulars, they'd have known it straight away. The size of the crime made it unlikely that anyone would have travelled very far to pull it off, and in any case the computer would at once have recognised similarity features from elsewhere in the county. No, the local people were probably right, and what they had to contend with was the most frustrating kind of investigation, that of a normally straight citizen who had decided to take up crime. If that was the case, he would probably get away with it again, or possibly twice more, and then they would have him.

This next case was a bit more promising, the one about the three youths doing the off-licence. Gardener read this with considerable professional interest, noting the way the moves of the various units had been co-ordinated, and approving everything that had been done. A very nice, neat little piece of police work all round, ending with all three culprits behind bars. He felt momentary envy for those officers out there in the dark of the previous night, going through motions that were so familiar to him, with that extra little bit of satisfaction that comes from a successful arrest. He could almost visualise them, sitting around a deserted canteen, drinking coffee and pulling each other's legs, before settling down to the boredom of committing all that excitement to a few typed lines on a multi-copied report, with a pink marked 'County H.Q.'

That was him. That was his involvement now. He was the end of the line, the embodiment of the pink copy marked 'County H.Q.', and the thought gave him little pleasure. That was when he yawned suddenly, and went to stare out of the window, his thoughts a strange jumble of the peaceful green scene which stretched out beneath him, and the concrete reality of his earlier existence.

Wait a minute.

That shopkeeper who'd been done the night before. There was something familiar about that. Nothing to do with Midchester or the computer. Something much earlier, from the Liverpool days. But what?

He went back to his desk, and took the pink report from his OUT basket, where it had been awaiting removal. Then he sat down, and read it all through again, racking his brains. Finally, he looked at the telephone, hesitating. He had his own outside line, but it was a rule of the department that he would use it only for calls within the county. Long-distance calls were to be obtained by the operator, and only then by permission of his departmental head. That would have presented no difficulty if he had been on the track of something big. A nice payroll grab, or a travelling rape-artist, and permission would be granted automatically. But he could just imagine the reaction he would get on a piddling little case like this. And, with no more than a vague recollection to back it, the justification for an expensive telephone call was difficult to sustain.

Gardener agonised on the pros and cons for a full minute. Then, with a guilty look around the room, he pulled the telephone towards him.

★   ★   ★

Detective Sergeant Hoo was a Liverpool-born Chinese who had made his determined way up in the world by sheer dogged perserverance, and the refusal to be put down on any grounds. Early setbacks in his career had made him ever more correct and precise in his approaches to those around him, whichever side of the law they inhabited. There was very little that could disturb his calm detachment, and very few people who could reach him on other than the most formal level. As he picked up the telephone that fine afternoon, he was unprepared for the voice at the other end.

'D.S. Hoo speaking,' he announced.

'Tishy? It's me, Frank.'

The Chinaman took the receiver away from his ear, and looked at it, as if hoping for some visual image of the impudent rascal at the other end. Tishy? There were only half-a-dozen people in the whole world who would dare to call him by that nickname, and none of those was called Frank. The only Frank who'd ever enjoyed such intimacy had been his old mucker Frank Gardener, now out to pasture in some village in the middle of England. It couldn't possibly be him.

'I think we have a bad line,' he replied coolly. 'Who is it you wanted to speak to, please?'

'Wake up Tishy, this is Frank Gardener,' came the brisk rejoinder. 'Have you been on the opium again?'

It was Gardener, all right, no doubt about it. He was the only one who would

100

dare to speak to Detective Sergeant Hoo like that.

'Frank, is that really you? How are you, and about two million other questions.'

The people in the outer office would not have recognised the animated face on their much-feared D/S as he chattered away to the distant Gardener. Finally, the caller came to the point.

'I'm on the cadge,' he admitted, 'and I think you're the only one who can help me out.'

'My life savings will be in the post tonight,' promised Hoo, 'what's your address these days?'

'It's not that simple, I'm afraid. It's your memory I'm after. I've got a case down here, silly little case, but there's something about it that's vaguely familiar. Let me tell you what I've got.'

Detective Sergeant Hoo listened carefully while his distant friend went through the details of the raid on George Thomas's little shop. Pencil in hand, he made a few notes as the story progressed. When Gardener was finished, he said carefully,

'Frank, my boy, I'm sure this is practically a crime wave down there. It's probably been described as the breakdown of law and order in Midchester, and what are the police doing about it, demands our editor. But Frank, think for a moment. Think about this end, will you? Today, I've got on my desk, brand new, four muggings, two rapes and a razor attack on some homosexual who might die. That's today. On top of that, I've got a list of Under Enquiry's as long as your arm, and as far as the burglar bridgade is concerned, I've got three D/Cs working round the clock. Even if we were in a position to help you, the Lord above knows where we'd get the time. Just what is it you think we can do, anyway?'

At the other end Gardener nodded, as though the situation was much as he had expected to find it.

'I didn't expect anything else,' he admitted, 'and I wouldn't have called you if I hadn't had one of those queer feelings. I seem to remember a case very like this one about two years ago on our old manor. Stocking over the face, gloves, elderly shopkeeper, no violence. Only cash was taken, and it was only two or three hundred quid that time as well. It was a neat job, very clean, and the reason I remember it is because I thought we had a new man just starting, and we'd be hearing from him again. Only we never did. We actually kept his file near the top as long as we could, we were so sure he'd be back.'

He sighed. An unsolved petty crime that might have happened two years back. He stared at the heaps of paper on his desk sadly. Much as he would have liked to help his old comrade, he really didn't see how it was possible. There were just so many hours in a day, and — wait a minute. His eyes fell on a flimsy Movement Sheet, and he picked it up, reading quickly.

'Frank, I can't recall this master criminal at all. Tell you what, though. I've got one of these cadets assigned to me at the moment. I can put him on to a bit of file searching for a few hours, see if he comes up with anything. No guarantees, you understand. And if the station super gets wind of it, I shall deny the whole thing.'

Gardener was highly relieved. He would have understood only too well if his friend had been unable to do anything, and any offer was to be appreciated.

'Don't worry about the super. Just look inscrutable, your lot are supposed to be good at that. Do you want to make a note of my number and extension?'

'I suppose so,' groaned Hoo. 'Fire away.'

The Midshire man read out his eight digit telephone number. Then he added,

'Extension 230. Thanks Tishy. Mustn't keep you. Got an important missing sheep case to follow up. Happy joss sticks.'

Detective Sergeant Hoo's reply was more Liverpool than Hong Kong, and they both chuckled as they hung up. Hoo went to his door, and opened it, calling out to the world at large.

'Somebody find Cadet Kerr. I want him in my office, now.'

Two minutes later an eager-faced youth

presented himself in the feared D/S's office, and was kept waiting while the seated man finished studying the file on his desk.

'Ah, there you are. Andy isn't it?'

'Yes, sir.'

'Not sir,' growled Hoo, 'Sergeant. What have they got you on, Andy?'

'Procedure Manual, sir — er — sergeant. I'm reading it up, trying to get it into my head.'

Typical, thought Hoo. As soon as somebody didn't know what to do with a newcomer, or couldn't be bothered with him, they simply handed him the Procedure Manual, and told him to bone up on it. Well, at least he wouldn't be taking the boy off anything valuable. Nothing of this showed on his face, or in his tone when he spoke.

'Good. A copper who doesn't know his manual is a menace to himself and everybody else. However, I've got a little something I want done, if you fancy a change.'

Kerr's face lit up. He'd been wading through the manual for almost two days, and the prospect of something different was welcome.

'Glad of the change, sergeant.'

Hoo explained what it was that needed to be done. It involved searching through all the unsolved small robberies for the previous two years, then, if there was no result, possibly having to go back further. At the end, he handed over his pencilled notes.

'These are the similarity factors we're looking for.'

The young man took the paper, glancing at it quickly.

'Could I ask a question, sergeant?'

'Certainly.'

But there was a grimness on the sergeant's face, despite his expressed willingness to answer the question. Kerr had heard all about the fearsome reputation of D/S Hoo, but the question seemed so obvious, he felt he had to ask it.

'Well sir — sergeant, surely the computer will feed this back in less than a minute?'

That was the trouble with everyone

under twenty-five, reflected Hoo. They couldn't add up an expense sheet without a calculator, and when it came to records, they couldn't get their minds above computers.

He nodded, as though agreeing.

'Very likely, son, but let me tell you one or two things about computers. About this particular computer. It's a very expensive item for a start. Has somebody ever told you about a little thing called computer time?'

'Not yet, sergeant. I'm to have two days at the centre next week.'

'Well, let me tell you something before you go. I'm not proposing to trot out all the statistics, you'll get enough of that next week. I'll stick with this one little problem we have here. The computer is a wonderful institution, and I don't know what we'd do without it. The trouble is, we are not the only people interested. Everybody wants to play with it. First thing anybody thinks of, when they want some information, is the computer. Everybody in the country seems to imagine all you have to do is push a button, and the answer comes up V.D.U.'

'But surely — '

'Don't interrupt me, son. Don't ever interrupt me.' He silenced the young cadet with one of his famous glares. 'Now then, the computer is a little bit like a telephone exchange in some ways. So many lines going in, so many coming out. You know what that means. Sometimes the line is engaged, and you try again later. But there's one major difference. With the telephone exchange, whoever gets through first, gets served first. Now, we can't have that with the computer, or there'd be chaos. Imagine the Chief Constable can't get something he wants in a hurry, because some P.C. is asking the computer how many bicycles were nicked the year before last. That can happen if you don't have a system, but we do have one. It's called R.F.A., which is short for Request For Access. We put in an RFA and we get an access time allotted to us. It's usually within twenty four hours, but we can't rely on it. Everything depends on the priority rating. But that's only one point. There's another reason why we don't involve the computer unless we have to. Computer time is money, real money, and it has to be accounted for. We just can't play with the magic box because it's there. We have to have a reason. Every month, there's a divisional meeting, and one of the items on the agenda is computer time. All the superintendents and chief supers have to explain exactly what their people are up to with every enquiry on the list, and Gawd help somebody if there isn't a good tale to tell. Am I beginning to make things clear, son?'

Cadet Kerr blushed.

'Oh yes, sergeant, thank you. Very clear. I just didn't know — '

The remorseless sergeant droned on as though the youngster hadn't spoken.

'So there's the scene, you see. There's the Head of Division sitting at the table looking at our Chief Superintendent. 'What's all this?' he says. 'What's this enquiry from your end?' You can imagine our gaffer's face. All he can say is, 'Ah well, sir, you see, Cadet Kerr thought it might save him a bit of bother.'' Hoo leaned forward, the naturally slanted eyes now no more than slits in his olive face. 'I won't tell you the rest of the conversation, because I don't think you're old enough to hear that kind of thing, but it would not be friendly. It would be down-right critical of our gaffer, take my word. But that's not the end. Our gaffer does not care to have his backside tanned at Division. He gets very resentful, and when he gets back to his own manor, he starts lashing out. It's very painful for people on the wrong end of it, and I don't intend to be one. Is that clear?'

The unfortunate Kerr, by this time quite convinced that he had been the direct cause of a major upheaval at Divisional H.Q., swallowed mightily.

'Yes, sergeant. This certainly wouldn't justify — '

'No, it wouldn't.'

Hoo was satisfied that he had made his case, with good logical reasoning. Everything he had said was quite true, and supportable, but he had omitted his major reason. Everyone on the force would think he was barmy, if they found out he'd taken notice of the odd request from Sergeant Frank Gardener. People would begin to wonder whether he was in need of a rest himself. They might even suggest he should be down there, helping Gardener to locate his missing sheep. He smiled briefly at the momentary vision of himself and Frank creeping about in meadows, looking for clues. A bit remote from the days when the same two men had gone up against the O'Leary's, all five of them, at the end of the supermarket, one wet Saturday night. Frank Gardener had almost certainly saved his life in the course of that memorable melée, and Hoo would not let him down over this seemingly crazy request, even if it meant a blistering from above in due course. Still, mustn't dwell on the past. This lad was standing there, waiting for instructions.

'Right then, off you go. Ask PCW Dalton to show you where to start.'

That got rid of him fast enough. Gwen Dalton was the prettiest girl in the station, and it would get Cadet Kerr started off in the right frame of mind. Hoo put the matter out of his head for the moment.

Now then, this razor attack. It was high time he had an up-to-date report from the hospital. Lifting the telephone receiver, he began to dial.

5

Adam Spencer Holden stepped out on to the platform at Euston Station and made his way through the shifting crowds to the underground. There was little point in going direct to the office. If he did that, he would arrive a few minutes before mid-day, which was a something and nothing time to be reporting back. Most of the junior staff would be getting ready to depart for the early lunch break, and the senior people would be immersed in their various tasks, or at meetings. He would sit in his own office, as he knew from experience, out of touch with what had been going on in his absence, and unable to catch up by using the internal telephone system, or dropping in casually on his colleagues. They would all have set themselves individual targets, to be achieved before lunch if possible, and they would not give the same reception he would have received had he arrived earlier. Holden had learned over the years that if he couldn't reach his office by eleven a.m., there was no point in going in until after lunch.

The underground was packed with the usual motley assortment of new arrivals in the capital. Hordes of young people with rucksacks, handgrips, airline bags, gathered loosely into groups, each group identifiable only by a common tongue, seldom English. Skin colours covered the whole spectrum between white and black, including olive, yellow, light brown, chocolate and intermediate shades. One group caught his eye in particular. They were very tiny people, the tallest being less than five feet three inches, with hair of shining jet, and the girls were all strikingly pretty, with their slanted eyes and parchment skins. Holden could not begin to identify their language, which was conducted at a high pitch, like the chattering of excited magpies. One of the young men stepped in front of him as he strode along the platform, bowed with considerable ceremony and smiled.

'Victoria, pliss?'

He was glad that he knew how to direct them, with much sign language and after several false starts. The group studied him as he frowned in concentrated effort, referring continually to the brightly coloured plan of the underground system which the young man held out to him. When he thought he had at last made it all quite clear he smiled encouragingly, and was astonished that they all bowed their thanks. He found himself bowing in return, which earned him a barrage of gleaming smiles from the visitors as he made his escape.

Victoria.

For a moment, he had been tempted to say that he was going there himself, and would be glad to escort them. Cheryl lived at Victoria, and would usually be home at this hour of the day, unless one of her rare modelling jobs had cropped up. If she was there, that would be the end of the day, so far as work was concerned, and Holden really ought to report back. It wasn't so much that his absence would be questioned, because he could always cover himself in such an eventuality. It was rather that it was not part of his plans for the day, and he was very much a man who liked to proceed in an orderly fashion. This day had been planned out in advance, so much time to his work programme, so much for the domestic side of life. It was not that he was not an adaptable person, indeed he prided himself on his ability to accept unexpected changes in routine, but these should come from outside sources. A sudden summons from one of the directors, an emergency meeting with overseas customers, these things would not find Holden lacking. But it was his firm conviction that such adaptability could only be effective if it emerged from a solid base of routine. There was a wealth of difference, in his view, between a man who could rise to a crisis situation from the confidence which stems from an ordered existence, and the man who faced the same crisis from a mishmash of disorderly procedures, or no procedure at all. Holden had sat at too many tables with people like that, having frequently to control his embarrassment as the familiar phrases were trotted out.

'Should be on your desk tomorrow.'

'Haven't got all the returns in yet.'

'Just on the last lap now.'

And others. They all boiled down to the same thing in the end. The speaker was not on top of his job, and the reason lay all too often in a slovenly overall approach. Those were the people, he told himself grimly, who would have led the little group of students to Victoria and gone looking for their Cheryls, if they had one. Well, much as the prospect appealed to him, he wasn't going to be diverted from the day's plan by the simple accident of being asked for directions by a bunch of foreigners.

Twenty minutes later, he emerged into the bright sunshine, and enjoyed the short walk from the tube station to his own house. On the way, he passed the little general stores which had first given him the idea for his grand plan, and smiled to himself at the recollection.

Turning into Melrose Avenue, he moved briskly along to Number 64, noting as he approached that the car was missing. Sheila was out then, and why not? Probably sitting around eating cheese on toast, and drinking sherry with half a dozen other young mums. That seemed to have become something of a pattern since Patricia had started school, and really, he reflected, who could blame them? It must open up a whole new horizon for any woman, when the smallest child finally starts school. Suddenly, after years of being virtually housebound, they find themselves with six or seven child-free hours, and the change must be drastic. True enough, there was a certain amount of work still to be done. Beds had to be made, there was cleaning work and shopping as always, but these assumed a new proportion too. Overnight, they became merely jobs. In the past, they had seemed endless chores, to be fitted in against a background of demanding children, toys everywhere, sudden crises, mysterious stomach pains and a hundred and one other distractions. In the new pattern, once the school bell clanged at nine, the endless draining demands of the household routine became straightforward tasks, with definable beginnings and ends. The lady of the house could decide what she was going to do, and when, then simply get on with it.

Sheila had always been an efficient person in her working days, and once she had come to realise that she had a whole new life-style, she had adapted to it with a will. The hours between 9 a.m. and three-thirty belonged to her. Once Patricia had passed safely through the school gates in the morning, there was no child-demand on her until it was time to set out in the car to collect the new schoolgirl. She soon found herself involved in coffee mornings with other young women in the same situation, and she relished the newfound freedom.

That was probably what she was up to now, decided Holden, as he inserted his key in the lock, and entered the house. They had agreed long ago that there was no point in Sheila remaining at home on those days when he may or may not arrive home at lunchtime. He was quite capable of making himself something if he was hungry, and for Sheila to disrupt her entire day for the half an hour or so he would spend indoors was really not worth it.

Hallo, the postman must have been very late. There were two letters lying on the mat inside the door, and Holden bent to pick them up. The post usually came between nine and a quarter past, so that Sheila would normally find it waiting when she returned from the school run. Change of shift at the post office or something of that kind. The letters were not very interesting. One was an invitation to a display of furniture at amazing new reductions, and the other was the annual report from the golf club, with the usual apology for the need to increase subscriptions for the coming year. Holden dropped both envelopes on the hall table, and went upstairs, placing his suitcase on the bed. Unlocking it, he pushed back the lid, and lifted out the thick shoes, then put them on the floor of his own wardrobe. The soiled shirt was deposited in the laundry basket in the bathroom, and his pyjamas tossed onto the bed. The woollen gloves he left, as always, stuffed in the pockets of the jeans, which, in turn, remained in the suitcase along with the sweater, and the sleeping tablets. After a final check, he locked the case carefully and placed it on top of the wardrobe until the following week.

Originally, Holden had assumed that his property was sacrosanct, and that no one would dream of interfering with it. He learned differently one evening when he arrived home from the office, to find that his son Graham was missing.

'Where's Graham?' he queried. 'At a party or something?'

Sheila shook her head.

'No, he's staying away tonight with that Cooper boy. Don't you remember, I told you about it the other day.'

'Oh, did you? No, I'd forgotten. What's the big attraction there, then?'

'Nothing special,' she shrugged. 'Seems to be some new phase, staying in other people's houses. It's our turn next week. I think we might get two at once. Patty says she doesn't see why Graham should have a friend staying the night if she can't have one of her friends.'

'Well, why not?' he said testily. 'If we really put ourselves out, we could probably take six or seven. Start our own camp, if you like.'

Sheila grinned.

'Don't be such a grump,' she chided, 'It's only one night, and we probably won't see them half the time. They'll be busy upstairs doing secret things. Hope you don't mind, dear, had to borrow your case for Graham. It's the only small one we have.'

For a moment he scarcely believed her.

'You — did — what? What do you mean by it? Supposing I wanted to go away tonight?'

She was obviously taken aback by his reaction.

'But you're not going away tonight,' she pointed out reasonably. 'And it's only a case. Why all the fuss?'

Holden's mind was racing, as he tried to recall what exactly had been inside the case on his last return.

'And what about my stuff?' he

demanded. 'Just chucked on the floor, I suppose?'

Sheila was not only surprised now, but rather hurt.

'Nothing of the kind,' she snapped. 'I put it in your wardrobe, and I was very careful with it. As careful as you can be with a miserable jersey and a pair of jeans. Really, all this fuss.'

Jersey and jeans, was that all it was? He couldn't remember, and cursed himself for being so trusting. Well, he wouldn't make that mistake again.

'I might have had papers in there. Confidential papers about the job,' he insisted. 'Really, if I can't trust my own family — '

'Oh come on, Ash, you're making a terrible fuss over nothing. After all, the wretched case only sits up on top of the wardrobe all the week, doing nothing. And there weren't any papers, anyway.'

'That's not the point,' he grumbled. 'My stuff is my stuff, and it is not to be chucked all over the house just because Graham takes it into his head to go off camping.'

'All right,' she capitulated. 'I'll buy another case. Today. Will that satisfy you?'

'It's a ridiculous situation to be in, anyway. We ought to have known this sort of thing would crop up sooner or later.'

'All right, all right, I'll get one today. Anyway, you're only cross because I found out your secret.'

The words seared into his ears like red-hot needles.

'Secret?' was all he could manage.

'The clothes,' she explained. 'One doesn't have to be Sherlock Holmes to work out that little lot. Now I know what you get up to when you're off on these jaunts of yours. You're jogging aren't you? Why on earth didn't you tell me?'

Jogging. His secret. Yes, that was it. Shame and fear and relief struggled mightily inside him for supremacy, but all that Sheila saw was confusion, which she misinterpreted.

'Caught you, didn't I?' she chuckled. 'Poor old love, what a shame. And here's me imagining you in all kinds of swanky gambling casinos, and dashing about with a lot of sophisticated women, when all the time you've been trotting round the country lanes, trying to keep your manly figure. Come on, why didn't you tell me?'

'I thought you'd laugh,' he confessed. 'Besides, I didn't know whether I'd be able to stick to it, and if I failed, I didn't want you to know.'

She eyed him impishly.

'It's more than that though, isn't it? You didn't want me nagging on about heart failure and so forth. Well, don't worry. I think it's lovely. But you won't overdo it, will you?'

Then, as she realised she'd started automatically to nag, she burst into laughter, in which he thankfully joined. It had been a narrow squeak, and one he would never risk again. Always careful with his suitcase and its contents, he now gave it first priority on reaching home. There had been occasions in the past when he had actually left his packing until he'd had a meal, or a bath. That must not happen again.

A final check round, and he looked at his watch. There was ample time for a sandwich and a cup of coffee before he reported to the office. He went down to the kitchen and inspected the contents of the refrigerator. The menu seemed to consist of a choice between pâté and cheese. Lifting out the pâté, he went to the breadbin and cut two thick slices, which he popped into the electric toaster. Then he switched on the kettle, and spooned some instant coffee into a mug. In the hall, the telephone began to ring.

Holden hesitated. The caller could scarcely be wanting him, at this hour of the day, and he didn't feel like gossiping with one of Sheila's friends. Still, there was always the chance that the office might be needing him urgently. Setting a plate by the toaster, he went into the hall and picked up the green leather receiver.

'Hallo?'

'Adam, is that you?'

A woman's voice, sounding surprised.

'Yes. Who is this?'

'Joy Hayward,' was the reply. 'Is Sheila not well?'

Joy Hayward. Yes. Bruce's wife. Pretty little thing with dark hair. Holden had met her a couple of times at other

126

people's houses, and knew she was one of Sheila's 'gang', as he called the young mothers' coffee brigade.

'Oh hallo, Joy. She's fine as far as I know. Not here at the moment. Matter of fact, I thought she was probably with your lot.'

'My lot?' and her voice was now puzzled.

'Sorry,' he apologised, 'clumsy expression. What I mean is, I thought she was probably out at one of your coffee sessions. Obviously not.'

She laughed.

'Our lot, indeed. A fine way to describe us. No, she's not with us, and that's why I called. She was to have come, but she telephoned to say she wasn't very well, and would probably stop in bed for an hour or two. I thought I'd phone, in case she wanted me to pick up the children from school.'

'Oh, I see.' Blast. Now he'd get himself involved in some female administrative network, a matter to be avoided at all times. 'Well, Joy, I think she must have got over it, because she's taken the car.

Probably doing some shopping, then going on to collect the kids. I've been away, and I only popped in to change, so I can't be more helpful, I'm afraid.'

'Never mind, she's obviously better than I thought. If she's out driving, she'll certainly go to the school. Well, I'd better get back to my lot.'

Holden grinned at the implied rebuke.

'And I'd better get off to work,' he rejoined. 'Thank you for the offer. Sheila will appreciate it.'

They each said goodbye, and hoped to see each other soon, and the usual meaningless exchanges. Holden went into the kitchen, in time to rescue his toast.

At the other end, Joy Hayward stood in the bedroom, still holding the disconnected telephone, the dialling tone buzzing insistently from the earpiece.

Sheila Holden had made it quite clear that she had the most splitting headache, and would be unable to join the others for their usual sherry and lunch session. That had been less than two hours previously, and Sheila was not one to cry off lightly. Indeed, she was one of the leading lights of their little circle. She and Joy, and two of the other young mothers, were sometimes referred to as the Gang of Four, and none of them would dream of missing a gathering without some very sound reason. A splitting headache was such a reason, but it seemed to have cleared. If it had, then Sheila's normal reaction would have been to get to Joy's house as fast as she could, complaining about the sherry she had missed. Since she had not arrived, it was obvious that there was something else which had priority on her attention.

But what?

A voice called enquiringly up the stairs. She shook her head, and put down the buzzing receiver.

'Coming,' she called.

★   ★   ★

Holden walked into his office at five minutes past two. Miss Bunting, the severe middle-aged woman who acted as his secretary, confidante, and fort-holder, looked up from her desk.

'Good afternoon, Mr. Holden. How was Midchester?'

'Hallo Bunty. Oh, about the same. Not much we can do to rush things in a sleepy place like that. What's been going on?'

'I'd better come through,' she replied rising.

Holden's office was small, but he was grateful to have it. So many people had been swept into these terrible open-plan arrangements, and he had been fortunate so far to escape. His plea was that he had to be able to hold very confidential conversations with clients, on the one hand, and also be free to castigate their people in the field when necessary, without being overheard by a lot of junior staff. The people in establishment hadn't liked it, but he had contrived to get his own way, much to the envy of many of his colleagues, who had been less persuasive.

Now, he sat down, looking at the papers neatly arranged for his inspection. He didn't bother to start work, being more interested to hear Miss Bunting's report first. There was clearly something of importance to be heard, as he knew from the special glitter which came into her eyes on such occasions. Sitting primly in the vacant chair opposite him, she waited for her opening.

'Bunting, it's quite obvious that World War Three is about to start, and you're the only one who knows about it,' he said, smiling. 'What's the big secret?'

'Well,' and she turned instinctively to ensure that the door was closed, despite the fact that she herself had made sure it was, less than ten seconds previously, 'it's Mr. Michaels.'

George Michaels was the head of the department, which made him Holden's immediate boss, and also required him to attend Board meetings in a non-voting capacity. Anything involving Michaels was a matter of keen interest to Holden and his three equal-status colleagues.

'Come on Bunty, let's have it.'

'Well,' she hedged, spinning it out as long as she dared, 'mind you, it's only a rumour, and I wouldn't want you to think — '

'All right,' he held up his hands. 'It's only a rumour, and I promise not to think. Now then, what is this rumour I mustn't think about?'

'He's leaving.'

She had been planning this announcement all morning, rehearsing various ways of imparting this vital piece of information. Finally, she had decided on the simplest statement, and, looking at Holden's face, she knew her decision was vindicated.

'Leaving?' he echoed, almost not believing the words.

'He's going to Nicholls and Ware, so I hear. As a director.'

Nicholls and Ware were their leading competitors. For someone in a position like Michaels even to contemplate moving over was in very much the same category as a Government official defecting behind the Iron Curtain. It was unthinkable. Anyway, she'd said it was only a rumour. There was probably nothing to it. People like Michaels didn't just —

'Where did this rumour come from?' he asked, and there was a new coldness in his tone.

Miss Bunting knew the signs, and how

to deal with them. She had a great regard for Adam Holden, both personally and because of his value to the company. She was not the woman to come to him with information which did not have some secure foundation in fact.

'There was some kind of row in the Chairman's office yesterday morning,' she began carefully. 'Mr. Michaels was in there with him alone, and, when the coffee went in, they both stopped talking together, and just stared out of the window until the door was shut.'

'That could have been business,' objected Holden. 'People often drop the subject when there's an interruption.'

'No,' she rejected. 'It wasn't that kind of silence. One gets to know. People don't as a rule stop talking altogether, because it's too pointed. What they do is to change the subject. Talk about golf, or where they're going on their holidays, something safe. Besides, that's not all.'

Holden found himself becoming irritable with the woman, and yet he knew he was being unreasonable. She hadn't had an item this juicy in years, and she was determined to extract every last drop from it. Could scarcely blame her for that.

'Well?' he asked, with considerable control.

'Beth Hotchkiss said Mr. Michaels hardly spoke to her when he got back to his own office. He shut the door, refused to see anyone, or take any calls. After half an hour, he came out and said he was a bit under the weather, and he was going home.'

That wasn't hard to understand, reflected Holden. A man who'd had some kind of row with the Chairman would certainly be feeling a bit under the weather. The Chairman, when crossed, was not a man to mince his words. There had to be something else, and he was damned if he was going to keep on prompting Miss Bunting. He simply sat and waited. Seeing that he was not intending to comment, she continued.

'Miss Hotchkiss went into his room to tidy up. She always does that, as a matter of course. There were two things missing. Mr. Michaels kept a Council of Design

Award on his wall. That was gone, for one thing. The other was that photograph of his children, which he always keeps on his desk.'

H'm, reflected Holden. It certainly began to sound quite serious. A man only removes very personal items like that if he thinks he's not likely to come back.

'I don't see where Nicholls and Ware come in,' he objected.

This was her last vital link in the chain, and she released it with evident reluctance.

'Well, Beth thought she ought to check his appointments diary — ' and the fact that Miss Hotchkiss had now become Beth did not escape Holden's attention — 'because it might be necessary to cancel some appointment or other. She found he had ordered a table for one o'clock at the Hilton, with the name Brooker beside it. So she called the restaurant, because it was getting on for one, then, and the head waiter thought it was some kind of hoax. Mr. Michaels was already there, in the bar with his guest, and would the lady please explain what she meant? He asked if she wanted to speak to Mr. Michaels, but she said no thank you, and put the phone down. So you see, despite his bad temper, and regardless of the fact that he said he wasn't well, he still went to keep his appointment for lunch, and Mr. Brooker is — '

' — Chief Sales Executive of Nicholls and Ware,' finished Holden. 'Yes, thank you. I know Mr. Brooker.'

It all fitted together, he had to admit. An outsider might put a dozen different interpretations on the recent events, but Miss Bunting was not an outsider and neither was Miss Hotchkiss. They had been steeped in the company's affairs for many years, and they were both highly responsible people, whose judgment in matters of this kind had to be given the closest possible regard. They were not a couple of youngsters in their first jobs, anxious to partake of office tittle-tattle. Indeed, he was mildly surprised that Miss Bunting had told him about it. She would not, in the ordinary way, bring him gossip, even well-founded gossip. Still, the fact remained that she had, and there was no doubt of its importance. If George Michaels had really gone, or was about to go, then the question of his replacement would be the next item on the agenda. There were really only four possible candidates inside the organisation, and he was one of them, no doubt of that. In fact, there was little doubt that he would be the most likely successor of the four, if past performance and personalities were to be the key factors.

'Mr. Holden?'

'M'm? Oh sorry, I was thinking about what you said. It's all very interesting Bunty, and we'll have to wait to find out the truth of it. Meantime, I strongly suggest — '

'Good Heavens, Mr. Holden, what must you think of me? You surely don't for a moment imagine I would repeat a word of this outside this room, do you?'

'No, no,' he soothed, 'of course not. Naturally not. Never entered my head, I assure you. I think we've known one another long enough, don't you?'

She nodded, evidently troubled about something.

'But there's something else, isn't there?' he probed. 'You haven't quite finished yet, I think.'

Miss Bunting had spent a sleepless night following the events of the previous day. Although she was not a demonstrative person, the six years she had spent as assistant to Adam Holden had been the best of her working life. She liked order and permanence, a settled way of things, and now it seemed in her judgment that there was every possibility of a drastic change. Her boss was the clear leader in any race to succeed George Michaels, and that would mean that he would move into Mr. Michaels' office, leaving her behind. It would be unthinkable that he would get rid of Beth Hotchkiss, just in order to make Ellen Bunting's life more comfortable. He wasn't that kind of man, and she wouldn't respect him even if he contemplated such an action, because Beth was also a good and loyal servant of the company, who had every right to expect to maintain her present role. Still, it was evident that Mr. Holden expected her to say something, so she had better try.

'I've — I've been thinking ahead, Mr. Holden. I know I shouldn't, and I know things have a habit of turning out quite differently from the way we thought, but I can't help it. What I see happening is your being offered Mr. Michaels' post, and me having to stay here with some new person.'

My word, thought Holden, the way these women go leaping ahead. She had it all worked out, as though he would be moving offices the following morning and she would be left high and dry.

'My, my,' he smiled. 'You really are thinking ahead. And as you say, things have a way of developing under their own steam. It's very early days for you to be even thinking about such things, let alone planning for them. I suggest we both put the subject from our minds for now. Nothing might happen for months, and I daresay the company will expect us to keep busy meantime. It is by no means a foregone conclusion that I shall be appointed in Mr. Michaels' place, indeed there is no guarantee the job will even be filled. Don't forget what happened in Shipping last year, when the number two died suddenly. Instead of replacing him, they simply parcelled out his duties among those four other chaps, and achieved an overall staff reduction. Anything can happen, and we'll simply have to wait. First thing, please, is to get my notes typed up from the Midchester visit.'

He held out the handwritten sheets, and she took them.

'Same as usual?'

'Of course. Why do you ask?'

'Well, you normally send the second copy to Mr. Michaels, but if there's not going to be anyone there to read it — '

'Come on, Bunty. Think now. This is not a question of people, it's a question of procedures. The procedure is for a copy to be sent to the head of the department, and we must follow it. Whether there's anyone to receive it or not, is not my concern. The report gets delivered as usual.'

'Yes, of course. I'll deal with this first.

Then I'll come back, if I may, and we can get down to the other things which have come in.'

'Right. Off you go. I'll start on this lot, get some priorities sorted out.'

But when the door closed behind her, he did not give his attention to the papers and files in front of him. He could have a serious problem on his hands in the next few days, if there was any question of his being offered George Michaels' post. The head of department seldom went out on provincial trips for one thing. Possibly every couple of months he might make what was in effect a state visit to one of the larger regions. These were tightly scheduled affairs, and the evenings were always in the shape of a dinner for the visiting dignitary, given by the half dozen most senior company people in the locality. There would be no opportunity for one of his 'jogging' expeditions, and the excitement that went with them. That was one objection, and a serious one.

Then, there was the question of money. He wasn't exactly certain of Michaels' salary, but it was not so much higher than his own, probably two and a half to three thousand. On that he would pay tax at forty per cent, which, even on three thousand, would leave him only eighteen hundred in pocket. On top of that he would be required to contribute the obligatory seven and a half per cent to the pension fund on the full amount. Seven and a half per cent of three thousand was, and here he picked up a pencil to do the sum, yes, two hundred and twenty five. Take that away from eighteen hundred and he would be better off finally to the tune of fifteen hundred and seventy five pounds.

His nocturnal exploits earned him an average of three hundred pounds, and, at twenty five jobs per annum, he was collecting seven and a half thousand pounds, all in cash, all tax free.

Financially, the upward move into Michaels' office would be a disaster, and there was no other way to look at it. It would cost him, in cash, about six thousand pounds per annum, and it would also cut out the wonderful excitement of that dark area of his life.

On top of all that, he would be required to carry greater responsibility. It was an appalling prospect.

The point was, how could he turn down the job, without antagonising the top brass, or possibly even making them suspicious of his motives. He was known to be something of a go-getter, a man who grabbed at his chances, and it would be totally out of character for him to do anything other than to accept such an offer gladly. It was going to be a serious dilemma, and one that he wished he could avoid. The only bright thought was the one he'd mentioned to Ellen Bunting. There could be some kind of internal reorganisation, the end product of which would be to leave his job very much as it was, with an extra couple of tasks which he was sure he could cope with.

The thing to do was to follow his own advice, and put it from his mind. Resolutely, he pulled the incoming mail towards him.

The telephone rang.

'Mr. Holden?'

He thought he knew the rather prissy

voice, but couldn't place it at once.

'Kitt-Walmers, from the Chairman's office.'

Of course. Slimy little chap with greasy hair and a manner to match.

'What can I do for you Mr. Kitt-Walmers?'

He narrowly avoided calling the fellow 'Feet-Warmer' which was the way he was normally referred to.

'The Chairman would be greatly obliged if you could arrange your diary for tomorrow afternoon. He would like a little chat at four o'clock, if you could manage that.'

That's what everybody meant by greasy. 'If you could manage that'. Did he think he was talking to an idiot? If the Chairman wanted him at four o'clock, he had bloody well better be there, and that was all there was to be said. Sudden death or a nuclear war might be accepted as excuses for absence, but even those would cause a question mark to be placed against his name.

'I shall most certainly be there,' he confirmed. 'Did the Chairman happen to

144

mention whether I shall need any papers with me? Will he be wanting some kind of report?'

'Not that I'm aware of Mr. Holden. If you could just present the body, please.'

'Right. Will do.'

He sat looking at the silent telephone for long minutes. Four o'clock tomorrow. Unless he could come up with some waterproof scheme for refusal in the next twenty-four hours, the days of his big deception were numbered.

6

Sheila Holden reached across the sleeping man beside her, and groped for her watch. Twenty past two. That wasn't so bad, she reflected lazily. She needn't leave until ten past three, which would give her ample time to meet the children from school.

It was an incongruous situation. Here she was lying in bed with some man in the middle of the day, and at the same time making certain that her children would be met from school. A strange man? Well, she could hardly call him that, after all these months. He was far from strange to her now. Sometimes, when she was alone, she would think back to their first meeting. It had been ordinary enough.

April had been deceitful that year. A few days after Easter, the sun had broken through the clouds and heavy rain of the previous week. Suddenly, it was false summer. Gardens and parks sprang into early life, and all the forecasters were happily predicting that this would be the longest and hottest summer for fifty years. People cast off their heavy clothes gladly, and welcomed the unexpected bonus. At weekends the roads were jammed with determined early revellers, and the catering trades prepared for record business. The doom and gloom brigade were also well to the fore. According to reliable sources, water would be severely rationed by mid-July. The visiting West Indies Test cricketers would be unstoppable on the hard fast pitches they would encounter. Crops would ripen too early, and there would be a shortage of fresh vegetables by the autumn.

None of these predictions was in Sheila Holden's mind when she drove over to Joy Hayward's house for coffee at eleven o'clock on a warm sunny morning. They still referred to their sessions as 'coffee' although the format had changed dramatically since the early days. A certain spirit of competition had crept in among the young mothers. What had begun as simple coffee and biscuits had somehow developed. The breakthrough had occurred one day when, at twelve o'clock, the hostess on that particular occasion had said:-

'Look, I don't want to break this up, but the fact is I usually have a glass of sherry at about this time. Won't some of you join me?'

Some of them had, and that had marked the beginning. Sherry became a regular institution, and before long someone else had invited them to stay for a makeshift lunch, which was an hilarious success. Makeshift lunches became elaborate three-course affairs, with the hostess-of-the-day trying to outdo the others in her choice of dishes. There were never less than six young women present, often as many as eight or nine. Wine appeared with the food as a matter of course, and one lady had even produced liqueurs with the coffee at the end, but it was generally agreed this was not a good move. One of the group had been quite incapable of driving at the close of that particular session, and had had to be put to bed, while others saw to her children. It was the general view that the liqueurs were responsible, and so they were dropped by mutual consent.

The sherry, and the table wines, continued, and Sheila was looking forward to the 'coffee' party as she walked up the drive to Joy's house. With the early advent of summer, she had put on a halter-necked sun-dress which left her arms, shoulders and back open to the welcome rays. Sheila was a summer girl really, who tended to flower rather in the way of the garden plants when the sun was shining, retreating into drab colours and unrevealing apparel each winter. She was thirty-two, and, despite her two children, had the figure and carriage of a girl ten years younger. Her face was too pointed in its outlines to be described as pretty. She had high cheekbones, a straight nose, and there was a strong line to her lean jaw. Her skin was almost olive-coloured, setting off the dark green of her eyes and the shining jet-black hair. No, it would not be correct to describe her as pretty, but, on her day, particularly when the sun was high, there were plenty of people who considered her beautiful.

She was the first to arrive, and Joy was waiting for her at the door, having seen her car pull up.

'You can go home as soon as you like,' was her greeting. 'You're not coming into my house looking like that. You'll make us all look like a bunch of old frumps.'

Sheila laughed, pleased.

'I've had this old thing three years, and you know it perfectly well. And look at you. Not exactly Frump-of-the-Year are you? That's a new dress, and don't tell me it isn't.'

Of them all, Joy Hayward was the one who seemed to have the most money to spend on herself. And, Sheila admitted, she certainly spent it wisely. The flowered sun-dress Joy was wearing was exactly like one that had been featured in the Sunday Times Colour Magazine a week or two earlier. She even remembered the price, which left little by way of change out of a hundred pounds.

They went inside, Joy leaving the door

open for the next arrival, and, as always, Sheila was struck by the opulence of the large living room. Joy's husband, Bruce, was something vaguely to do with television, but not in front of the cameras. He worked in the background some-where, on what Joy referred to as the 'business and financial' side of things. Whatever it was, it seemed to pay him well enough. There were always new cars in the garage, and Joy herself was a walking advertisement. Now, reclining in a deep armchair, Sheila watched the sun striking brilliant colours from the crystal sherry glass. This was undoubtedly the life, she decided. For the next three hours at least, there would be no children, no husband, and no work. She would probably give Joy a hand with the serving when the time came, but that didn't classify as work. More a labour of love.

'First today,' announced Joy raising her glass.

'Cheers,' responded Sheila, raising her own, and sipping at the amber liquid. That was another thing about going to Joy's house. Most of them produced sherry, and it was the same for everyone. Joy had three choices, and always remembered that Sheila preferred the dry. As she peered over the rim of her glass, she wondered whether it really was the first today for her friend and hostess. There had been a glitter in Joy's eyes when she first greeted her, and an air of relaxed excitement about her. Perhaps there was some new development to be learned about.

'How's Bruce?' she asked casually.

Bruce Hayward was something of a mystery man in the community, because very few people had actually met him. His work took him away for days at a time, occasionally weeks, and, on his visits home, he stayed inside the house mostly, and had been known to spend all day in bed. With such an unpredictable work programme, it was clearly difficult for the Haywards to be able to forecast their commitments, and so it was a rare occasion indeed when they attended a function together. Sheila had met him only once, a tall rather aloof man, with an abstracted air which suggested his mind was busily occupied with matters else-where. She had been trying for about five minutes to find a subject which would provoke some kind of response from him, other than that of polite inattention, when suddenly he cut across whatever it was she was saying.

'You have the most amazing shoulders. Breathtaking. Have you ever thought of doing anything with them?'

It was so totally unexpected that Sheila was at a momentary loss for words. Then she made a weak response.

'Shoulders? What do you mean? What can one do with shoulders?'

'Model them, naturally,' was the curt reply. 'There are plenty of girls earning a good living from it, whose shoulders are simply not in your class.'

Sheila was non-plussed. What was the man talking about? She'd never seen an advertisement for shoulders. Eyes, hands, whole bodies, yes. But what would anyone want with just shoulders?

'I've never seen anything concentrating on shoulders,' she rejoined, beginning to feel rather foolish.

'Of course you have. It's just that you're not aware of it. When you see a girl getting out of a bath, or washing her hair, the camera spends a lot of time on shoulders.'

'Ah yes,' she agreed, 'but then, the girl in the advertisement has been given the job because of her whole body, or a beautiful face. The shoulders are an afterthought.'

He gave her an odd look, as though to make certain she wasn't pulling his leg, then decided she wasn't.

'My dear lady, Sheila isn't it — ?'

' — Yes — '

'My dear Sheila then, you don't know much about the advertising business, especially television commercials. What you call 'the girl' is frequently two different girls, and I have known as many as five used for just one ad.'

Sheila was now intrigued. Bruce Hayward was actually talking to her about what went on behind the scenes, and she was as fascinated as most people to hear more.

'Please tell me more,' she urged.

He smiled for the first time, and it made a great difference to his otherwise taciturn features.

'Very well,' he conceded. 'Let's take a typical case of a girl getting out of a shower. They're trying to sell you some body rub, or talcum powder. What's the first thing you see?'

'Her head?' ventured the listener.

'Yes. Either the head, or her feet stepping out. Can't just have a picture of an entirely naked women in front of the kiddi-winks. So you get a bit of her, close up, or rather one part of her. Then you see a hand reaching for a towel. It's always a good, finely shaped hand, and the chances of it belonging to the same girl whose face you've seen are pretty slim. The hand belongs to someone else. Then they show you the spray, or the bottle of oil, or whatever it is. The last shot is probably the girl arriving to meet some young ponce in a white dinner jacket, and often you only see her back as she walks towards him in a backless dress. The back is flawless, and the idea is that all the women will rush out and buy the product. Seems to work, too, from what they tell me.'

Sheila was sceptical. Unable to decide whether he was joking or not, she made a mental resolve to study the commercials more closely in future, to check whether what he was suggesting was possible.

'It always seems like the same girl,' she objected.

'It's supposed to,' he retorted. 'If anyone spots the substitutions, somebody is going to get fired. You could do it.'

The direct return to the matter of her own shoulders left Sheila feeling some-what flustered. She was wearing a strapless evening gown, which left her shoulders and most of her back open to inspection, but to have this near-stranger making such pointed observations made her faintly uncomfortable. They became separated shortly afterwards, and he made no attempt to seek her out and renew the subject. Sheila was uncertain as to whether she was relieved or faintly annoyed. When she got home that night, she inspected herself carefully in the full-length mirror. She'd never really thought much about her back, concentrating on face, hair and hands, with occasional disparaging examinations of her figure. No, she wasn't perfect, not by any means. But there might be something in what he'd been saying about her shoulders. They really were rather nice. Smooth and well-proportioned.

'Are you going to be much longer?' demanded a sleepy Adam.

That had put paid to the shoulder episode, but Sheila made up her mind that, the next time she encountered Bruce Hayward, she was going to raise the subject again. After all, if he was serious, there might be some good money to be earned, and it would be a new excitement in any event. It had been weeks ago, and Bruce was as elusive as ever. Now, here she was once again, in Joy's house, and her enquiry about him would not be taken for anything other than polite conversation.

'Oh he's fine,' said Joy carelessly. 'At least, he always seems that way whenever I see him, which isn't often.'

'Poor old love,' she commiserated.

'Where is he now, in the States or somewhere?'

'Got back yesterday from Hong Kong. Been asleep ever since. More than ten hours already. Still, I shouldn't complain. He brought me some lovely silk. I'll show you later. Ah, doorbell.'

The others began to arrive, and soon they were all chattering freely, and the wine flowed, just that little faster at Joy's than at other people's get-togethers. Later, in the kitchen, Sheila was helping with coffee, when she realised Joy was far from well.

'Look, are you all right?'

Joy leaned against the breakfast bar, rather pale.

'Not really,' she admitted. 'It's the heat in there, I think. Do you think you could manage here, if I go and take a quick shower?'

'Yes, of course. Shall I come with you?'

'No, no. Be all right.'

Sheila watched, as Joy Hayward weaved her way out of the room. There was something more than the atmosphere affecting her, she decided, and it had a lot to do with the gleaming array of bottles in the other room. Sheila was herself conscious that she'd drunk more than she ought, and would have to be careful with the car. It was half an hour later when someone asked what was keeping Joy.

'She was feeling a bit faint,' explained Sheila, 'I'll go up and check on her in a minute.'

There were a few caustic remarks about the wine-flow, and, soon after that, people began to drift away. Eventually, Sheila was alone downstairs, and she decided to go and make certain her friend was comfortable before she left. That red wine had really been very much more full of body than the usual supermarket plonk, and Sheila knew she ought to have stopped sooner. Well, too late to worry about that now. Got to see about Joy.

She found her in the bathroom, stretched out on the carpeted floor, and dead to the world. Try as she might, she could not rouse her from the drugged stupor into which she had fallen, and she knew she hadn't the physical strength to carry the unconscious woman. She was kneeling beside her when a man's voice sounded from the doorway.

'Oh Lord, not again.'

Looking up, she saw Bruce Hayward standing there, naked to the waist, and wearing only pyjama trousers. Sheila hadn't realised before how broad-shouldered he was. Odd that. It struck her suddenly that shoulders seemed to be their main topic of communication, and she giggled.

'Glad you think it's funny,' he grunted.

'Oh, it's not that,' she assured him hastily. 'I was just thinking that you and I aways seem to be on about shoulders, and now here you are — er — well, here you are. You probably don't remember what I'm talking about.'

He looked at her more closely now.

'Yes, of course I do. You're the girl with the shoulders, I remember very well. Did you ever do anything with them?'

Sheila got up from her kneeling position.

'Don't you think we ought to do something about Joy before we start on other subjects? We can't just leave her here.'

'I'm tempted to, sometimes,' he said sourly, 'but I suppose you're right. Would you mind opening that second door along? That's where I normally dump her.'

Sheila went to the indicated door and went inside. It was obviously a spare room, sparsely furnished, and with a single divan against the wall. What did Bruce mean when he said that was where he usually dumped her? Was Joy always passing out like this, and, if she was, oughtn't somebody to be doing something about it? Her thoughts were interrupted by his arrival in the room, carrying the unconscious Joy in his arms. He laid her on the bed, none too ceremoniously, and stood looking down.

'Welcome home,' he muttered, as if to himself.

She pretended not to hear.

'Will she be all right?' she asked.

Bruce turned then, and looked her full in the face.

'All right?' he repeated. 'Oh yes. She'll be all right. Till the next time. This is how she was when I arrived home in the small hours. With one thing and another, it took me over thirty hours to get here, and this is what I find.'

He seemed to find nothing unusual in the fact that he was standing there with almost no clothes on. The odd thing was that Sheila felt none of the embarrassment she would normally have experienced under such circumstances. After all, as she reminded herself, her own body was scarcely more covered.

'What time do the kids get out of school?' he asked.

'Oh, not until half past three,' she assured him. 'Don't worry about that. I'll collect yours when I get mine. There's over an hour yet.'

'Thanks. That'll be a help. Well, I'd better have a wash or something, I suppose. Will you do something for me?'

'Yes. Yes, of course.'

'Would you mind getting me a drink? There's a rather good brandy down there somewhere. You look like a girl who can tell one from another.'

She found herself going downstairs without question, and making for the drinks cabinet. Brandy was just brandy to her, but she had accepted the implied compliment that she would know the good from the inferior, and now she was stuck with it. Without much difficulty she isolated two bottles and stood staring at them uncertainly. Well, she decided, the only way to select one was to reject the other, and the only way to do that was to take a small nip of each. The one she liked best would be the one Bruce Hayward would get, and if she got it wrong, well, that would be just bad luck. Finding a small glass she poured out a teaspoonful from the first bottle, and drank it. For a moment she thought her mouth must be on fire, then the back of her throat burned, and finally it seared its way down to her stomach. With tear-filled eyes, she looked around for some water, but the nearest thing was a half empty bottle of Chablis, and she reached gratefully for it to get rid of the fiery sensation. Then she stood for a moment, fanning at her mouth with one hand, and wondering what to expect from bottle number two. Gingerly, she tipped out her second sample, closed her eyes and put the glass to her lips. For a moment she wondered whether the label had been wrong, and then a warm mellowness came into her mouth as the smooth spirit took its effect. She looked gratefully at the bottle, and there was no doubt about her choice. Finding a clean glass, she poured out a generous measure for Bruce. Then, before taking it to him, she decided to treat herself to a little more. It must be the right stuff, she decided, making a note of the name for future reference.

When she got back upstairs, he was drying his face with a large soft towel. He took the glass from her, and sniffed at it, then sipped it.

'Oh good girl,' he approved. 'I somehow knew you'd get it right.'

It came as a mild surprise to realise how important it had become to her that she should not make a mistake. And, of course, she hadn't. It really was a most pleasant drink, and its warmth was spreading inside her, making her languorous after all the wine. It seemed the most natural thing in the world that he should take her by the hand and lead her into the bedroom.

'We — we mustn't forget about the children,' she found herself saying half-heartedly.

'We won't, but there's a whole hour yet.'

That had been months ago, and there had been many meetings since then. Sheila was certain in her own mind that they were hell-bent for disaster, but she seemed unable to do anything about it. No, she corrected herself in her more honest moments, it wasn't that she was unable to do anything about it. She didn't want to, and that was the truth of it. Bruce Hayward fell far short of the image of the fantasy lover she had conjured up in her imagination over the years. Strong, but not handsome, he was frequently off-hand and inconsiderate, yet he aroused a passion in her that she had thought long dead.

So far as her relationship with Joy was concerned, she felt no deep guilt. Joy did little to retain her hold on her husband. She was far too preoccupied with her own life, and in particular with her drinking, to provide a background which was deeper than decoration. Her own position with Adam was not dissimilar. He seemed to live primarily for his work, and his absences from home were marked by two days of tension beforehand, with feverish activity upstairs in his room. It was her private conviction that the job was too much for him, since his whole reputation seemed to be under threat with every trip out to the regional offices. His return home was little better, since he appeared to be drained of energy, and usually went early to bed. It worked out that four days of each week were lost to the marriage, with Adam really only available to the family at weekends.

She had never planned to deceive him, never set out to find someone who would give more meaning to her existence. It had simply happened, and no amount of post-analysis was going to avail. The odd thing was, she no longer felt particularly guilty about it. Adam wanted for nothing, the house was always tidy, the children well-cared for. She had no intention of doing anything foolish, anything that would bring disgrace to them all. She and Bruce had become scrupulously careful lately about their assignations, and it was now understood that these were subject to last-minute cancellation if there was any hint of risk involved. They had not been quite so methodical when it all began.

Another look at her watch told her she had been daydreaming for over ten minutes. That still left forty minutes before she had to go. If she allowed ten minutes for getting dressed, there was a full half an hour remaining.

Turning to the sleeping Bruce, she began gently to arouse him.

'M'm? M'm?' he muttered.

'I must go,' she murmured in his ear, 'time to get up.'

That was usually sufficient to have him prevent her, in his own special way.

This time was no exception.

7

Like many insurance men in the field, Alun Griffiths operated from home. What had once been a spare bedroom, with his papers pushed into one corner, had developed gradually into a properly equipped office, complete with answering machine and copier. With the children now grown up and left home he had no longer any need to feel guilty about using the living accommodation. There was even a woman who came in part-time on two days each week, to help him control the volume of paper.

On this particular Friday he had returned home for a quick bite of lunch, and to see if anything of importance had come in during the morning. The message that intrigued him most was a message to call a Detective Sergeant Gardener at County Police Headquarters. The only business he had had during the previous few days which involved the police, had been the robbery at old Thomas's little shop, and he'd already talked to Inspector Dalton about that. It was hardly important enough to claim the attention of County H.Q. He dialled the number at once, asking for extension 230. The man at the other end simply said,

'Gardener.'

'Detective Sergeant Gardener? My name is Griffiths, Alun Griffiths. I had a message left on my answering service to call you back. What can I do for you?'

Frank Gardener frowned. There was another officer using the spare desk in his office, and he didn't want any publicity about what might turn out to be a wild goose-chase.

'Very good of you to call back so quickly, Mr. Griffiths. I wondered whether we might meet for a few minutes' chat. Look, it's almost my lunch hour. Is there a pub near you where we could have a little chat? Promise you it won't take very long.'

Mr. Griffiths hesitated. He wasn't a great one for visiting public houses at any time, and certainly never in the middle of the day.

'Well,' he hedged, 'I don't know. Could you give me some idea of what it's about?'

'Not really, not over the telephone. It's a bit confidential.'

Confidential, was it? And from the County Headquarters, no less. Well, a man could scarcely refuse to co-operate with people at that level. Besides, Mr. Griffiths was finding himself vastly intrigued.

'In that case, do you know the Bull? It's in Roman Road, near Woolworth's.'

'Yes. I could be there at — let's see — ten to one. Would that suit you? Saloon Bar.'

'How will I know you?' came back the query.

'Good point. I'll be carrying a brown brief case. Oh, and I'm wearing a dark grey suit. Ten to one?'

'Yes, yes, I can manage that. I shall be there.'

As they put down their telephones, each man was wondering about the other.

At just after twelve forty five, Frank Gardener parked his car in the concrete square behind the Bull Hotel, locked it carefully, and made his way round to the entrance to the saloon bar. Evidently Mr. Griffiths was not a regular patron of the Bull on Friday lunch times. He could scarcely have selected a place less suitable for a quiet and private conversation. The bar was jammed with young people from the nearby offices and shops, crowding ten to a table, and making sporadic raids on the snacks counter. Gardener paused in the doorway, taking in the scene. Once he advanced into that mob, he realised, he would become a part of it. Short of actually waving his briefcase in the air, he couldn't see what chance there was of his making contact with Alun Griffiths.

'Excuse me.'

Turning, he found a shortish square man looking at him expectantly.

'My name is Griffiths,' announced the newcomer. 'Are you by any chance a Mr. Gardener?'

'Yes. Frank Gardener. How d'ye do?'

Gardener stuck out his hand and

Griffiths shook it, at the same time looking disparagingly over his shoulder.

'I'm afraid I didn't realise it was going to be like this,' he apologised. 'Not much of a pub-goer, you see. Do you think there might be somewhere a little quieter?'

The policeman didn't really know too much about the pubs in the centre of the town, but they couldn't all be this bad.

'I don't know, to tell you the truth,' he admitted. 'But I think we ought to go and try, don't you? Could scarcely do worse, could we?'

They went outside, and looked at the busy shopping centre.

'Let's try one of the side roads,' suggested Gardener.

Walking away from the crowds, they came across a small pub which had no car-park. They looked enquiringly at each other, nodded, and went inside. The place was half-empty, and Gardener suggested his guest find a table while he ordered the drinks. Soon, they were seated in a corner, close to a fruit-machine which bore the welcome notice 'Out of Order'.

'You know, Mr. Griffiths, I've seen you somewhere before, and I'm trying to remember where.'

'Oh dear,' replied the other in mock horror. 'That doesn't sound very good does it? Not coming from yourself, like. Not on some list of desperate criminals, I hope? You wouldn't be a musical man, Mr. Gardener?'

Musical? No, reflected Gardener, he wasn't especially musical. Then he realised he was being given a hint, and racked his memory.

'Yes, that's it,' he recalled, with triumph. 'You're the Mr. Griffiths who conducted the Messiah at the Town Hall last Christmas. I remember now. I enjoyed that.'

Alun Griffiths glowed. He had worked very hard to coordinate the various musical groups in the city, and the Messiah had been the successful outcome.

'It seemed to go well, didn't it?' he acknowledged modestly.

'I thought so. I'm from the North, you know, and we judge our Messiahs very harshly up there. Tend to regard them as our own property.'

'Yes, I know. I have travelled up twice in the past. Learned something each time.'

They were friends now, a couple of music lovers on common ground, and they sat in companionable silence for a few moments. It was Gardener who next spoke.

'Mr Griffiths, I'm going to have to ask you to regard this as an unofficial conversation. I haven't told anyone that I intend to speak to you today.'

'Oh. Sounds very mysterious. What's it about?'

Gardener put down his glass, rested his elbows on the table and spoke in low tones.

'I've got a bee in my bonnet, and it won't go away. I was hoping to get you to help me.'

The insurance man was intrigued.

'Naturally, I'm always glad to help the police if I can,' he volunteered. 'But you'll have to give me some idea of what it's about.'

174

'Let's start with the robbery at a shop called Thomas's the other day.'

Griffiths felt disappointment. He'd been into that already with Inspector Dalton, and they had privately agreed there was little to go on.

'I have told Inspector Dalton all I know about that matter,' he said carefully. 'Is there something new?'

Dalton. Frank tried to place the man, and cursed his lack of local knowledge yet again. Yes, he had him. The Park Street Station.

'Not really,' he admitted, 'and I know the inspector has the matter well in hand. No, this is a little private theory of mine, and I'd like to tell you about it. As I told you, I'm from the North, from Liverpool in fact, and I haven't been down here all that long. Now, this little case at Mr. Thomas's, it seems to ring a bell with me. I can't get it out of my mind that we had one very like it about two years ago, up on my old patch. Very like it indeed. The man in the stocking, the gloved hands, elderly shopkeeper late at night. Quick in, quick out, cash only.

Do you see what I mean?'

It certainly sounded very much the same, admitted Griffiths to himself, but he didn't see where he came in. Bit off his route, Liverpool.

'Sounds very like it,' he agreed. 'But how can I help you?'

'With that one, probably not,' was the unexpected reply. 'But let me go on a bit. You see, I have a kind of theory about it. This is only a little job by our standards, and yours too, I fancy. Comes under your Small Claims arrangements, I daresay?'

'That's true, yes. Authority to settle locally, details to Head Office of course, but really it's left up to me to satisfy myself.'

'Quite. As I say, your position is rather like ours. Up to a certain point, local matters are left to the local coppers, otherwise we'd end up with everyone tripping over everyone else. And, like you, details are sent up the line for information, but nobody higher up is expected to do anything except keep records. Do you take my point?'

Griffiths frowned, unable to see where

this was all leading.

'I understand what you're saying, certainly,' he agreed. 'But I'm afraid I don't see yet what you are driving at, Mr. Gardener.'

Gardener sipped at his bitter. This could be an important moment for him, and he was anxious not to lose the listener's support.

'I have this feeling,' he began, 'that these two jobs were carried out by the same man. Luckily, I still have some friends up there, and they are having a look round for me. It's all unofficial, you understand. Nobody in real authority is liable to thank me for taking up valuable police time on a couple of piddling little cases like these.'

Griffiths felt a growing disappointment. He hadn't known what to expect when he started out, but he'd hoped for something a little more exciting than another small claim two hundred miles away, and years in the past. Probably not even covered by his company.

'With the greatest of respect, Mr. Gardener,' he said carefully, 'it does all seem a little bit remote.'

Good word that, remote, he decided. Didn't carry any offence with it. Detective Sergeant Gardener nodded.

'Yes, it does. But I've been giving it a lot of thought. If there had only been the one report, the one you're dealing with, I shouldn't have thought twice about it. But, having it stir up my memory the way it did, I've been letting my imagination loose. Suppose I'm right, Mr. Griffiths? Suppose it is the same man? What does it suggest to you?'

The man from the Trusty thought about it for a while.

'Well,' he said doubtfully, 'I would think the man has probably moved down this way. He'd hardly travel a journey like that just to grab a few hundred pounds, would he?'

To his surprise, Gardener nodded enthusiastic agreement.

'Exactly,' he beamed. 'You are absolutely right. It wouldn't be worth his while. As to moving, I doubt it. Here we have a man, a planner, who worked out a nice clean little caper. No violence, no witnesses, no trace. Let us assume he is the same man who pulled that little job in Liverpool, all that time ago. Got clean away with it, just as he expected to. Do you think he'd let it rest there? Can you honestly see him thinking to himself, 'Ah. That seemed to go down all right. Next time I move my house, I'll do the same thing again.' Can you really see him doing that? Leaving it two years, or more? Because I can't, Mr. Griffiths, and I've got an entirely different explanation.'

Despite his earlier disappointment, Alun Griffiths began to feel some of the other man's excitement communicating itself to him.

'Well, go on man,' he urged.

'Right. We're granting our man intelligence. He's thoughtful, methodical and effective. So why doesn't he pull off something big, like a bank or a post-office, a payroll? I think I know why. Because they are big, and big crime attracts big attention. Little crime doesn't. It gets investigated, of course. The local police give as much time to it as they can, but they're overworked, Mr.

Griffiths, everybody in the country knows that. Overworked and under-manned. That's not just a copper complaining, it's statistical fact, and you must know it perfectly well, in your business.'

The insurance man nodded, thinking.

'I think I'm beginning to see what you're driving at, sergeant. I have a feeling that you are next going to point out that you and I are in much the same position. Deal with it locally, do the best you can, copy to headquarters. Nobody up there is very interested, although the reasons are different. Your people are worried about murder, rape, bullion robberies. My people are more interested in fraud, big fires, and,' permitting himself a small joke, 'also the bullion robberies. My top level has no more time to waste on three or four hundred pounds than your top level.'

Gardener leaned back, feeling rather smug. There was more to this little man from the Trusty than his ability to conduct the massed choirs. He'd obviously cottoned on very fast to the general trend of Gardener's thinking, and his tone suggested he did not disagree with it.

'Precisely, Mr. Griffiths. Now, then, back to our man. Suppose he is always on the move? An intelligent man, always moving about the country, in connection with his work. Plenty of people like that. Construction workers, auditors, salesmen, all kinds. One night here, a couple of nights there, home for the weekend. If such a man decided to go bad, and keep it small, he'd be the very devil to trace, wouldn't he? Especially if he avoided pulling two jobs in the same town. There's no-one to build up a history on him, no-one who rates him any higher than a one-time nuisance. In fact, so far as your side of it goes, there'll be even less on record than there is with the police.'

Alun Griffiths was uncertain whether this might be some kind of reflection on his company's procedures.

'I don't know about that,' he objected. 'Everything is properly recorded, you know. The system is very thorough.'

The policeman realised he hadn't made his point.

'I'm sure of it. In fact, I know very well it is from my past experience. What I should have said was, the chance of the information coming together is so much less in your case, because of the number of companies involved. I mean, just guessing, how many insurance companies are carrying this kind of small trader? Ten? Fifty?'

Accepting the point now, the insurance man shrugged.

'I wouldn't like even to guess. All the big ones, like my own, and heaven knows how many small ones. You're absolutely right, Mr. Gardener. This chap could do a dozen jobs like this, without even affecting the same insurance company twice. By George, I begin to think you really might be on to something here. But the point is, what do you propose to do about it? It's all theory, and anyone could shoot holes in it. Even at the end of the day, even if you managed to get all the police forces interested, and all the insurance companies, what are you going to end up with? Not a mass murderer, not a bank robber. You're going to land a man who's going to be the very devil to convict on more than one or perhaps two little charges. Hardly seems worthwhile, does it?'

The glum look on Gardener's face reflected the truth of what had just been spelled out. There was going to be no major trial for this man, even if they caught him. Gardener was a practical working policeman, not a theoretician, and he knew well the problems of involving other forces in a prosecution. It had to be something pretty big to justify joint action, even by two authorities. In the case of this man, if he existed, the problem would be astronomical. It would be necessary to convene, at one point, police officers and prosecution witnesses from probably half the forces in the country, if not more. And for what? To secure the conviction of one man, who stole a couple of hundred pounds here, and three hundred there, and whose identification by people involved was well nigh impossible.

Gardener had been all through this discouraging thinking fifty times in the past couple of days. He knew there was no way he could stir up any interest in his theory, let alone support. At the same time, he felt unable to let the matter rest. If he was right, and there was such a man, he was roaming about the country, thumbing his nose at the authorities at large, and some way must be found of stopping him. He simply couldn't be allowed to get away with it.

Well, he'd better say something, or he was going to lose his audience.

'Mr. Griffiths, believe me, I have no argument against what you say. Not against the logic. You are absolutely right, and I knew it before I asked to meet you. But let me try another tack, one that I think might appeal to you.' He took another sip of his drink, watched by the expectant Griffiths. 'Before I start, let me explain to you that I'm not an office man. I've been given this job here in Midchester for a temporary period, and I'm very grateful for it, don't misunderstand me. But really, I'm a working copper, always have been. I'm trained to catch thieves, and I've been doing it for years. Thieves are there to be caught, prosecuted and locked up. It makes my blood boil when they get away with some of the strokes they pull. Take this man, now. To have him poncing about, doing what he likes, that's wrong, and I want to do something about it. You've been in insurance a few years, I would guess?'

'Twenty-two altogether,' affirmed the other. 'I was eight years with the company before I transferred here. That was fourteen years ago.'

'There you are, then,' nodded Gardener. 'Twenty-two years. A lifetime. I'll bet you've lost count of the people who've tried to put one over on you in those years. Dozens of 'em. Hundreds, probably.'

This brought a tiny smile to his companion's face.

'Hundreds would be nearer,' he admitted. 'You develop a kind of feel for it, you see. You can usually tell.'

That was the answer the policeman had

been hoping for, and he nodded with enthusiasm.

'Of course you do. I'm sure you do. And you don't stand for it, do you? It's wrong, and they're out to swindle your company and you're not going to stand for it, right?'

'Certainly not. The company expects me to spot that sort of thing, and I think I usually do.'

'I'm sure you do, Mr. Griffiths. Sure of it. We're the same, you see. You're not going to stand for people robbing your company, and I'm not going to stand for people robbing the public. We're alike, you and me. And this man, whoever he is, has just done the Trusty out of four hundred quid.'

'Three hundred and ninety four,' amended Griffiths automatically. 'I adjusted the figure downwards after consulting Mr. Thomas.'

'All right then, three hundred and ninety four. Not much to a company your size, I admit. Drop in the ocean. But how many times has he done it before, I wonder? In other cities, other counties. And why should he go on getting away with it? Who knows what the total figure is, after all? Tens of thousands, perhaps more. This man, Mr. Griffiths, is as much your concern as he is mine, when you look at the broader picture. Do you begin to follow me?'

The little man fiddled with his glass.

'Oh, I follow you all right, and I don't like it, any more than you do. But we still come back to the same question. What do you propose can be done about it?'

His tone was not dismissive, as Frank Gardener noted with relief. He did not put the question as though it were unanswerable, but rather in the more positive manner that suggested he would be willing to listen to a solution — perhaps even to help find it.

'What can be done about it? To tell you the truth, I'm damned if I know, at this moment. But I have a proposal for you. The first thing is to establish that the whole thing isn't just my imagination. To prove that this man exists. I was thinking about your own Head Office, Mr. Griffiths.'

'In what way?'

'You're a man who must be in very good standing with the people up there,' coaxed Gardener. 'There must be occasional meetings and conferences. Is there someone up there you know well enough to ask him about this? What I mean is, someone who could ask your computer for some kind of national analysis?'

Griffiths looked doubtful now.

'I don't know about that,' he demurred. 'There isn't much to go on, is there? All I have is just the one case.'

'At the moment,' reminded Gardener, sensing that he could be in danger of losing his man. 'But don't forget I'm hoping for good news from Liverpool. If that's positive, it should make a difference.'

The little man nodded, half-convinced.

'It would certainly help,' he admitted. 'Even if I could persuade somebody, and I don't guarantee it, what would you be hoping to find? You pointed out yourself, we are only one of many companies.'

He was beginning to buy it, and his questioner began to feel the same kind of excitement that was so familiar from the past. The dawning certainty that a suspect was about to crack.

'That's true,' he acknowledged, 'but only half-a-dozen of them are truly national in the same way as Trusty. If this man has been operating for a long time, and Liverpool will confirm that it's at least two years, he might have done fifty or even sixty jobs like this. The chances of your company carrying the cover in five or six cases are fairly high, statistically?'

'I would say that's a fair assessment.'

'Right. Then if your computer proves he exists, your people would become interested in finding him. They would probably be interested enough to ask the other big companies about their experiences of him. I know they are small cases, but enough small cases build up in the end to a big one, and I don't imagine your people at Head Office will like the idea of him getting away with it, any more than I do. They must have links with the other big firms, over just this kind of situation, surely? I know they are all in competition, but they have mutual interests in certain fields.'

Griffiths frowned. His knowledge of the company's procedure was incomparable, but as to what went on at H.O. at this kind of level, his information was skimpy, to put it mildly. Racking his brains, he seemed to recall that there was something called the City Liaison Committee, or something of the kind. As to its functions, he was far from clear. Still, he reminded himself, it stood to reason that the people in London must at least know each other at some high level. There were, after all, areas of natural self-protection where some degree of cross-fertilisation would be required. Yes, he decided finally, it had to be possible. And he'd already decided on the man he would talk to. The Head of Small Claims was someone he'd met a number of times, and with whom he had established a good relationship. A man named Walden.

'It might be possible, Mr. Gardener,' he conceded. 'I make no promises, you understand. I don't deceive myself about how important I am at Head Office. But yes, I do know one or two people, and I could broach the subject. Before I do, though, I'm going to have to be certain about your man in Liverpool. You can see the sense of that, I'm sure. One case is no case at all. Two, with years in between, and hundreds of miles apart, are far more likely to get me some attention.'

It was as far as Gardener had hoped to get at this first meeting, and he well understood the fairness of the insurance man's condition.

'Absolutely,' he agreed, meaning it. 'After all, if I'm wrong about that, then the whole theory collapses anyway, doesn't it? So, I thank you for listening to me, and the moment I hear from my friends up North, I'll give you another ring. Same again?'

He pointed to their now-empty glasses.

Alun Griffiths smiled and shook his head, as he rose from his seat.

'Not for me, thank you. Middle of the day. I'd be asleep all the afternoon. I'll wait to hear from you, then? One way or the other?'

They shook hands and Gardener watched him leave. He had taken quite a liking to the man from the Trusty, and had a feeling he would prove to be a valuable ally, always assuming that anything transpired from the Liverpool end.

The answer to that outstanding query came before the end of that same afternoon. The telephone rang, and he picked it up, responding automatically.

'Two three O.'

A familiar voice sounded at the other end.

'Guess who?'

Gardener grinned. It had been a long time since he and his old colleague Sergeant Hoo had played this particular game. The reply was pre-determined.

'Who is that?' he enquired.

'Yes it is,' was the acknowledgment, and the word-game was now complete. 'How are you Frank?'

'Not too bad. Did you find anything?'

'Matter of fact, I think I have. Do you happen to have any elephant blood, by any chance? Only this little tickle was two and a half years ago, and you don't need me to tell you how much paper's been dumped on top of it since then. Still, it looks good. You ready?'

Gardener sighed with relief, picking up a biro.

'Never more ready,' he confirmed.

The Liverpool man began to read out the facts of the case, and Frank Gardener scribbled quickly at the sheet in front of him.

'Well, that's it,' announced his friend finally.

'Er, just one little favour,' responded Gardener quickly. 'Any chance of a copy?'

'A copy?' came the incredulous reply. 'Got an all-stations circular about photo-copies. Did you know, once you add in the officer's time, station overheads and everything else, a photo-copy is now costing twelve pence? Bet you didn't know that. Quite apart from which, can you imagine what they'd do to me, if they caught me sending a copy of an official form outside the county? I should probably get life, my son.'

'You'll just about catch the five o'clock post, if you get a move on,' Gardener replied smoothly. 'Oh, and if they lock you up, I'll come and see you.'

'Won't be necessary,' he was assured,

'I'll make bloody certain you're in the next cell. Can't stop now, got some illegal copying to do.'

'Cheers then, and thanks. Hooever you are.'

'Hoo too.'

Frank Gardener cradled the receiver, tapped at it with thoughtful fingers, then picked up his written notes. The job was almost a carbon copy of the one already on his desk.

The raid had been carried out at twenty minutes to ten on a Wednesday evening. The shopkeeper, a sixty-three year old widow, had been alone on the premises when the man with the stock-inged face had suddenly appeared. The description of his clothes was identical to that supplied by George Thomas. The raider had hardly spoken, and when he did he sounded hoarse. Only cash was taken, three hundred and eleven pounds in all, and the elderly woman had been forced down by a gloved hand in exactly the same way. The only difference was that in this case there was no reference to the cutting of the telephone wire, but that

was not necessarily significant, decided
Gardener. There was nothing in the
report to suggest that there was an
instrument inside the shop anyway.
Probably at the back, or even upstairs.
No. It was all too familiar, and it had to
be the same man. He read it again and
again, to be absolutely certain he was
overlooking nothing because it might
spoil his theory. There was no doubt
about it, he decided finally.

He now had two cases, plus his
scribbled notes, and they needed to be
kept together. Opening a bottom drawer,
he took out an empty file cover, and
slipped the papers inside. Closing it, he
stared at the blank cardboard. Ought to
have some title, he decided. Picking up
his pen he tapped at his teeth a few times,
thinking. Then, he smiled to himself and
wrote the legend 'Mr. Gloves.' Not as
good as a full name and address, but it
would have to do for now.

The point was, ought he to wait for the
copy report to arrive, before contacting
Alun Griffiths again. No, he realised, that
wouldn't do. He had no reason to distrust

the man, but it was taking an awful chance to let him see a report from another county. No, that report must remain in his own possession, for his own confirmation, and no-one else's. In which case, he thought, there is no point in further delay.

Now, where had he put Mr. Griffiths' number?

8

The Claims Division of Trusty Assurance occupied the upper four floors of a concrete steel and glass monstrosity, with a clear view of the Post Office Tower. Roger Trevitt looked at his watch and groaned as he stared out of the window. He had to see Sir Keith at three sharp, and he would need every second if he was going to be able to present his brief coherently. Nevertheless, his calendar stated firmly that he must review the progress of this graduate student fellow at half-past two. Sir Keith himself had been adamant on the point that these new recruits were not to be fobbed off on running errands and helping in the post room. They were there to learn, and it was up to every man in the organisation to see that they received every opportunity. If he learned of any case where a graduate was being misused, it would be the head of the department he would blame.

In this case that meant Trevitt, so there was no way he could avoid the necessity for at least ensuring the chap was doing something worthwhile. There was a tap at the door and Freddie Brant breezed in, as full of confidence as ever. Brant was Trevitt's number two, and it was his job to ensure that everything outside went smoothly, also that only essential matters reached Trevitt's desk. They had been together now for four years, and Trevitt had learned, gradually and to his astonishment, that Brant really did feel it was his task to back him up. In that position, so many people would have seized on any opportunity to reveal his weaknesses, leave him short of vital information, little things that would undermine the top man in the long run. But that was not Brant's style. He set himself out to be the best number two in the Division, and his loyalty was beyond question.

'Sorry chief,' began Brant, 'but you've got to give this graduate five minutes at least. However, I have a suggestion.'

'Ah,' Trevitt's eyes gleamed. 'Come on then Freddie, be suggestive.'

Brant placed a file in front of him.

'You remember I told you about Walden's scheme the other day, chap from Small Claims. Thought he was on to something?'

'Walden, Walden, yes, I remember. What about him?'

Leaning across the desk, Brant tapped at the file.

'This graduate, Peter Barrett, absolutely shone at statistics. Thought you might fish that out accidentally, then get a brain-wave, and push him over to Walden. Should be three or four days solid work involved. Get him off our back for a while. And who knows? He might come up with something.'

There wasn't time for argument. Trevitt nodded his head.

'Fine, Freddie. Is he outside? Well, whistle him in, and let's get it over with. Afterwards, you get back in here and let's both have a final polish at this other stuff before I see Sir Keith.'

'Right sir.' Brant opened the outer

door. 'Come in, Peter.'

Trevitt looked over at the newcomer. Peter Barrett was five feet eleven, with well-trimmed fair hair, and a controlled moustache. He didn't slouch or lurch about the place like so many nowadays, but walked upright, in almost military fashion, wearing a neat grey suit.

'Sit down Peter, sit down. Let me just have a quick glance at your departmental progress.'

Barrett sat on the high-backed chair which was popularly known as the hot-seat. Brant stood beside the desk, his face impersonal, while they waited for the great man to complete his scrutiny.

'I see you're twenty-seven,' muttered Trevitt, 'that's pretty late to be coming into the scheme, but — ah — yes, I see, you were almost three years in the army. How'd you come to give that up?'

Barrett grimaced.

'I think it would be more true to say that it gave me up, sir. I caught a booby-trap while we were peace-keeping in the Middle East. I have a false hip as a result, and so I had to leave the service and look for something rather less strenuous.'

Trevitt cleared his throat, grinning.

'Are you suggesting we don't keep you busy enough?'

'Lord no, sir, far from it. I've been kept hard at it all the time I've been here. No, I meant in the physical sense. No more leaping in and out of tanks, that kind of thing.'

No more rugby, either, noted the other sadly. This chap had once had an international trial. Rotten luck.

'You seem to be making good progress,' he praised, turning quickly over the section reports. 'Mr Brant and I have been talking about you, wondering whether you might like to take on a little special project for us.'

Barrett didn't hesitate. In the army he had learned one golden rule very quickly. Never volunteer. In civilian life, if you were aiming to achieve something, as distinct from merely plodding along, the precise opposite applied. If the top management made a suggestion, you grabbed at it. It could be a unique opportunity, which would never come your way again. On the other hand, it might simply be something which was convenient to them at that moment. There was no way of telling, and you went for it anyway, looking cheerful in the process.

'I'd like it very much, sir.'

'Good, good.'

Trevitt closed the file, and handed it to Brant, who now spoke.

'If I may suggest it, sir, it might be as well to let Mr. Walden explain matters to Peter. All the files and records are to hand out there, and it would save a lot of fetching and carrying.'

Good old Freddie.

'Yes, that would seem sensible. All right Peter, if you'll go along with Mr. Brant, he will introduce you to Mr. Walden, who will have all the details. You seem to be doing very well. Keep it up.'

Brant looked enquiringly at the young graduate, who realised the interview was ended, and stood up.

'Thank you very much, sir.'

Outside, he walked beside the hurrying Brant.

'I don't think I've heard Mr. Walden's name before,' he asked hopefully.

'Small claims,' grunted his escort. 'Some people think of it as a bit of a backwater, but don't you listen to them. Far too much attention paid to the big jobs, at times. They are more exciting, it's true enough. There's a lot more glamour to being involved in a department store fire, which might cost us ten or fifteen million, than there is in fifty quid for a burnt carpet. But make no mistake about it. Straightforward life insurance and small claims are the backbone of this business, the real hard rock on which the whole thing is founded. People like Walden do invaluable work.'

Barrett listened politely, but with a sinking heart. This wasn't going to be his golden opportunity after all. All this chatter about the backbone of the business didn't deceive him. He was going to be given some boring assignment, which would keep him out of harm's way for a week or two, and out from under the management's feet.

The sight of Walden's office did little to restore his confidence. It was no more than a glass cubicle at one end of a giant open plan office, complete with compulsory greenery at stated intervals. Brant left him outside, while he went in, after the most perfunctory tap on the glass. Barrett could see Walden rise from his chair as Brant entered, looking surprised. Why should he look surprised? Surely they must have told him there was a trainee on the way? No, perhaps they hadn't, he decided. Perhaps this so-called 'special project' was as much of a surprise to Walden as it was to himself.

'Come on in, Peter.'

There wasn't much room for the three of them, in that confining space.

Walden was in his early fifties, a tubby five feet eight inches of good humour, with thick fronds of white hair either side of a large bald patch on his head. He held out his hand to the newcomer.

'How d'ye do?' he greeted.

Peter took the proffered hand, smiling and replying.

'I'll leave you two alone,' announced Brant. 'I suggest you listen carefully to anything Pop has to say, young Peter. He's been twenty-six years at the game, and there's not a lot he doesn't know.'

Twenty-six years. Almost as long as he'd been alive. And with this glass cubicle as the end achievement. It sounded like a life sentence. There was Brant, disappearing through the door, and they were alone.

'Sit down Peter, sit down,' urged Walden, looking him over.

Brant had only given him the briefest outline about his new charge, and had taken the file with him when he left. Pop Walden was not sufficiently up in the hierarchy to be entrusted with a trainee's personal file.

Peter Barrett was also taking in his new surroundings. There were several old-fashioned green filing cabinets, well-worn, and the desk itself was a clutter of paper. The visual display unit, that essential tool for immediate access to company records, was almost blanked off by files, and a disrespectful vase containing three daffodils rested on the top.

'Let's have a bit of a chat,' suggested his mentor. 'Have they told you about my idea? My 'hare-brained' idea, as they were kind enough to call it?'

Barrett fought to keep disappointment from his face. Was this to be his special project? An idea which had emanated from these uninspiring surroundings, and already dismissed as hare-brained?

'No,' he replied. 'They thought it would save time if you told me about it direct.'

'I'll bet they did,' was the laconic comment. 'Cigarette?'

'I don't, thank you.'

'Good. You'll live longer.'

Despite this sage comment, Pop Walden lit a cigarette for himself with every indication of enjoyment.

'This job,' he announced, waving an arm about, 'is what you make of it. It can be just a lot of figures that have to be sorted out, or it can be interesting. Up to the individual. To me, it's fascinating. Do you know what pours into this office?'

Peter called on his scanty experience in

an attempt to make an answer which sounded intelligent.

'District Reports?' he hazarded. 'Regional Summaries?'

Walden listened impassively.

'Technically, yes,' he agreed. 'If you choose to think about them that way. That's how most of those people out there regard them. Just so many figures, to be totted up and analysed. That's not the way I look at it. Not at all. To me, it's a flood of human experience. You have to look behind the figures, use a bit of imagination. That's where the truth is.'

'The truth?' encouraged Peter.

'Behind the figures,' repeated Walden. 'What can you tell by looking at a pageful of columns? 'Comparison with previous quarter'. 'Comparison with same quarter in previous year'. 'Five year projection'. What does any of that mean in human terms? I'll tell you. Nothing. All it tells us is what our claims experience is, what it used to be, and whether there's any prospect of a change in the future. So that we can determine next year's premiums. Get our sums right, in short. Huh.'

Peter listened to this homily in respectful silence. What was the man blathering on about? Getting the sums right, surely that was what was so important to the future well-being of them all? And if this chap didn't think so, how had he come to be put in charge of this life-blood side of the job? Puzzled as he was, he thought his best policy would be to keep quiet and listen, as had so often proved to be the case in the past.

He contented himself with a look of polite enquiry, and made no comment. Pop Walden recognised the expression. He'd seen it before, many times, and it normally signified that his words were going in at one ear and out of the other. Too bad. This was his philosophy, and people passing through his hands were going to have to listen to it.

'This business,' he went on, 'is an essence of what is happening in the world outside. This recession the country's been going through, for example. It's all there, in the small claims summary. Happens every time. Increase in the number of claims, resulting in increased premiums, and a slight fall-away in new business. Does that tell you anything?'

The trainee hesitated, thinking.

'Well,' he began, 'I suppose any increase in premiums acts as a kind of brake on new business.'

'To an extent, but it's scarcely measurable as a rule. It only reflects the increased income people are receiving anyway, and they ought to be able to afford it. But let's take the larger number of claims first. All of a sudden, when there's a general recession, people break more windows, crack more washbasins and so forth. That's on the domestic side. There are also more break-ins, more theft, all the petty crimes that our policies cover. These things are not coincidential. They are a direct reflection of what is happening in the world outside. If you try to think of our paperwork in those terms, instead of as rows of figures, you'll find it all much more interesting, and therefore more rewarding. Your personal profit will be twofold. You'll be a better insurance man, and a more informed citizen.'

Despite his reservations, Peter found

himself warming to the older man's enthusiasm. In his training hitherto, he had not encountered this kind of approach. It made a pleasant change from the coldly analytical lectures he'd been given at his introduction into the various departments he'd visited so far.

Walden carried on expounding, but he knew his little speeches by heart, and he was anxious to get through the preliminaries as soon as he decently could. Pop Walden had a job for this young man, and he was keen to get him started on it.

When their man in Midchester, Alun Griffiths, had first spoken to him about the idea, his first reaction had been to wave it away. But, being the polite person he was, he had heard the regional agent out to the end, then asked for time to think about it. The request was certainly unusual enough, a distinct change from the normal day-to-day of the department. Pop Walden had spent several years out in the field, before joining the Head Office staff, and it was a pet theory of his that an effective H.O. man was normally a man with local experience behind him. Far too many youngsters came in direct from school or university, knew nothing of field agents' problems or difficulties, and cared even less. Walden was not like that, and he had never forgotten those invaluable years in the outer darkness. He often missed the tight schedule of appointments, in all weathers. Missed, too, the human contact, the wide range of people in all walks of life, whom he would deal with in the course of a normal week.

It was against this background experience that he was able to weigh up his conversation with Griffiths. Sound chap, that. Not given to flights of fancy, by any means, and in fact considered by some to be a rather stolid sort of person. That may be as it may, but he contrived to retain his place in the Top Fifty, and that alone meant that any request from him merited special consideration.

Besides, it had police origins. Not officially, of course, he'd made that quite clear. The request had originated from some police officer for whose opinion Alun Griffiths appeared to have some regard. That again was a pointer. Griffiths was by nature a careful man in his dealings with others, and by no means the type to be bowled over by a smooth talker. As to why the policeman was hamstrung through his own channels, Pop Walden understood that only too well. Had it not been he, and another colleague, long retired, who had first put the police on the track of a highly organised gang of mobile bicycle thieves, many years before? That had been an early triumph for Walden, and one which had made a favourable impact at Head Office. The outlines of the case were not dissimilar in some ways, from the insurance point of view. The details were very different, naturally, but there were quite enough echoes from that old case to compel him to pay special attention to the man from Midchester. When he had first broached the subject with Freddie Brant, his reception had not been encouraging. Brant was a Head Office product, qualified up to the eyeballs, as Walden privately categorised him, and with no knowledge of insurance whatever. He could be transplanted at will to a similar post in banking, steel or one of the ministries, and be equally effective inside a week.

'I don't know, Pop,' he demurred. 'If it was just a question of asking Gertie, well, I'd be inclined to say go ahead. But you say it's not that simple?'

Gertie was the name by which the officers of the company referred to the computer.

'Afraid not, Mr. Brant. You see, our interests are not the same as those of the police. We wouldn't take up valuable Gertie time by recording the kind of thing that interests them. Description of the intruder and so forth, that's not our business. A theft is a theft, and that's the way we memorise it.'

'Quite,' rejoined Brant, a trifle stiffly. He didn't need this old boy to give him a lecture on the insurance business. 'So it will entail a lot of manual digging, eh? The point is, can we justify it?'

Meaning, thought Walden inwardly, can I justify it?

'The truth of that is, Mr. Brant, that I don't know,' he confessed. 'If we get a result, the answer is probably yes. Unfortunately, I can't guarantee that we'll get one.'

'Well, there you are, you see. And all your people are hammer and tongs at the half-yearly figures, aren't they? Are you sure you won't be cutting your own throat? There can be no question of these summaries going past the deadline, and you don't need me to tell you that.'

No, I don't, thought Walden irritably, and I didn't come in here to have you chuck that at me. The summaries had never yet been late, and they wouldn't be this time. Aloud, he said,

'Oh quite, sir, quite. What I wondered was, whether you could shift the training periods around for one of the graduates? I'm due one next month, anyway, and there's no real reason why I couldn't have him before Admin. is there?'

Damned cheek, reflected Brant. The movement of trainees was a matter for his decision, no one else's. As for shifting them about — just a minute. There was one chap, Bartlett, Brent, no Barrett, that was it. Barrett was due for his periodic review with Roger Trevitt, Head of Claims, the very next day. It was a nuisance, because Sir Keith had called for a special report on a vastly more important subject at three in the afternoon. The man Barrett was due for interview at two-thirty. If he could tell Trevitt that there was a special project ready and waiting for the young man, it would save him invaluable preparation time for the three o'clock appointment.

'A trainee, you think? H'm. Let me see.'

He made a great show of opening a file and studying it for a few seconds, leaving Walden to watch hopefully.

'Matter of fact, there's one chap I could divert,' he murmured, as though talking to himself. 'Mind you, Pop, he's a sharp chap. Better not be wasting his time.'

'I don't think we'll be doing that, Mr. Brant,' and Walden made deliberate use of the 'we', 'whether anything comes of it or not, he'll get first hand knowledge of what our field people are really doing out there. Invaluable.'

Brant was never quite certain whether Walden was forever drawing attention to his own lack of field experience, but he had long since decided not to let it ruffle him. After all, as he reminded himself on such occasions, he was the one behind the desk, while Walden stood respectfully on the other side.

Now he smiled, having decided.

'O.K. I'll see if I can talk Mr. Trevitt into it. He wouldn't do this for everyone, you know, Pop. But since it's you, I think he'll probably look at it quite favourably.'

'I'm much obliged, Mr. Brant. Let's hope I'm not on a wild goose chase.'

That was how it had started, and now here he was with the necessary pair of hands, ready and waiting.

'How would you like to help the company catch a crook?'

The young man's face lighted up. This sounded promising.

'A crook, sir? You mean someone's cheating the company?'

Pop Walden laughed.

'No, not in the sense you mean. People are trying that on every day, and we have

216

our own little procedures for keeping tabs on those gentlemen. And Ladies,' he amended. 'Mustn't be chauvinistic eh?, not even when it comes to cheating the company.'

Barrett smiled politely at the small joke, wondering when they would get to the point.

'No,' resumed Walden. 'I mean a real live crook. Chap who wears a stocking over his face, and steals from shopkeepers. Real life drama stuff. He also wears woollen gloves. That's how we think of him. Let's call him Mr. Gloves.'

'It sounds exciting,' admitted Peter Barrett. 'But isn't it more a matter for the police?'

'Indeed it is, but, if we're right, he's contrived to spread his little activities over such a wide area, that the police haven't really had a chance to cotton on to him. That's where we come in. Or rather, you do. You and Gertie, working together, might come up with some very valuable information. Do you fancy it?'

'Very much,' enthused the trainee. 'I see what you mean about putting flesh and blood on to some of the paper work. How do I set about it?'

Walden nodded, satisfied. This young feller showed the right attitude. Might even make an insurance man of him.

'Well,' he began. 'It originated in Midchester. We have a very good man out there, by the name of Griffiths, Alun Griffiths — '

Peter Barrett leaned forward to listen.

9

Holden stayed late at the office, completing with meticulous care his report on the Midchester visit. Having recommended certain procedural changes, he also stated that he intended to make an unannounced routine visit before his normal six-monthly inspection. It was one of his innovations into the regional inspection system, that these should not necessarily be hide-bound as to their regularity. The local people were given too much opportunity to present a nice tidy picture, and it was his view, borne out by results, that the occasional unplanned visit produced a more accurate assessment of the local scene. It would mean two nights away from home instead of one in that week, because his planned arrangement in another area would still go ahead.

He had also decided to say nothing yet to Sheila about the forthcoming interview with the Chairman.

It was almost seven-thirty when he arrived home, and Sheila had just begun to agitate about the evening meal. He kissed her perfunctorily, and learned that the children were engrossed in some television programme.

'How was Midchester?' she asked, as he followed her into the kitchen.

'Oh, not bad, but it could be better, I think. I shall do one of my Big Daddy trips up there in a few weeks' time.'

Sheila was glad her back was to him, as she stirred furiously at a saucepan. A Big Daddy visit meant that he would be away for two nights instead of one, and three whole days. If she could manage to park the children with friends, it would be a golden opportunity for her to be with Bruce.

'That means you'll be missing half the week again,' she grumbled. 'Any idea when?'

'Too early to decide yet. Besides, I'm doing one next week, you know, didn't I tell you?'

She forgot to stir for a moment, and the saucepan sizzled ominously. Next week? No, he hadn't mentioned it, she was sure. She wouldn't be likely to forget something so important. Mustn't make it sound important, she realised.

'You may have done,' she admitted. 'If you did, I've forgotten. Where is it this time?'

'Plymouth,' he replied, chewing on a piece of celery. 'I was a bit bothered about a couple of things the last time I was there. So I'll go there on Tuesday, then go over for my regular stint at Swindon on the following day.'

'Well, I'm glad you've told me in time. I'll make sure your shirts are in order.'

The mention of Plymouth had taken her mind off at an entirely different angle. She even forgot about Bruce Hayward for the moment.

Adam always had the local newspaper sent to the house after one of his trips. He always read it in his room, and usually threw it away the next morning. It hadn't been so many weeks since his last trip to Plymouth, and she could recall seeing the newspaper on top of his wastepaper basket when she came to empty it. In the ordinary way, Adam was very good about emptying it himself, but on this particular week the dustmen were calling a day early. She noticed that he'd cut an item from the front page of the paper, and wondered idly what it could have been. Bound to be something to do with his job, she realised, because everything was. She took the basket down to the dustbin, emptied it inside, then carried it back upstairs, thinking.

What could it be on the front page that would be of interest to Adam, or the firm? Might be a photograph of him having lunch with the mayor or something. Typical of him not to bother to mention it. Well, he'd cut it out, so it must be important. He'd have stuck it in that clippings book he kept locked up in his desk. He was always locking things up, ever since the children were little, because he didn't trust them not to go poking what he called their sticky little fingers into everything.

Well, that was all right for the children, but they were bigger now, and yet he still did it. And she wasn't one of the children, after all. If there was a photograph of him in the newspaper, she naturally wanted to see it. Adam always kept his keys with him, because of the car and the front door, but the locks on the desk were scarcely the latest Chubb design. They were simple in the extreme, and surely she could find something that would fit. There were enough keys around the house, gathered over the years, and Sheila collected a few, trying them in turn until one of them moved smoothly round. For a moment she paused, irresolute. Then she told herself not to be so silly, and pulled the drawer open. There was a book of clippings, and all she had to do was lift it out. Even so, she felt slightly guilty as she did so, even looking towards the door to be certain Adam wouldn't walk in and find her at it. What rubbish. She rested the book on the desk, and sat in his chair, staring at it. With uncertain fingers she turned to the first page. It contained an item from the Glasgow Herald, dated four years earlier, and the headline struck her as odd.

YOUTH DIES
IN MOTOR CYCLE TRAGEDY

Andrew McLeish, 24, a garage fitter died tragically on Tuesday last, when ....

Sheila read the item in utter bewilderment, totally unable to find any connection with the accident and Adam Spencer Holden. The next page only added to her confusion. This was from a Bristol paper, two weeks later than the previous entry. It read: —

PEACE MOVEMENT
MARCHES ON TOWN HALL

and there followed a description of the incident, including interviews with those taking part.

The third page contained a clipping covering an outbreak of fighting at a local football match, the fourth, a report on a royal visit to the city. Thoroughly bewildered by this time, Sheila turned page after page, unable to find any reference to a single subject which would be of particular interest to either Adam Holden, or his employers. It was a very thick book, and soon there were two and sometimes three clippings on each page, but still no connecting thread. They were all matters of purely local interest and importance, and covered every conceivable human activity. She gave up after ten minutes of this, and turned to the last entry, the one which had prompted her curiosity at the outset, when she found the mutilated Plymouth newspaper. The headline this time read: —

DRUG ENQUIRY — VICAR'S DAUGHTER QUESTIONED

and she read it with rapidly failing interest. So much for her hope of seeing her husband shaking hands with some civic dignitary.

All that flooded back into her mind as she lifted the saucepan from the cooker, and left it to cool. Well, if he said he needed to make a quick return visit to Plymouth, no doubt it was necessary. She would have to find some way of letting Bruce know as early as possible.

'How's your head?'

The question came out of the blue, and she was unprepared for it. Turning, she looked at her husband's enquiring face.

'My head?' she echoed.

'Yes. Joy Hayward told me you had a headache. Is it better?'

Joy Hayward was the very last name Sheila wanted raised in conversation, well, she amended, the last but one.

'How did you happen to run into Joy?'

'I didn't,' he denied. 'She telephoned while I was here at lunchtime. Wanted to know how you were.'

Of course, she realised. As soon as she arrived home she had known Adam had been in the house. He had left a plate and coffee mug on the draining board to be washed up.

'Oh, it was nothing,' she laughed. 'I'd forgotten about it to tell you the truth. One of those come and go things, you know.'

'Good,' and he nodded casually. 'Then why didn't you go over to the lunch party? Not like you to miss one.'

Sheila shrugged, anxious to end this particular conversation.

'Well, it was getting late, and I didn't want to get all dressed up at that time of day. I went out and did some shopping instead.'

Adam crunched on his celery, and turned away, apparently satisfied. In fact, he was wondering why she should be lying to him over something so unimportant. The post seldom varied in its delivery time, and only on very rare occasions was it late. The latest he could ever recall had been nine-forty-five in the morning. Yet today, when he had arrived at lunchtime, the post had been on the doormat, and clearly Sheila must have left the house before it was delivered. She could no more disregard the incoming post than she could ignore a ringing telephone. So, she had been gone, at the latest, just after half-past nine, and yet here she was, claiming that her headache had not cleared until it was too late to go to her friend's luncheon. Odd, that. Very odd. Particularly since she claimed to have gone shopping. She hadn't returned to the house by the time he left, which meant that she had been shopping for at least four hours. What was she saying now?

' — and I thought we could have them for dinner one week-end, if that's all right with you?'

'Who?' He must have missed something important.

'Oh Adam,' she sighed, 'I've just been telling you about these new people, the Powells. He's something to do with market research, I think she said, so I'm sure you could find plenty to talk about.'

'Oh, them. Yes, the Powells. Well, why not? Who do you think they'd go well with?'

That was always a sensible question, because it set Sheila off on one of her analysing jaunts, while she tried to match up suitable people for a dinner-party. She would chatter away, requiring only an occasional grunt or shake of the head by way of his participation. It left his mind free to think about Swindon. That had been one of the jobs he'd had to abort owing to a last-minute hitch. He'd had the premises picked out for some time, and it met all his usual minimum requirements. Unfortunately, he had been about fifty yards from the shop when a gang of youths had roared up on motor-cycles, and disappeared inside. It would have been a simple matter for Holden to have walked the streets for another five or ten minutes, to let the motor-cyclists get clear, but he stuck to his rule. If everything was not one hundred per cent at the exact moment he expected to act, then the whole operation was postponed. It always annoyed him, and he was still surprised to find that a dropped operation produced the same physical reaction as one which had been successfully carried out. Next week, he would try the Swindon shop once more. If he should be prevented that time, he would cross the job off his list for good. What with that, and the unlooked-for summons to the Chairman the following day, Holden could hardly wait to escape to his own room.

Later that evening, after the children

had gone to bed, he finally went up to his study, leaving Sheila to watch one of her favourite television programmes. Once she heard his door close, she turned down the volume, and settled down to a quiet think.

Much as she did not want to face the fact, Bruce Hayward had not been so anxious to see her lately, not nearly as keen as in those early days. At the beginning, he had made all the running. He had been forever on the telephone, urging an early meeting, compelling her on more than one occasion to take certain risks in order to see him. Caught up in the marvellous excitement of it all, Sheila had given little thought to the eventual outcome, and when danger signals appeared she would dismiss them from her thoughts. But in recent weeks, there had been a subtle shift in the relationship. He had sometimes left a period of several days without telephoning, and something inside her had prevented her from asking the reason. She knew about his unpredictable work, which occasionally took him away for days at a time, but he had always contrived to let her know, even if he was not in a position to telephone.

Bruce was called an investigative reporter. From what she could gather, his job consisted of ferreting out information about people or situations, while others were doing the same kind of work in other areas. Eventually, all their findings were assembled, and someone would decide whether they had sufficient material to make a programme from the result. Journalism with cameras was his own description of the job, which he affected to loathe. The end product would be a twenty-six minute exposé of the subject, which could be banal, such as a tour with a pop group, or exciting, like the one she'd seen recently, which drew attention to the life-style of a certain M.P. by comparison with his known income. Sometimes the job involved danger, physical danger, when organised prostitution was the subject. Bruce had narrowly escaped being knifed during the course of that particular investigation.

And so, knowing the kind of job it was, she did not press him for explanations of his new unaccounted absences. Deep down, she was afraid that he was paving the way to severing their relationship, and any undue histrionics on her part would only accelerate things. It wasn't that she loved him, she admitted sadly. This odd feeling she had for him could not be excused under that heading. But, whatever it was, she wanted to hang on to it. Bruce Hayward had brought a whole new dimension into her life, and she was not going to do anything foolish, which might bring it to an end.

She had told him about Adam's odd book of press clippings one day, soon after she had discovered it. They had been lying in bed, drowsy after their love-making, and they often talked over a wide range of things in those circumstances. To her surprise, Bruce had not given her the series of acquiescent grunts, which normally indicated his lack of interest in what she was saying. He had actually roused himself sufficiently to question her.

'And you've really read it all very carefully?'

'Well, no,' she admitted. 'Not all of it. There's far too much. But I saw enough to be certain there's nothing that binds them all together.'

'How many?' he pressed. 'How many did you actually read?'

Gratified that she at least had his attention for once, she thought about it.

'Seven or eight,' she decided. 'Quite enough, anyway.'

'Is it? How many pages do you think there were?'

'Oh, I don't know. It's quite a big book. Perhaps eighty, a hundred, I don't know. I'm not very good at that sort of thing.'

He sighed, with near-exasperation. In other circumstances, the exasperation would have been more forcefully expressed.

'But there was one every week. Every week he's been away?'

No, she recalled, that was one thing which had struck her as curious. There had been a gap in the sequence, the omission of the odd week here and there. She told her not-so-sleepy partner about it.

'Ah yes,' he nodded. 'That would

account for the weeks when he doesn't go away. Nothing queer about that.'

'That's just it,' she contradicted. 'There is never a week when he doesn't go away at least once. Unless we're on holiday, of course.'

'Well, perhaps he doesn't always have a paper sent,' he suggested.

'Yes, he does. Without fail. The envelopes don't always come, though.'

Bruce Hayward felt the sleepiness falling away from him. Sitting up in bed, he reached for a cigarette. Sheila frowned her disapproval, but he ignored that. This was an odd situation she was describing. Adam Holden had a local newspaper sent to his home from whatever city he was visiting at the time. Sometimes he took a clipping, and sometimes not. There was no connection between the clippings, or rather, nothing that the untrained Sheila had been able to spot. Now, there was this added ingredient about envelopes. What was the man doing?

'You didn't mention the envelopes before,' he pointed out casually. 'Tell me about those.'

She shrugged, and her handsome breasts bobbed up and down. Bruce concentrated hard on his cigarette.

'Nothing to tell really,' she asserted. 'He posts stuff to himself at home. They're quite thick envelopes as a rule, obviously full of papers.'

'But they don't come every week?' he insisted.

'No. Most weeks, but not all. Why do you ask?'

'I don't know,' he confessed. 'I suppose I just can't let mysteries alone. It's in my blood. The answer's in the clippings you know. Must be. You just haven't spotted it.'

She turned to him with some asperity, or as much as she could muster in their circumstances.

'I may not be an investigative reporter,' she said huffily, 'but I'm not an out and out cretin. I tell you there's no connection.'

He twisted her nose playfully.

'And I'll bet you there is,' he assured her. 'Tell you what. You bring the book some day, and I'll find the connection.'

She paled at this proposal.

'Oh no,' she stammered, 'I couldn't. Couldn't possibly. Adam would skin me alive if he thought I'd been at his precious desk.'

'But he's away a lot,' he countered reasonably. 'He'd never know anything about it. You'd have it back in his desk inside a few hours. I don't believe you're concerned about that at all. You don't want me to show you up, that's about the size of it.'

'Rubbish,' she dismissed. 'And what's all this about sizes, Mr. Hayward?'

That had ended that particular discussion, but now, sitting alone, and making vague plans for Adam's two-night absence in the coming week, the book of press cuttings came back into her mind. Bruce had certainly seemed very interested at the time, and perhaps she could now use the book as a bait to persuade him to take her away somewhere for a couple of days. The thought of the actual deed, of taking the thing from Adam's desk, and actually leaving the house with it, filled her with apprehension, but she resolved to be firm

236

with herself. Tomorrow she would telephone Bruce.

★ ★ ★

At five minutes to four on the following
afternoon, Adam Spencer Holden presented himself in the small ante-room to
the Chairman's suite, which acted in the
dual capacity of office for its occupant,
the well-located Kitt-Walmers, and a
buffer against unwelcome intrusion.

Kitt-Walmers rose from his desk, smiling. Odious creature, reflected Holden,
wondering yet again how the man had
ever got himself appointed.

'Ah, well on time then. Good. Master
will buzz when he's ready. Do take a seat.'

Holden dropped on to one of the
shining black leather lounging chairs, and
hoped the Chairman would send for him
before he dozed off. The chairs were more
suited to a high-class bordello than to a
working office, and there were those in
the organisation not above suggesting that
Kitt-Walmers had probably brought them
with him from his previous appointment.

The object of his speculation made no attempt at conversation, but was engrossed in the Financial Times. Holden was not especially wounded at the implied rudeness, since he had no wish to talk to the man in any case. What surprised him was the lack of sophistication in the ploy. Anyone who read the celebrated pink journal as part of the day's normal routine, had extracted everything they needed to know long before the morning coffee break. If Kitt-Walmers was trying to make an impression by reading it at four in the afternoon, he'd have done better to acquire a copy of the Beano. Assuming, Holden amended, that the favourite comic of his own school days was still printed. He made a mental note to check the point with Graham when he got home.

A soft rasping noise cut into his thoughts, and the ingratiating tones of the Chairman's P.A. announced,

'Ah. The Chairman is ready for you.' They both rose, and Holden followed the other man to the hallowed door. A brief tap, and it was opened.

'Mr. Holden, sir.'

Holden went through and was struck at once by the peace of the room. Every architectural and furnishing device had been employed to ensure that no unwanted sounds broke into the atmosphere, and once the door closed softly behind him the absence of noise was total.

'Come in, Holden. Come and sit down.'

Edmund Peronne was a short, powerfully-built man in his early fifties. Brought in six years earlier to revive a flagging group of companies, he had achieved wonders, and at the same time acquired a fearsome reputation for his direct methods. Holden, though suitably in awe of the great man, had no particular fear of him. His own performance would withstand any scrutiny, as well he knew. The only people who needed to fear Peronne were people who failed to shape up.

The Chairman did not rise to greet him, but sat quite still, watching, as he settled himself into the indicated chair.

This was a more robust affair than the one he had vacated outside, and he was thankful for the firm support of the heavy back and armrests.

'You'll have heard about George Michaels?'

Directness was another of the Chairman's characteristics. There was no time to spare for enquiries about his health or his family's well-being. Carefully, he replied.

'Only rumours, sir.'

'Which are?'

'That he may have left us, and gone elsewhere.'

'Do you believe it?'

There was no emphasis in the Chairman's tone, no hint as to what reply would please him. Holden looked at him coolly.

'A big organisation like this, sir, is full of rumours. I never believe anything until I see it on the Appointments Bulletin.'

'Hah.'

The brief explosive noise was an indication of approval. The Bulletin, a monthly circular setting out all staff movements, had been one of the Chairman's own innovations.

'Well, you can believe it. I sent out a Press Release at two o'clock. Here's a copy.'

Holden had to lean well forward to take hold of the proffered green sheet, which he read quickly. It was true then, he realised, as he scanned the first paragraph. But when he came to the second paragraph, his heart jumped, and he had to read it twice.

'As a result, the Board have announced a minor re-shuffle among its senior executive staff. A new post is to be created, that of Chief Sales Co-ordinator, and the man appointed to the post is Adam Spencer Holden, at present . . . . . . '

It was typical of Edmund Peronne that he should break such news in this dramatic fashion, and his method had the desired effect. Holden's composure was in tatters, when he finally looked up.

'Do you still want to wait for the Bulletin, or is my word good enough?' he was asked.

At that, he contrived a faint, embarrassed grin.

'I don't know quite what to say, sir.'

The Chairman held up three fingers.

'You say three things. One, thank you very much. Two, how much does this new job pay? Three, what are the new duties?'

Holden nodded, hanging tightly on to the sheet of paper, his mind in a whirl. Had he only stopped to think, he realised, he ought to have known the Chairman would do something like this. There wasn't to be any discussion, any negotiation. His promotion was a matter of fact, a foregone conclusion, and known by now to every financial editor on Fleet Street.

'Thank you very much, sir,' he said meekly, 'I'm a bit taken aback.'

Peronne nodded, the thick bull-neck disappearing between his shoulders as he did so.

'Been wanting to make this change for a while now, but George Michaels wasn't the man for it. You are, and it's worth an extra five thousand.'

Five. Almost twice what he'd been expecting. Holden's initial shock began to evaporate in the face of this new revelation.

'Expect something for it, mark you. Now then, what I want from you is this . . . '

10

When the internal telephone rang, Freddie Brant clucked with impatience. The half-yearly figures were causing the usual flood of last-minute questions and Roger Trevitt was pressing him for results. It was at once a relief and an irritation to hear Pop Walden's voice at the other end. Relief, because it could not mean another new enquiry. Irritation, because there was no time to waste on internal matters. He could scarcely believe his own ears, when Walden said he wanted five minutes of his time.

'Can't it wait, Pop? I'm very tied up at the moment.'

'Quite understand, Mr. Brant, and of course it will have to, if you say so. What shall I do with the trainee, meantime? There's nothing else for him here, I'm afraid.'

The trainee. Blast. Keeping Pop Walden waiting was one thing. Having an expensive trainee twiddling his thumbs was precisely the kind of thing calculated to send Sir Keith off into one of his famous fits. Brant grinned wryly to himself. Cunning old sod, was Pop, knew where to apply the pressure.

'Look, if you're sure it won't take more than five minutes?'

'Absolutely. In and out before you know it,' was the answer.

'All right. Come now, and bring young Barnett with you.'

'Barrett, Mr. Brant,' was the firm correction, 'Peter Barrett.'

'H'm.'

Brant was already lost in a jumble of figures when the tap came at his door. At his shouted invitation, it opened, and Pop Walden came in, followed by the trainee.

'Ah, there you are. Have they been keeping you busy, Peter?'

The younger man was embarrassed, since Brant had more or less ignored the senior staff member with him.

'Very, sir,' he confirmed.

'This young man has done a splendid job, Mr. Brant,' announced Walden, holding up some papers. 'You will recall that I mentioned to you my little theory about a robbery at Midchester the other day?'

Brant had dealt with dozens of different subjects since then, but the presence of the trainee helped him to recall.

'Yes, of course. Chap wore a mask or something. What did you find?'

Pop Walden wished the whole business didn't have to be hurried through in this fashion. Ideally, he would have liked time in which to expand on the background, to underline the tremendous application brought to the boring routine of search by young Barrett. But he knew the signs, and when Brant had allowed him five minutes, he had meant precisely that, and no more.

'The man has attacked us before,' he said crisply. 'To be exact, we have had eight such claims over the past four years. In each instance, the method, the timing, and the circumstances are practically identical, and so is the claimant's description of the intruder.'

He paused there to permit his listener

to absorb the information.

Brant knitted up his forehead.

'Eight? In four years? Total cost to the company?'

'Two thousand six hundred and eighteen pounds.'

A bit over six hundred and fifty pounds per annum, reflected Brant. Here he was, trying to explain six-figure trends under various headings, and this chap seriously expected to take up his time with this cops and robbers business. Unconsciously, he echoed words which had been used elsewhere, by people he didn't even know.

'Not exactly the Great Train Robbery, is it? You can drop a note to the local police, ask them what's going on, if you like. I'll sign it.'

It was tantamount to dismissal. But Walden made no attempt to leave. Instead he said,

'Mr Brant, there are eight different police authorities involved. I don't think any one of them would appreciate a letter on such a small matter. However, I have another suggestion.'

Well, there it was, the chap admitted it himself. Small matter was right. If anything, it was an exaggeration. Trivial would be nearer the mark. What other suggestion?

'Come on then Pop, let's hear it.'

'This man, whom I shall refer to as Mr. Gloves — '

— bloody melodrama, thought Brant —

' — seems to cover a wide range of territory. He is very methodical, and obviously researches his victims thoroughly beforehand. Therefore, he has a job which keeps him on the move.'

Brant saw an objection to that straightaway.

'Why? Why can't he just be a thief with a car?'

Walden shook his head.

'The profits are too small, Mr. Brant. Nobody's going to travel two hundred miles to steal three hundred pounds. No, I'm certain he must have a proper job of some kind.'

A casual criminal? And only eight jobs in four years? It didn't sound very plausible to the listening Brant.

'I don't necessarily agree with you, but I fancy you're not quite finished.'

Despite the politeness of the enquiry, it was being made clear that Mr. Brant had not very much more time to spend on this nonsensical kind of speculation. The company dealt in millions, not hundreds.

'Mr. Brant,' began Walden, 'there is nothing to indicate that this man is a particular enemy of this company's. In fact, I think it would be rather a wild assumption.'

'And?'

'Owing to the different ways in which our competitors prepare their accounts, and the many different presentations of annual reports, it is not possible to make accurate comparisons in performance. Nevertheless, as you well know, we have concluded over the past years, that our share of the small shopkeeper market is somewhere between eight and nine point five per cent of the possible maximum.'

Brant could see the direction in which this kind of thinking might lead them, and he rested his elbows on the desk, hands clasped together. Although he was not aware of it, this was a clear indication to others that he was giving matters his full attention.

'Go on.'

'Right. If we accept those figures, and they are the best we have, then it could mean that the world of insurance generally is suffering. In other words, if we take our eight claims as representing eight per cent of the total — '

'Yes, yes.'

Brant waved him to silence. Walden's thinking was sound, as he was quick to recognise. Eight claims for Trusty was the statistical equivalent of one hundred for all companies. Two thousand six hundred pounds would then become — and here he did a rapid mental calculation — about thirty-three thousand pounds. Suddenly, this chap — what did Pop call him? Mr. Gloves, that was it — Mr. Gloves became a very much more interesting character. Even so, he didn't see what Trusty could be expected to do about him. A police matter, this.

'Got your point, Pop,' he conceded. 'But it's all theory, isn't it, and I don't see where we go from here.'

Pop Walden had gathered his thinking together before seeking this interview, and he knew he would not be given another chance.

'As you say Mr. Brant, it is only theory at this moment. I was wondering if it might be put to the Mutual Interests Committee.'

Brant frowned. The Insurers' Mutual Interests Committee was an extremely high-powered body, and he scarcely felt that this Mr. Gloves business could justify taking up its valuable time. What was Walden saying now?

'Matter of principle, you see. No one is suffering very much, but this man is laughing at the industry as a whole. We always say that small business is the lifeblood. This chap of ours, Mr. Gloves, is draining it off, and nobody's even noticed. So far as we know, that is. It could be that the Pru, or Alliance or somebody else has already spotted this, and is doing something about it. It just seems it would be a pity if some other company were to raise it first.'

Despite himself, Brant could not resist a small grin. Old Pop knew his man all right, when he quietly dropped in the suggestion about their competitors.

'All right,' he smiled. 'Supposing we were to confirm that other people are having the same kind of experience? What is supposed to happen then? We're not policemen. We can't catch this feller.'

'Agreed, sir. But I respectfully suggest that the police are in much the same situation as this company. I doubt whether their procedures will have cottoned on to the fact that this man exists. You yourself make the point. It's all so trivial that no single authority has had any need to get excited so far. There has been no violence, no use of weapons, nothing to bring any of these cases into prominence. I'd take a small wager that no county force would waste the time of its neighbours by circulating information as unimportant as this. In fact, I'd go further. I doubt, in many cases, whether a division would bother to circularise the other divisions. If they were to pester each other with this sort of stuff, they'd spend all day reading each others' reports. The police have far too much paper-work as it is.'

That was all true enough, reflected Brant, but he still couldn't see where it led them. He shrugged.

'Well, there you are. You seem to be blanking off your own arguments Pop. It's not important enough for us, or the other big companies. It's not important enough for the police. I don't quarrel with either of those points. So where does it take us?'

Pop Walden knew the weakness of his own case. By any normal business measurement, the Mr. Gloves mystery was not worthy of the time of a lot of senior people. On a time-involvement basis alone, it would be a costly business, far outweighing the expense of letting Mr. Gloves get on with it. But he was resolved to dig in his heels.

'I think we have to stick to the principle, Mr. Brant,' he stated firmly. 'Here is a man of some intelligence, if I judge him rightly. He has worked out this scheme, rather than some dramatic large-scale raid, simply because it is all so unimportant. He is banking on the police not comparing notes. He is banking on the big companies not realising his existence. In short, Mr. Brant, he has been gambling on the precise conversation we are having at this moment. Mr. Gloves is, in my opinion, a real clever bastard.'

It was as much the sudden unexpectedness of the bad language as the import of the words, which gave Freddie Brant pause. Never, in all his dealings with the mild Pop Walden, had he ever heard him swear.

'The principle, eh?' he muttered.

'Absolutely,' confirmed the unruffled Walden. 'This man is laughing at our business, and he's laughing at the law at the same time. He knows we're all too busy, and that's what he's banked on. Now that we know he exists, I can't believe that there isn't somebody, somewhere, who's prepared to take this on, and find him.'

Time was getting on. Brant drummed his fingers in a rapid staccato on the desk top.

'I'll go this far,' he conceded. 'I know you have chums in most of the big offices. If you can get just one of them to conduct a little enquiry of his own, and if he comes up with a similar result, I will look at this again. If I agree with what you find, I'll put up a paper for the Mutual Interests Committee. Is that fair enough?'

'More than fair,' beamed his visitor. 'I know just the man, and I'll phone him straightaway.'

As the door closed behind the jubilant Walden and young Barrett, Freddie Brant smiled to himself. Then his eye caught the face of the clock above the door. Gawd.

The half-yearly inquest.

★   ★   ★

It was a few minutes before five-thirty when the telephoned invitation to dinner came. Frank Gardener had already commenced to tidy up his desk, a habit which was a hangover from earlier times. In the past, the desk he always thought of as his own was in fact shared by the relief officer. The simple economic reason was that the force operated around the clock, and could not afford double space and double equipment. Everything had to be in use continually, and by whoever happened to be on duty at the time. It was therefore essential that an officer going off duty should ensure that all his case-papers and other bits and pieces were cleared away for the benefit of the incoming man. This situation did not apply in the comparative luxury of his new surroundings, but it was an old habit, and one that he quite deliberately held onto. It was no part of his long-term plans to remain in this quiet backwater, and already he was beginning to wonder how soon he dare make approaches to his superiors for a review of his position.

Now, when he picked up the telephone, he recognised at once the lilting accent of his caller.

'Oh hallo,' he greeted. 'Any developments?'

At the other end, Alun Griffiths was containing his excitement with some difficulty.

'As a matter of fact,' he admitted,

'something rather important has come up. It isn't something we can really discuss on the telephone. I was wondering whether you might be free to come to my house tonight for dinner? My wife would be very glad to welcome you, and I think you'd find it rather more comfortable than the public house.'

Not only that, reflected Gardener, but he'd also get a damned sight better meal than one of his boring ready-to-heat affairs, which was his normal routine.

'Delighted,' he agreed rapidly. 'Very good of you to ask me. What sort of time do you want me, and what's the address?'

At seven-fifteen, freshly laundered and presentable, he rang the doorbell at a neat semi-detached house on the outskirts of Midchester. Griffiths had evidently been watching for him, because the door was opened at once.

'Come in, come in,' beamed the insurance man. 'Right on time. Dinner's just about ready. It's Frank, isn't it? Please call me Alun.'

The house was immaculately tidy, and Gardener felt the usual momentary envy of a solitary flat-dweller. Mrs. Griffiths appeared in the hallway, a pleasant-faced woman of about fifty. She held out her hand to him, smiling.

'How d'ye do Mr. Gardener. Very nice of you to come at this short notice.'

Gardener shook the proffered hand, and at the same time wrinkled his nose, sniffing appreciatively.

'My dear lady,' he assured her, 'a man who lives alone never turns away the opportunity for some real home cooking. I'm very grateful to be asked.'

She blushed.

'Oh, it's nothing fancy, you'll see.'

'Nonsense,' chuckled Griffiths. 'My Megan is the best cook I ever met. Main reason we got married, it was.'

Later, as he sat sipping his coffee in the living room, the policeman reflected that it had been many a long day since he had enjoyed such excellent food. Nice people, the Griffiths. Hard workers, both of them, and immensely proud of their children, now out in the world, and doing well by the sound of it. It was then nine o'clock, and there had been no talk of business since he arrived. He was reluctant to raise it himself, but the problem was suddenly solved by the lady of the house.

'Well,' she announced, rising. 'I must be off for a while. In case I don't get back until late, I'll say goodnight, Frank. Please come and see us again, and Alun, you see he does.'

'All right, my love.'

Both men rose as she went out, Gardener expressing his thanks, and her husband going with her to the front door. He was quickly back, and poured more coffee before resuming his seat.

'There's an old lady, four doors down,' he explained. 'Megan likes to pop along last thing at night to make sure she's all right, and find out if she wants any little bits of shopping the next day. She'll stay a bit longer tonight, so that we can have our little chat.'

'She's a very fine lady,' offered Gardener. 'You're a lucky man, Alun. Makes me quite envious.'

The little man smiled his pleasure.

'Well now, I must admit, she is not that bad at all. Looks after me, and that's a fact. You'll have to be thinking about getting your own Megan, you know. Can't be good for you, living on your own too long.'

Gardener had no wish to embark on a discussion of that kind, so he dismissed it, and got down to business.

'You find me one exactly like your missus, and I'll give it very serious consideration,' he promised. 'Now then, what's been going on that you couldn't tell me over the telephone?'

Griffiths finished his coffee, and sat back.

'Your theory seems to have been proved,' he began. 'My head office people carried out some research, and it appears that your Mr. Gloves has been at the root of eight claims over the past four years. Statistically, bearing in mind our share as a company of that particular market, it would indicate that if everyone else's claims experience is in line with ours, the man has been responsible for about one hundred cases, all told.'

'I knew it,' exulted Gardener, 'and so — '

' — let me finish,' interrupted his host. 'Once the people in London got interested, they had an informal chat with another big company. Their experience proved to have been about the same. When I say the same, I mean proportionately. They have about eleven per cent of the total, as near as we can estimate. They came up with twelve similar cases. Again, over four years. If you put the two together, it's fair to assume that the real total is somewhere between one hundred and one hundred and ten. In cash terms, again we're having to do very rough averages per claim, we would seem to be talking of about thirty to thirty-five thousand pounds. All tax free, of course.'

Gardener nodded with satisfaction.

'And that's how the acorn became a tree,' he mused. 'There's nothing trivial about that sort of money. The point is, will your people do anything about it, or will it just die the death?'

Alun Griffiths hesitated before replying. He wasn't certain of his visitor's reaction to the next little bit of news.

'Well, that's just it, you see. No single

company has suffered enough to warrant any particular action. More a matter for the police as my people see it.'

'D'you mean they're just going to drop it?' queried Gardener, showing the beginning of exasperation.

'No, no that isn't it. Matter of fact, I believe someone in my company, at a very high level, is going to raise it with a very senior policeman. I hope you're not going to mind this, Frank, but they insisted on my telling them how I got started on all this. There had to be more to it than just my one little claim. I really didn't have any option.'

'So they know it was me,' ended Gardener flatly.

'I'm afraid so, yes. Do you mind?'

The policeman thought about it. Did he mind? No, he decided, not really. All he had done was to make a friendly enquiry in the right quarter, which any copper would have done. Well, not quite, he admitted. There had been more than a touch of the unorthodox about it. In the first place, he had not referred the matter to any of his superiors, either before or after taking action. He had also moved without consulting the officer in charge of the local enquiry, which again would not make him very popular. And now, by the sound of it, his name was being bandied about in London. He had better get busy the next morning, he realised. Those little omissions would have to be repaired before somebody gave the chief constable a ring, and the big guns came into play.

Then, realising he'd gone into a reverie, he smiled at the waiting man.

'Mind? No, not really. Glad you told me that though, Alun. Gives me a chance to put a few people in the picture, just in case there are any noises from London. Tell me, you don't have a breakdown on these cases, do you? I mean, a list of dates and places, hard facts?'

Griffiths shook his head.

'Why, no,' he admitted. 'I suppose head office could produce it if they were willing. Why do you ask? I mean, your point has been made, surely?'

It was Frank Gardener's turn to shake his head.

'Not really. The basic point, yes. It has

now been confirmed that Mr. Gloves exists, and if the only reason for that was to make me feel like a very clever man, well O.K. But it doesn't end there. Can't have him becoming a statistic, can we? We've got to catch him, that's the real point.'

The insurance man looked mystified.

'Granted, that would be very nice. Nice for everybody concerned. But you can't exactly alert all the police forces, can you? You said yourself, they haven't the time or the manpower to waste on a little thing like this.'

Gardener was now leaning forward, anxious to make his point.

'I said that,' he agreed, 'and I stick to it. But what we're talking about here is a proper analytical approach, don't you see? If we could chart all these jobs, dates, times and places, we shall very likely find ourselves looking at some kind of probability pattern.'

Then, seeing the mystification on the other man's face, he went on rapidly.

'If we could chart the historical position, we might come up with some idea about his movements. That, in turn, would give us a probable notion of where he'll act next. Look, have you any graph paper? I'll try and show you what I mean.'

'Yes, I use it sometimes. I'll go and get some.'

Gardener sat in quiet exultation while his host went away, to return a few moments later with a pad of blank graph paper in his hand.

'There we are,' he announced.

'Could we sit at the table for a minute?' Gardener did so without waiting for an answer, a biro already in his hand. 'Let's try this. Look, down the left hand side we'll put the months of the year for four years. Along the bottom we'll put the names of towns, any old towns for now, since we haven't got the proper facts.'

He began to make entries on the sheet, and Griffiths quietly pulled up a chair, so that he could sit and watch.

The policeman was bent over his work, frowning as he tried to remember sufficient town names to enter on the bottom line. Finally, after twenty place-names, he sat back.

'Now then, let's try it out. First job, say Newcastle, four years ago. Next one, Bristol, following month.' He made crosses at the appropriate parts of the graph, and slowly completed an extremely rough chart. Then he joined up all the crosses with a thick black line, and moved the pad to where both he and Griffiths could see it clearly.

The little insurance man stared at it.

'Not very informative, is it?' he queried. 'Goes up and down like a mad thing. If that was a temperature chart, you'd have all the doctors running round in circles.'

Gardener rubbed at his jaw, nodding agreement.

'You can't tell much from this, I admit, but that's because I had to invent all the place names. If we had the real facts, I'd lay odds we'd get something very different. Remember that this man's job is the deciding factor. It's the job that takes him to these places, not the robberies. And it's my guess he pays two visits to each place. The first time, he susses out the likely locations, but doesn't do anything. Then he takes a close look at what he's found out, decides which is the most favourable, from his point of view, and does the job on his next trip.'

'You're assuming rather a lot there, surely?' protested his listener.

'No, I don't think so. None of these little capers has been carried out on the spur of the moment. If they had, Mr. Gloves would have been nicked long ago. There's always a chance of getting away with an impromptu raid, I grant you, but the risk element is very high. If we were talking about two or three cases, it would be possible to accept that we're dealing with a very lucky man. But we're not. We're talking about somebody who's got away with it perhaps a hundred times, and there is no luck in the world that stretches that far. These jobs are all pre-planned, and that has to mean an earlier visit.'

Griffiths nodded, half convinced.

'Even so, you couldn't chart the visits where he doesn't do anything,' he pointed out, reasonably. 'Unless he does something, we don't know he's even been there.'

'That's true, but to a real mathematician it could be important. You see, this job of his, whatever it is, operates on a certain pattern. There are reasons for him to be in a certain part of the country at certain times each year. We're lucky, because we have four years' history to work on. If we can do a real chart, we'll get a real picture. There are people at the computer centre who could log all the information we have, and by clever programming they can get the computer to give us a fair estimate of his future movements. It won't be one hundred per cent, of course, because of the unknown factors we can't feed in. But it'll be close, and every now and then it will be spot on. Alun,' and Gardener turned to look directly into his new friend's face, 'what we need is all the facts, and from all the companies. Is that possible?'

'H'm.'

Griffiths made a doubtful sound, staring again at the graph.

'I don't know,' he admitted. 'You have to bear in mind that I'm only an area rep. for one company. I've been lucky so far, because the people in London were willing to humour me, but as for approaching all the companies, well, that's way over my head. It could be done, I suppose, but not at my level. This kind of co-operation is practically board-room stuff. You'd have to convince somebody well up the tree before you could get anything like this.'

The words only confirmed what Gardener had been thinking privately.

'You're quite right, of course,' he replied grudgingly. 'You are only a local representative and I am only a local copper. We might be a couple of bright lads, but it's not exactly a combination to shake the world of finance, is it?'

They would both have been a lot less dispirited if they had had a crystal ball which could look into the future, and thus enable them to eavesdrop on a certain conversation which would take place in London during the next forty-eight hours.

As it was, they parted that night with a feeling that the whole thing would probably die. Frank Gardener was resolved to clear his position with his local superiors, and also with Inspector Dalton of the Park Street station, but that was merely a tidying-up process, to forestall any call that might come from London, which was highly unlikely.

Or so he thought.

11

More than one man turned his head to look at the attractive woman who emerged from the gloom of the underground station into the sunny London street. She walked with the confident, swinging grace of someone who was headed for an important destination, and there was an appealing radiance about her which marked her out, even on that busy morning.

Sheila Holden waited impatiently for the traffic signal to change to green, then went quickly across the zebra, clutching the airways bag as it swung from her shoulder. Left at the lights, then second left, was what Bruce Hayward had told her. Number eleven didn't look very impressive, just a scarred wooden door between two shop-fronts, but she pushed it open and went inside, climbing the dark narrow stairs.

It was odd, the way one could become

accustomed to using houses and flats which belonged to perfect strangers, she reflected. Bruce seemed to have acquaintances all over London who were 'away for a couple of days', and who had no objection to his using the premises in their absence. This man, Lionel McEwan, was away in North Africa somewhere, and was not expected back until the end of the week. That meant she and Bruce could stay until Thursday, although she must be certain she returned home in time to collect the children that day. The stairs seemed endless.

At the end of the street a man stood outside a newsagents, watching Sheila's progress, and noting carefully the doorway into which she had turned. Once the door closed behind her, he walked slowly along, ready to turn quickly away if she should emerge suddenly. But the door to number eleven remained firmly closed, and he was in something of a dilemma about what to do next. People in London are famous for minding their own business, but he couldn't loiter for very long without someone beginning to wonder what he was doing. Then, another thought struck him. For all he knew, Sheila could be standing at one of the many windows of number eleven, and she could scarcely fail to spot him if she did, since he was about opposite the place. What he must do was to get out of sight, and he stared along the row of shopfronts. There was a tea and sandwich bar fifty yards along, and he walked gratefully inside, collected a cup of tea, and sat on a high stool by the window.

The building which had swallowed up Sheila Holden consisted of four storeys. The ground floor was taken up by shops, and the next two floors were business premises. There was lettering on the window, which he could not read from the angle at which he sat, so he had no way of judging whether she was calling on one of the companies involved. The top floor was clearly used as living quarters. There were curtains at the windows, and a television aerial on the chimney, so perhaps one of the shopkeepers lived on the premises. After thirty minutes of waiting, he realised that the proprietor of the café was eyeing him, so he ordered more tea and resumed his vigil. Twenty minutes later he was still there, and had decided that there was no point in continuing the surveillance. He left the café, ducking his head and walking swiftly across the street, then approached the door through which Sheila had vanished. There was no outside indication as to the occupants, merely a faded brass number plate, and the number was eleven. He pushed at the door, and when it opened slipped inside, adjusting his eyes to the sudden gloom.

The wall to his left proved a little more informative. According to the mixture of wooden and metal plates, the first floor was occupied by an import and export firm. There were two firms on the second floor, one an advertising agency and the other a company dealing in greetings cards. The third floor, which he had concluded was occupied privately, simply bore a name, Lionel McEwan. He looked up at the worn stairway, unable to decide for a moment what he would do next. Then an idea came to him. He went out of the building, and retraced his steps to where he had observed a freshly painted telephone kiosk outside a small sub post-office. Digging in his pockets for change, he went in, to find that there were no directories left in the space provided for the purpose. What did people do with them, he wondered? Picking up the receiver, he dialled Directory Enquiries, and almost at once a voice announced,

'Directory Enquiries. Which town please?'

'London.'

'Name of people?'

'McEwan.'

'Is that M-A-C?'

'No. M, small C. First name Lionel.'

'Just a moment.'

There was a pause, during which he continued to watch the entrance to number eleven, ready to abandon the call if his quarry should re-appear.

'Have you an address please?'

He called over the address, and the operator replied at once with the number, which he scribbled quickly down, and repeated. Then he thanked her and hung up, staring at the seven digits on his piece of paper. It was all very well to have this man's phone number, but now that he had it, he wasn't quite sure what use he could make of it. If Sheila was indeed with this man, as he suspected, the most obvious thing to do was to go to the flat and confront them. But something held him back, and the something was caution. There was a chance that he was entirely wrong, and that Sheila's visit was perfectly innocuous. He was going to look a complete fool if he revealed that he had taken all this trouble to follow her, only to learn that she was visiting an old friend. For all he knew, this man McEwan could be married to one of her old schoolfriends or something. Well, at least he had the telephone number. There was a lot of telephone canvassing these days. It would be quite unremarkable for a salesman to want to speak to the lady of the house. Our New Summer Range, Madam. Something like that.

Slowly, he dialled the number. It was a long time before anyone answered, and it was a man's voice, guarded.

'Yes?'

'Mr. McEwan?'

'No. He's not here, I'm afraid. Who is this?'

Adam Holden's mind raced. Somehow or other he had to find out the name of the man on the other end. Probably he shared the flat with the absent McEwan or something of that kind. There was only one way he was likely to be given that information.

'Metropolitan Police,' he announced crisply. 'Sergeant Atkins speaking. When is Mr. McEwan expected back please?'

Police? At the other end, Bruce Hayward, drowsy from his recent encounter with Sheila, suddenly cleared his head.

'Not for several days, I'm afraid.'

The bogus policeman put a tinge of suspicion in his tone when he next spoke.

'I see. That's very unfortunate. Who is this speaking, please?'

Hayward hesitated. What the devil had old Lionel been up to, for the police to want to talk to him? And the last thing he wanted was to have some great flatfoot walking in on Sheila and himself.

'I don't see why you want to know

that,' he countered. 'I'm not involved in Mr. McEwan's affairs.'

There was no cordiality in Holden's tone now.

'That was not suggested, sir, but you are in the gentleman's flat, and I must have a name for the record.' The next words were half-joking, half-menacing. 'After all, you could be a prowler for all I know. How would I explain that to Mr. McEwan, eh? What would I say to him, if he came in to report the premises had been burgled, and I was to tell him 'oh yes, I know. I was chatting on the telephone to the man who did it'. Perhaps it would be better if I sent a man round?'

That put an end to Hayward's hesitation.

'No,' he said hastily. 'No need for that. Mr. McEwan has kindly let me stay here while he's away. My name is Hayward, Bruce Hayward.'

Hayward. For a moment 'Sergeant Atkins' stared at the telephone as if willing it to produce an image of the scene at the other end. Joy's husband. Television chap, or something. Then remembering his role, he queried,

'And your home address, Mr. Hayward?'

He had no need to use the waiting ballpoint. He knew perfectly well where the Haywards lived.

'Thank you,' he replied. 'Would you please tell Mr. McEwan that we called, and we'll try again at the weekend?'

Hayward, greatly relieved, confirmed that he would do that. Both men put down their respective receivers, and stood for a few moments in thought. Holden was interrupted first. There was a fierce insistent tapping on the glass of the telephone box, and he looked out to see a very fat woman glaring at him, and waving her watch. Pushing open the door, he stepped out into the sunshine, and walked slowly away.

Bruce Hayward was still standing by the telephone, cogitating about the call, and wondering whether any possible harm could come from the police having noted his name and address. They might well call his home, of course, to confirm with Joy that he was staying in London at present. That might cause a bit of embarrassment, since he'd told her he was off to Holland for the next couple of days. Still, forewarned was forearmed. He'd think up some yarn to explain his having called in at McEwan's place on the way. He ought to be able to —

'What was all that about, darling?'

Sheila's sleepy voice drifted out from the bedroom.

'Eh? Oh, some policeman wanting Lionel. Probably about his car or something. No big deal.'

He went back inside and looked down at the recumbent Sheila, who opened one eye and held out her arms to him.

'Your friend is probably wanted by Interpol,' she murmured. 'Trust you to get us involved in a bank raid or something. Come and tell me all about it.'

Taking her hands, he tucked them firmly under the bedclothes.

'I'd better call Joy, I think. I had to give the sergeant my name. If he calls home she'll probably think I've fallen under a bus or something. Worse still, she might decide to come up to London to make sure I'm all right. We can't have that, can we?'

She grinned impishly.

'I can just see her face, if she did.'

'H'm,' he grunted. 'It might be amusing to imagine it, but it wouldn't be so funny if it actually happened. Best to be on the safe side. Anyway, you'd better get some rest, my girl. You are in for one hell of a busy evening. I've got it all worked out.'

'Doesn't involve going out, does it? I was rather thinking we could keep pretty busy where we are,' she countered.

'That's all part of it,' he agreed, 'but yes, we are going out, and no, I'm not going to tell you where. It's all a big surprise.'

Sheila made a face, and burrowed into the pillow.

'Oh well, if I'm not wanted — '

But he wasn't to be drawn.

'You'll eat those words before the night is out,' he promised. 'Right now, I'm going to make that call, to prevent the balloon from going up.'

He went softly out of the room, closing the door gently behind him. Then he crossed to the telephone and dialled his home number. It was simply too early in the day for even Joy to have got plastered. She must have been standing by the telephone, because it only rang once before she picked it up.

'Bruce? Thank God. What on earth is going on? I've had some policeman on to me to confirm that you're away from home at present, and so forth. What's it all about? Are you all right? Where are you calling from?'

'Perfectly all right,' he assured her. 'I was afraid you might be getting a call and that you'd start worrying unnecessarily — '

'Well, of course I'm worrying,' she snapped. 'Thought you'd be in Amsterdam by now.'

'I had a message at the airport,' he explained. 'There were a couple of things to see to in London before I could get away. One of them was to come to McEwan's place, and pick up some documents. You remember him. You met him at — '

'What's all that got to do with the police?' she demanded.

'Nothing, dear, nothing at all. His car's been pinched or something. The police telephoned to talk to him about it. I thought it was probably my people calling, or I wouldn't have answered at all. They wanted to know who I was, which is natural enough, really. Could have been some burglar, for all they knew. Obviously, they did a quick check at your end, just to satisfy themselves.'

Joy considered this for a moment.

Then she said,

'So I can stop worrying? You're really all right?'

'Absolutely,' he confirmed. 'Matter of fact I'm just off. One more call to make, then I catch a plane at one o'clock. With any luck, I'll be back some time on Thursday.'

They told each other to take care, and hung up. Hayward was relieved that Joy had taken it so calmly, and also that he'd taken the precaution of making the call. Having established that he was on the point of leaving, he'd forestalled the possibility of Joy making the journey into London to see for herself.

Very carefully, he opened the bedroom door and looked. Sheila was sound asleep, as he'd hoped. When she had first called him about her husband's plans to be away, his reaction had been to fob her off, but he had remembered in time about the book of clippings. Bruce Hayward was, by instinct and training, a man who could not resist any kind of mystery, and he had been very intrigued by what she had told him. Adam's trip provided the perfect opportunity for him to have a look at those newspaper extracts, and he had persuaded her to bring them with her. Now that she was asleep, it was an ideal opportunity for him to study them. Opening the roomy sling-bag she'd been carrying, he hefted out the bulky volume, and carried it across to a table, where he sat down and began to leaf through it.

He, too, met the same baffling range of local stories that Sheila had described. He was much more thorough in his approach, reading every single word with great care, but in the end he had to admit she had been right. Turning back reluctantly to the front page, he stared at the first story, the one about the young man who had been killed in the motor-cycle accident. He still had this feeling there was something not quite right about the presentation, and then he saw it. The cutting itself was too big. The normal procedure, when anyone cuts an article out from a newspaper, is to extract only the relevant material, often with damage to adjacent columns. Holden had not done that. There was almost a complete advertisement for a well-known washing machine at the right-hand side of the story, but no extraneous material on the left. Now, why should he do an apparently untidy job like that? The next sheet was the same, except this time there was extraneous material above the head-line, making it again look untidy. An idea struck him. The clippings, all neatly taped at the top, were free at the bottom. Carefully, he lifted the top extract, and folded it back. Then he turned the book round so that the printing was the right way up. There were pieces of several smaller stories on the reverse, but only one was complete. It was a single column report of a raid on some grocer's shop by a man wearing a stocking mask. A small-scale affair, in which the thief had made off with some three hundred pounds in cash, and Hayward was disappointed. Nevertheless, he turned the page, and repeated the process. Once again, there were several news items, but the only complete story concerned a similar theft, almost a carbon copy of the first. Hayward checked the headings on the two newspapers, and the dates. The first was from a Glasgow newspaper, the second from Bristol, and there was a fortnight's gap between them. It could be no more than coincidence. Certainly the two crimes appeared identical, but there were hundreds of miles between the two cities. This hooded villain would scarcely make such a long hop simply to pick up such small sums. Puzzled, he turned to the third entry. Sure enough, there was the hooded man again, in an entirely different part of the country, and the puzzlement was replaced by excitement.

The next cutting was the same, and the next. He would have to abandon the random approach, he realised, and bring some system to bear on the search. Taking a sheet of paper and a pen, he started at the first entry and began to make a list. Town and date. It took him the greater part of an hour, and, at the end of it, he was on his third sheet of foolscap paper. Now, sitting back, he closed the book and stared at the list. There was no room for any doubt. The thief, described variously as the Hooded Intruder, Masked Man, Stocking-Face, and so forth, was touring the country, carrying out these small-scale operations. Why weren't the nationals clamouring about him? Bruce Hayward had been a television journalist long enough to know the answer to that. Nobody had noticed him. He had done nothing important enough to bring him to the notice of anyone higher than an inspector in the local police station, and, as the list revealed, he'd never visited the same locality twice. There was no reason why anyone should spot him, or even take anything more than a purely local interest.

No, that wasn't entirely true, he admitted.

There was one man very interested in the masked bandit. A man named Adam Spencer Holden was taking a very close interest in his movements. Close enough to have the local paper sent to his home. Close enough to cut out the newspaper clippings, and secret enough to disguise his interest, by keeping them face-down in the scrapbook.

Now, why should he go to all the trouble? How had he got on to this villain in the first place, and been so successful in tracking his movements? What was the connection between Holden, a man with a good steady job, and this back-street marauder? Then, the other half of the equation came to him. Sheila had told him there was a self-addressed envelope which arrived at the house most weeks, and it was usually thick with paper. But what kind of paper? Not business material. Holden would have a brief-case for that. Not newspaper, because that came separately.

Bruce Hayward ran his eye once more down the lists, hoping for some consistency of pattern to emerge, but there was none. What was it Conan Doyle had once said?

'When you have eliminated everything which is possible, you are left only with the impossible, which is therefore the solution.'

It had been something like that, anyway. He certainly had the gist of it right, if not the actual words. And, any way one cared to look at this present situation, there was only one impossible explanation. It was impossible that a man in Holden's position could do anything so bizarre as to roam the country, robbing small corner shops, all dressed up like some East End villain.

Impossible.

But inescapable.

What a story. What a lovely, beautiful story. Hayward was not remotely concerned with the moral aspects of the case. He would have to turn the chap in, of course, but that was not his main worry. He had somehow to ensure that he retained the journalistic advantage of bringing the case to public attention. There were thousands of pounds to be had here, in newspaper coverage alone, but everything would depend on the timing of his revelation.

Hayward was so deep in thought that he did not hear the door open behind him.

'What are you doing out here, darling?' came Sheila's voice, close by his shoulder. 'And that's Adam's book.'

Her question ended on an accusing note.

Hayward swiftly brought his mind back to the present. The very last person to be entrusted with any of this was Holden's wife. She might be willing to betray him, in the purely physical sense of the bedroom, but this greater betrayal would come into an entirely different category. This constituted a threat to her entire domestic background, the children, hearth and home syndrome. Faced with the possibility of any danger in that area, a woman who, only moments before, had been so yielding and complaisant, could be transformed into a snarling biting enemy. That was the probable outcome of his relationship with Sheila Holden, in any case, but he wasn't ready to have it happen quite so soon.

Turning, he smiled over at her, patting at the hand which now rested on his shoulder.

'Much as I hate to admit this,' he confessed, 'the ruddy thing has me baffled. It makes no sense at all.'

'Ha, ha,' she scoffed gently, 'so much for your poor little woman theory. Let me have it, you said. I'll show you a great big reporter at work. In fact, you haven't done any better than me, have you? Come on, say it.'

'I haven't done any better than you,' he repeated. Then he pushed the closed book away from him, and moved round to take her in his arms. 'Are you quite certain we're safe, darling? No chance of your old man changing his mind about Scarborough, or whatever it was you said?'

'You don't listen,' she complained, mock-seriously. 'I never mentioned Scarborough.

Plymouth, was what I told you. Plymouth tonight, Swindon tomorrow night. Scarborough doesn't come into it.'

'But he could change his mind,' he pressed. 'Decide to leave it for another week perhaps, and come home.'

'Change his mind?' she echoed scornfully. 'About work? You don't know Adam Spencer Holden. He can change his mind about a lot of things, like anyone else, but work, never. What do you think you're up to, now?'

Her voice was barely audible, with her head against his neck.

'Just investigating,' he assured her softly. 'You've hurt my manly pride, with your cracks about the scrap book. More around here to be investigated than a bunch of newspaper clippings, you know. Have to re-assert my authority.'

'Oh lovely,' she sighed, 'I take it all back. You really do investigate rather well. Shouldn't we go back to the investigation room?'

'I think we should,' he agreed, leading her away.

12

Frank Gardener stood in the sparsely-furnished room, staring down into Victoria. In his early days as a policeman, he had on occasion enjoyed a mental image of himself as a big man, real top brass, directing massive police operations from his luxurious office in New Scotland Yard. That was before he had a proper understanding of the real workings of the country's police forces, and the role played by the Yard. Nowadays, his projections into the future tended more to the prosaic, and he knew that it would take a lot of good fortune, in addition to zealous application, if he could ever hope one day to don a superintendent's uniform.

Mind you, he admitted to himself, the good fortune seemed to be running for him at this moment. Only the day before he had sent in a request to see his own chief superintendent, a request which had been met within the hour. At first, the senior man had been inclined to scoff at the theory which Gardener outlined to him. But, as the story unfolded, with the addition of the information which Alun Griffiths and his London associates had been able to provide, the chief super had paid close attention.

'All right, Sergeant Gardener, this is all very interesting, but two points arise. One, why are you telling me all this, and Two, are you expecting me to do anything about it?'

'As to the first question sir, I thought it was my duty, as a member of your team, to let you know what was going on. It all started out in a very small way, just a chat between me and the local man from the Trusty. Now that he's got the London end to take an interest, there's no telling what they might decide to do. They wouldn't for a moment consider referring to Mr. Griffiths, or even telling him what's going on. I wouldn't want this to come feeding back to you from some other source, and you being in a position of not knowing what one of your own staff had started.'

'H'm.'

Good. Yes, very good answer that, decided his chief. There was nothing more infuriating than having people going off on their own, and leaving their superiors uninformed.

'As to question two, sir, I don't honestly see what you can do. It would cost a fortune to contact all the forces involved, and I can't see anybody being all that grateful. They're such tuppenny ha'penny little crimes, when you take them singly.'

'H'm. Still, it all adds up to a tidy sum of money at the end. I'll have to think about this. Anyway, you did the right thing by putting me in the picture. If I decide to do anything at all, I'll let you know.'

It was a dismissal. Gardener thanked him and left the room. His timing, although he had no way of knowing it, could scarcely have been better. In a London office, two very different people were discussing the same problem.

The Mutual Interests Committee, in which all the leading insurance companies had a representation, maintained a very small permanent staff, one of whom was nominated as Police Liaison Officer. His job was to keep in close contact with an Assistant Commissioner at New Scotland Yard, one of whose special responsibilities covered the field of insurance. The A.C. was one Donald Saunders, an urbane and polished man of forty-three, and he had just finished listening to the story outlined to him by the insurers' representative, George Carson, known inevitably as Kit.

'Well, what do you think, Donald?'

Carson leaned back, lighting one of his obnoxious miniature cigars.

'Think?' repeated Saunders softly. 'What do I think? Well, let's see. I think you're a bloody fine chum to have, dumping a thing like this on me. This chap, the one you call Mr. Gloves — my God, wouldn't the Sundays love that — is already giving me a pain in the proverbial. What do you imagine I can do about him? This isn't television, you know. I envy those fellows, sometimes. In a situation like this, the chap in my chair would flick down a lot of switches and yell out orders. Police cars would go screaming out from all units, and your Mr. Gloves would have every copper in the country on his tail inside an hour. Life isn't like that, Kit, and you know it. I mean, look at what you've brought. This comedian has been making mugs of us all for over four years. Frankly, I don't see what's to stop him making it five, or even ten. We're on the losing end of this, any way you look at it. My only access to all the forces is the Conference of Chief Constables. I don't propose to tell you what the average agenda consists of, but you can probably imagine some of it. Narcotics, smuggling, Interpol, stuff like that. The agenda's far too long always, and those people are hard-pressed enough with vital work. If you think I'm going to face them with your Mr. Gloves, picking up three or four hundred quid every now and then, you must think I'm a lot braver than I really am. They'd kick my rear end from here to breakfast, and, in their place, so would I.'

Carson nodded sympathetically. He had expected this reaction, before he even raised the subject. However, he had not quite finished.

'There is a small ray of sunshine,' he offered.

'Oh yes? A signed confession? That would be nice.'

'No, not that, but I think we may have worked out something which will interest you.' Carson opened his briefcase, and removed some papers from it. 'We have some rather good chums in the computer world, and we decided to make use of them. We approached the three biggest, and told them about our problem. Then we handed over the complete documentation on every case we could positively identify. There are one hundred and eight, all told. The documentation varies from company to company, but only on minor points of detail. The basic essentials are always the same. We asked the computer boys to put their respective geniuses to work, with the object of producing a pattern, if there was one.'

He began to smooth out the papers on

Saunders' desk, and the A.C. leaned forward to inspect them.

'Come on Kit,' he encouraged. 'Get to it. I've seen a printout before.'

'Quite. Well, these people have all come up with the same answers. There has been no collusion, you can bet on that. They're all competitors. By plotting all these lovely details, and of course we're very lucky in the sense that they had over a hundred cases, they have been able to establish a pattern. From the pattern, they have been able to extrapolate Mr. Gloves's probable future movements. His job, whatever it is, takes him all over the country. At first sight, his movements seem to be just at random, but when you have over four years on record' — and at this Saunders winced — 'it becomes possible to isolate the root movements. Mr. Gloves tries to avoid visiting these places on a quarterly basis, or anything so obvious. That is not, we feel, in order to fool the authorities, but probably because it suits the nature of his job. We tend to think of him as being some kind of visiting supervisor, and the reason he isn't too regular in his habits is so that the local people can't be absolutely certain when he'll turn up.'

Saunders nodded, thinking.

'See what you mean, and it makes sense. Bit like the army. If everybody knows it's a C.O.'s inspection, they scrub everything up. This is beginning to sound good, Kit.'

'I hope you'll think so,' returned Carson smoothly. 'Well now, although the visits are not regularly spaced, they still have to be made, and with such a long period of time, and such a great number of logged cases, a pattern has to emerge, irregular or not. All our whizz kids are agreed. Mr. Gloves will be in action this coming Wednesday, or the Wednesday after, and he will be either in Swindon or Blackburn.'

Saunders made a face.

'Is that it? Two towns, hundreds of miles apart, and two different days. Not much to go on, is it?'

'I disagree,' replied Carson, somewhat stiffly. 'I think these chaps have done very well. Don't forget, until this morning, you wouldn't have had even that much advance information.'

Saunders grunted.

'I think it's you who's forgetting something. Until you turned up, I didn't even know we had a bloody problem. Ah well,' and his tone was now more conciliatory, 'can you tell me roughly how many premises we shall have to cover?'

The visitor shook his head.

'I'm afraid not. You'll have to rely on local knowledge for that.'

'Local knowledge? I should have thought your people would have had plenty of that. After all, it's their customers we're talking about.'

Carson coughed slightly, looking embarrassed.

'Unfortunately, my members, whilst naturally anxious to give every possible assistance, do not see their way to providing details as to their saturation in any given locality.'

'Gawd help us,' breathed Saunders. 'What you mean is, they don't want each other to know how well they're doing. Or badly.'

'I don't think you will find many industries where companies are prepared to divulge trading details to their competitors,' Carson pointed out, reasonably. 'Personally, I think they deserve a lot of credit for coming up with this historic material. Without it, there would be no way any of us could even have guessed at the future. Come on now, Donald, be reasonable. They've co-operated damned well, and you know it. After all, catching crooks is not really their job, you know.'

'Huh. Don't bother to finish. We all know whose job it is. Can I keep this stuff?'

'Certainly, those copies were prepared for you. Well, I must be getting along. I wish you luck.'

After Carson had gone, Donald Saunders sat for a while in deep thought. Then he put through a call to the Chief Constable of Midshire. The result, less than twenty-four hours later, was that the man Saunders regarded as the cause of this nuisance problem was waiting in his outer office, wondering what the summons to London was all about.

'Sergeant Gardener?'

Frank turned from the window to find a pretty blonde-haired wpc looking at him enquiringly.

'That's me,' he confirmed.

'You may go in now.' She pointed to a door. 'The A.C. is ready for you.'

Assistant Commissioner? Nobody had told him to expect to meet anyone at that level. Gardener thanked the girl, walked across and tapped at the door. At a barked invitation, he opened it and went inside.

'How d'ye do sergeant. My name is Saunders. Have a chair.'

'Thank you, sir.'

The man from Midshire did not know a great deal about the personalities at the Yard, but he could tell at a glance that Assistant Commissioner Saunders was not a man to be trifled with. Too many people, as he well knew, were inclined to write off the Yard these days. Something told him that this man Saunders would not be so easily written off.

'Have they told you why you're here?'

The question was suddenly shot at

him, before he was properly in the chair.

'No sir, not really. I was just told to get on the fast train to London, and report here. I imagine it has some connection with these small robberies, which have been going on all over the country.'

No use in sitting there like Simple Simon. Obscure police sergeants do not suddenly find themselves summoned to London on somebody's whim. It had to be connected with Mr. Gloves. Not that a man could learn much, by staring at the inscrutable features of the Assistant Commissioner, who now nodded.

'I've had a quick look at your history, sergeant,' he intoned. 'You seem to have the makings of a first-class copper.'

He waited, as though for a contradiction.

'Er, thank you very much, sir.'

'You also have the makings of a first-class bloody nuisance.'

'Sir?'

'This bandit of yours,' explained Saunders. 'But for you, we wouldn't have known he existed. He's been making fun of the entire police system for years. And getting away with it. Until you dug him out, and got every insurance man in the country steamed up. Can you imagine what Fleet Street will do, when we catch him? They'll have a field day with your Mr. Gloves. I'd like to know who dreamed that up, but I'm not going to ask. I suppose it's a bit better than the Hooded Terror, but not much. Anyway, thanks to you, we now know about him, so we'd better catch him, and quick. It's obviously a job that has to be done centrally, because he hops about so much. That means the Yard, or, more specifically, me. This is a one-off job, and you might think I've got people just sitting around, waiting for something like this. I haven't. Most of my people work all the hours God sends, and this little lot is the last thing they need.'

The great man paused, and Frank Gardener hoped his own eyes were expressionless, as he stared across the desk. He didn't like the turn of the conversation, and was already beginning to formulate his own ideas as to how it might end.

'So, you see,' resumed the Assistant Commissioner, 'I find myself with a problem. I don't like people to bring me problems, unless they also bring solutions. The way I'm looking at this, you're the one who started it off, and you're a bit of a spare part over in Midshire. Your Chief Constable has kindly agreed to loan you out for a while. You can go and net this villain, make everybody happy. What do you say to that?'

The man from Midshire shifted on his chair. This was his chance to get back to some proper police work, even though it wasn't what he would have chosen.

'I'd like it very much, sir,' he admitted. 'Only thing is, I don't know where to start.'

'Don't worry about that. The insurance companies have produced some forecasts for us. They have a pretty good idea of this chap's pattern, irregular though it is. I would think your chances are about fifty-fifty, but I expect a one-hundred per cent result just the same. Go and see a man named Carson. His address and the rest of it is all in these papers I shall give you. You report to me, and no one else, that must be clearly understood. I want to know exactly what you're up to, all the time. This is going to need some careful handling when it breaks, and I don't want it left to a Detective Inspector.'

So there was going to be someone else. Gardener was disappointed.

'Which Inspector is that, sir?'

'Eh?' Saunders glowered at the interruption. Then his brow cleared. 'Ah, see what you mean. I'm out of sequence. That's you. The outside world doesn't think things are being properly handled if there isn't a magic inspector on the job. You are promoted as from this morning, for one month, initially. After that, we'll see. My budget can just about stand one additional inspector, for a while. There are other vacancies, of course. Plenty of work for constables, supervising school crossings in the suburbs. I think you take my drift, Inspector?'

Gardener knew a threat when he heard one.

'Yes indeed, sir. Point taken. Thank you

very much. I'd rather like to be an Inspector — '

' — bloody good job, since you already are — '

' — but I've got reservations about the school crossings. I think I'd better catch this Mr. Gloves.'

'I think you had, too. Now then, as to the local people — '

The Assistant Commissioner began to outline the tactics his new appointee was to employ, and Detective Inspector Frank Gardener paid very close attention.

In another part of London, Bruce Hayward sat in Lionel McEwan's kitchen, smoking thoughtfully, and planning the use he intended to make of the windfall information Sheila had brought to him. He was also working out the details of his now inevitable parting from the woman who was cheerfully tidying up the sitting room.

In fact, all the principals were in London on that particular day. Adam Spencer Holden was staring incredulously at the impassive features of a man who had just given him some rather surprising news.

13

Wednesday 10.45 a.m.

'Three hundred pounds?'

Holden repeated the sum, as if half-hoping he may have misunderstood the man the first time.

'That's what I said, Mr. Holden,' was the calm reply. 'I don't understand why you look so surprised. You didn't think this company worked for nothing, did you?'

Holden shook his head.

'No, of course not. Naturally not,' he denied. 'But I expected to pay a lot less. A hundred pounds would have surprised me, frankly, for just a couple of hours work.'

The other man was squarely-built, and wore a well-fitting suit of tweed, with a quiet Paisley tie. His appearance was that of a comfortably-off but otherwise undistinguished member of society, not a man people would remember. It was part of his job to melt into backgrounds without attracting attention, which was what made him valuable to people who needed his services. People like Holden. When he smiled, it was without mirth.

'A couple of hours work?' he repeated. 'Mr. Holden, I think you really have very little idea of what's involved in a situation of this kind. There were three men on this surveillance, from seven last evening until two in the morning. Two cars were used, one by the camera team, and one by the man watching the front door. There was expensive equipment, too. This camera,' and he rested one hand lightly on the intricate assembly beside him, 'cost twelve hundred pounds. You insisted on absolute discretion, with no possibility of our activities being spotted. That meant setting up the camera at a high point from which we could see down into the flat, without being seen. We weren't taking holiday snapshots, Mr. Holden. This infra-red equipment is the last word in modern technology, and the results speak for themselves. The shots were taken from a block of flats nearby, and we had to slip the security man twenty pounds just to let us on the premises. That's not additional, by the way, it's included in the three hundred. I think, when you start to add all that together, you can begin to see that the charge is not at all unreasonable.'

Holden chewed his lip. He didn't know much about private investigators, not real ones. In his mind, he retained a vague mental image of fearless, indestructible men, who prowled the bars and dark streets, smoking endless cigarettes and always ready for a rough house or a silky woman. This smooth-looking character, with his infra-red cameras and his manpower deployment, was a far cry from that picture. But, as he thought of pictures, his eyes fell once more to the glossy blow-ups which had been turned towards him on the desk. There was no arguing with the efficiency of this man, nor with the ugly reality of the evidence. How stupid of Sheila and this fellow Hayward not even to bother with the curtains. Still, who would? They were on the top floor after all, with the lights out, and nothing but the dark night sky to observe them.

So they thought.

So they very obviously thought, he admitted savagely, staring down. Well, someone was in for a surprise. His immediate impulse was to storm round to this man McEwan's flat, and confront Sheila and Hayward with the damning evidence he had been given. What was that the other man was saying?

'Sorry, I was miles away,' he admitted.

'I was asking whether you would be requiring our service any further?'

Further? What for? He had quite enough already, surely, and what with these prices —

'Don't follow what you mean.'

His inquisitor was well accustomed to this kind of reaction to evidence such as he was now staring at.

'Sometimes,' he explained, 'a client likes us to build up a run of evidence, showing the couple involved against different backgrounds, so that there can be no challenging of identity when the case comes to court.'

'Challenge of identity?' repeated Holden, aware that he must be sounding rather foolish.

'Oh, yes, it has been known,' he was assured. 'People involved sometimes set up elaborate alibis for the occasion in question. It is much more convincing to the court, if a series of quite separate photographs are produced, which demonstrate that the couple are often together. Restaurants, theatres, that kind of place. If this is the only evidence produced, and the guilty parties decide to brazen it out, they can even go so far as to claim that actors have been employed. People who look sufficiently like them at a distance. These are not exactly studio portraits, you must understand. You know perfectly well who these people are, but you might not find it an easy matter to convince a court of law on these photographs alone, not if those concerned make a case for total rejection.'

But Holden had heard enough. And seen enough. All this nonsense about challenging the evidence was so much sales talk to persuade him to spend more money. He stood up, shaking his head, and shuffling the pictures into a tidy pile.

'No, I don't think so,' he announced. 'By the time I'm finished with these two, there won't be any nonsense about denial.'

The investigator rose too, and they faced each other across the desk.

'As you wish, Mr. Holden. If you should change your mind later, we are always at your service. Now then, as to our account — '

Fifteen minutes later, Holden was seated in a small coffee-bar, trying to assemble his thoughts. His first impulse had been to burst in on Sheila and Hayward, and have it out with them on the spot, but he had successfully resisted the temptation. Now, in the semi-darkness of the coffee-bar, listening to the muted chatter around him, he knew he had done the right thing.

This was not something which could be dealt with quite so easily and quickly. There was far too much at stake, so many complications, all of which needed to be reviewed in the light of this new and damaging information.

First and foremost was his marriage and home background. Holden no longer thought about love in any conventional sense of the word, but he was comfortably settled with Sheila. They got along with each other fairly well, and there were no major upsets in their comfortable routine. Certainly, he had no cause for complaint with the way she looked after him, and the children. The house was reasonably tidy, and she wasn't a spendthrift. All in all, he reasoned, he was not anxious to bring about the termination of his marriage, despite this enormous provocation. That was not to say, he reminded himself, that those responsible should be allowed to get off scot-free, but for the moment he did not want to take precipitate action. He held the whip hand, after all, and he could apply that whip whenever he chose. That was the important factor. His position was in no way weakened by deferment. If anything, his own situation was made stronger by the mere possession of the knowledge he had, as exemplified by the photographs now tucked away inside his briefcase.

The thought of the briefcase reminded him of his job. His new post, with its concomitant additional responsibilities, was going to require all his mental efforts. He had little doubt of his ability to bring it off, but he would be putting a great additional strain on himself if he were to be in the process of breaking up his marriage during those first important months. There had been interference already, and he was only too conscious of it. His intention of making a surprise visit to Plymouth on the previous day had gone by the board. Today, Wednesday, he was due for Swindon, but he had already decided not to make the trip. His mind was in too much of a jumble for proper attention to the job. A telephone call to the office would quickly take care of that. He wouldn't even need to claim that he wasn't feeling well, he realised with a wry smile. As Chief Sales Controller, he had no one to make excuses to. He would simply say there were one or two people he wanted to see in London, and no one would dare question it. Besides, if he claimed sickness, someone might telephone home, and he had no intention of being there. Sheila might be returning today, for all he knew, and he was not yet ready to face her. Apart from which, she thought he was safely away on his trips, and he did not want her to know otherwise. No, tonight he would stay in London, go to a concert or something, returning home tomorrow as if from Swindon. With all the thinking he would be doing during the next twenty-four hours, he would be very much more in control of the situation by then.

Which left only his last raid.

From the moment the Chairman had told him of his new, already publicised, appointment, Holden had known that his secret life must come to an end, and for sound, unanswerable reasons. There would be one final job, a kind of farewell performance, and then he would retire. It had been a good idea, soundly applied, and enormously successful, but now it must cease. His decision to cancel the current two away trips, for quite other reasons, brought with it the inescapable conclusion that even that final raid must be abandoned. The realisation of this, as he quietly poured a third cup of coffee, brought with it an almost childish additional resentment against Sheila and the man Hayward. The raids had supplied an outlet for one side of Holden's character, and the realisation that they had to be brought to a close was an unwelcome development in any case. But at least he had, until now, the keen anticipation of the final drama. The last, adrenalin-pumping entry into the little shop, the last fearful journey back to the hotel, the last experience of that enormous relief when it was over. Then, the plump envelope coming through the letter box for the last time, the final clipping from the local newspaper. The end of an era.

That was the way he had intended it to be, and his hand trembled with frustration as he stirred unnecessarily at his coffee. They had no right to deprive him of that final excitement, he thought savagely, and it was one further item on the account which had to be settled.

When?

Well, it was too early to say. Perhaps tomorrow, perhaps in a month's time. He wouldn't make up his mind quite yet. He was still too disturbed, too immediately angry and hurt. These things were best dealt with when the mind was clear, and the emotions cool.

No, for the moment, he would do nothing.

Wednesday 12 noon

Detective Inspector Gardener of New Scotland Yard found himself admitted quickly to the presence of Mr. George Carson, of the Mutual Interests Committee. The young woman in the outer office had been quite gratifyingly interested when he announced himself, and already he was enjoying the transition to his new role.

'Ah Inspector, how d'ye do?'

Carson was a capable-looking man, decided the visitor, and not the kind to be wasting his time.

'How d'ye do, Mr. Carson. I believe the Assistant Commissioner will have explained to you my interest in this case?'

'Indeed he has,' confirmed Carson. 'Told me you were the one who started all this off, and we're damned lucky to get you. Now then, please come and sit down, and let's talk about how we can be of service to you.'

Gardener took a chair, and took papers from his case.

'Well, sir, these forecasts suggest that our Mr. Gloves could be on the rampage again tonight. The likelihood is that he'll be either in Swindon or in Blackburn. I can't be in two places at once, so I shall go to Swindon this afternoon. The A.C. will be alerting the Blackburn people, at the appropriate level of course, and I don't think we need to worry about that end. I'm sure they'll do everything they can. He's also clearing the path for me at Swindon, so that I don't have to cut through a lot of procedural tape before I can get busy.'

Carson's eyes twinkled.

'I imagine there is occasional resistance to the man from the Yard among local forces?'

'Perfectly natural, sir,' replied Gardener. 'I've been on the other end myself in the past. There's bound to be a certain resistance to having some Savile Row tailored actor-type turning up in a real police station, and telling everybody what to do. I like to think that when they see me, they'll realise that isn't my style at all.'

Carson stared at him shrewdly.

'Yes, I think they probably will. Now then, your move.'

The new inspector leaned back.

'The reason I'm here, and it's my own idea by the way, is to give you a rundown on how I propose to set this observation up. The companies you represent have a big stake in this, and I think it's only fair you should be told what's going on. Also,' he added, 'it gives you an opportunity to make suggestions before the event. You see, if our Mr. Gloves does try his hand tonight, and gets away with it, it would be a natural reaction from your people to say, 'Ah yes, but they didn't do this, or they didn't to that.' This way, by my coming to you first, you have a chance to make those proposals beforehand.'

The insurance man grinned slightly.

'In other words, inspector, you are locking a few stable-doors before we are even certain we have a horse.'

'I wouldn't put it quite like that, sir,' countered Gardener. 'It's just that we have a common problem. Your members are the victims, and it's our job to catch the man responsible. Easier said than done. There are fifty two police authorities in this country, and our friend Mr. Gloves is very careful about spreading his work around. There are already more than forty of those authorities involved, and it would be a major exercise to co-ordinate all their records alone, quite apart from the follow-up work, detailed questioning of officers concerned, witnesses etc. It might become necessary in the end, of course, but I'm hoping we'll avoid it. With this short-cut, this excellent piece of analysis produced by your statistical people, we may have the answer. You will have done a lot of our research for us, if it works, and we're more than grateful. The least we can do in return, is to tell you what we're up to, and listen to anything you have to say.'

Carson nodded. He was rather taken with this man Gardener. If anyone was going to catch this thief, then his visitor had as good a chance as any.

'Fair enough. What steps are you proposing to take in Swindon?'

'Well now, here's a large scale map of the town centre.'

Gardener opened the map and spread it out in front of Carson, covering almost half the desk.

'I've marked the central police stations with these red stickers,' he explained. 'Now, at each central point — '

He began to outline the details, with Carson interrupting from time to time for clarification. It took twenty minutes to explain, and at the end Carson was satisfied. It was a thoroughly workmanlike and sensible scheme, and if Mr. Gloves escaped the net, then he would be a very lucky man.

'My congratulations, inspector. All I can say is, I'm very thankful it's not me you're after. Look, it's almost one o'clock.

Have you time for a quick lunch, nothing fancy?'

The policeman shook his head. Getting to his feet, he began to fold up his papers.

'Very good of you, but I'd better be off. I'll get a sandwich on the train. The sooner I get to Swindon, and start putting things into operation, the better I'll be pleased.'

Normally a phlegmatic man, Carson found himself mildly excited at the thought of the evening's police activity. Insignificant though it might be, in the monetary language of the insurance world, the strange case of Mr. Gloves had captured his imagination. As he wished the departing inspector good luck, it was with a touch of envy. Gardener was setting out to put theory into practice, and his next few hours would be filled with positive action. He, Carson, could do nothing more in that quarter. Nothing but wait, and carry on as usual. He had been hoping to keep the afternoon free, so that he could devote himself to clearing up his desk, but this television reporter man had been very insistent.

There was now a blue ring around the three p.m. entry in his diary. What was that name again?

Hayward. That was it. Bruce Hayward. What could he want?

Wednesday 3.15 p.m.

Bruce Hayward sat back.

He had explained the whole case to George Carson, and was now waiting for the reaction. Cool customer, he reflected. There was nothing on Carson's face to indicate whether he was interested, disbelieving, or simply dismissive of the whole thing.

Interested, he certainly was. Not to say astounded. He was going to have to make several decisions in the course of the next few minutes, and in the meantime it was important not to let this man Hayward know that his news was other than brand-new.

'An extraordinary story, Mr. Hayward,' he conceded. 'Indeed, if it were not that I know your programme, Inside Page, and have seen some of the astonishing pieces of journalism you have pulled off, I should have stopped listening early on. You must agree, there is more than a touch of the Boys Own Adventure about this. And yet, you've actually inspected this book of clippings?'

'I have. And I have no doubt whatever that it is authentic.'

'H'm.' Carson pursed his lips. 'At the same time, if I understand you correctly, you are not prepared to divulge the name of this mysterious criminal. Why is that?'

Hayward had rehearsed his answer in advance, knowing the question to be inevitable. In the ordinary way, he was far from reticent about claiming credit for his activities, but this was out of the usual run. Not only did he know the suspected man, but he was sleeping with his wife, through whom he had obtained the evidence. The people who ran Inside Page were not too scrupulous about the obtaining of information, but they certainly would not thank him if that little item were to leak out. In addition to which, there was his own domestic position to be considered. If his affair with Sheila Holden became public knowledge, he would be making Joy a present of a ready-made divorce, with himself as the sole guilty party. Hayward had plans of his own for getting rid of his wife, but not under those circumstances, which would include a prohibitive financial settlement.

He was quite ready with his explanation.

'His identity, Mr. Carson, is what gamblers call my hole card. Before I leave here, I intend to tell you where he plans to make his next raid. Even if you believe me, there will not be sufficient time for you to convince the police, and to set up a proper surveillance. This man will get away with it, we can be reasonably certain, looking at his past performance. Tomorrow, you will require no further convincing, and it will be your turn to approach me. It's my only advantage, you see.'

Carson pressed his fingertips together and rested them on the bridge of his nose, inspecting his visitor over the top.

'The puzzling thing is,' he explained,

'why you should be here at all, instead of telling all this to the police. Catching criminals is their business, not mine.'

'Quite agree,' rejoined Hayward smoothly. 'But if I went to them, they would simply pick up this chap, and I would have no story. The members of your committee are the sufferers in all this. They are the only ones who are really being robbed, in the long run. The police haven't exactly shone in this affair, so far. I have no intention of handing over my case to them on a plate. Inside Page is going to have the full credit for this exposure, and that's why I've come to you. Tomorrow, when you have actual proof that what I tell you is true, we can discuss the handling of the details, safeguarding my programme's interests.'

'It doesn't sound very public-spirited,' objected Carson.

'That is precisely where we differ. The best interests of the public will be served by the revelation that such a man exists, and that the police have failed to catch him for four years. It will draw national attention to the lack of co-operation between the various police authorities in the country. This is the kind of thing the public are entitled to know, not to mention your own members. One or two of them will look a bit askance, I fancy, when all this breaks.'

He had a point there, and his listener was only too aware of it. George Carson was as public-spirited as the next man, but the public did not pay his salary. That was met by the joint contributions of all the companies served by Carson and his staff, and he could forecast only too readily the reaction from certain quarters. It enabled him to appear to be persuaded by Hayward, and that was the important point at this juncture. The reporter, at the end of this discussion, must be convinced that he had persuaded Carson over to his point of view, and that they were joined in a conspiracy of silence until the following day at least. If Mr. Gloves, as predicted, did attempt a raid in Swindon that evening, then the chances were very strong that the police would land him. This man Hayward would then have no story, no revelations to make. If the projected robbery failed to materialise, then Hayward's position would be considerably weakened, and Inspector Gardener might be able to bring pressure to bear on him. Withholding information, or something of the kind. There was also the third possibility, but Carson had no wish to dwell on that, at present. Mr. Gloves might escape the police, in which case the circumstances would change. Time enough for that when it happened.

'Well, Mr. Carson?'

He'd delayed too long in making his reply, he realised.

'I don't care for it,' he said reluctantly, 'but, in all the circumstances, there seems to be no harm in leaving this for one more day. My reasons are not the same as yours, but I'll tell you what they are. In the first place, it's almost three-thirty in the afternoon, and, as you say, I could never convince people at a high enough level in the time available. In the second place, I'm by no means convinced about your information, which is all in retrospect. If you prove to be right after this evening, then we shall have a whole new ball-game, as they say.'

Hayward nodded. He didn't necessarily believe what Carson gave as his reasoning, but he didn't care. The important point was that things should go his way.

'Then we are agreed. There will be a robbery tonight, in Swindon. I don't know which premises are involved, and I wouldn't tell you if I did, but it's certain that one of your members will carry the cover. All you have to do is to contact the local police in the morning, and get the details. You'll need a little time to follow it up with the company concerned, but I'm sure you'll put the pressure on. How would it be if I came back here at the same time tomorrow?'

Carson thought quickly. He didn't want Hayward in the office again, if he could help it. With any luck at all, Inspector Gardener would be taking Hayward off his hands.

'Might not give me enough time,' he demurred. 'It could be one of the smaller companies, and some of their area people have a lot of miles to cover. If you'll give me a telephone number where you can be reached in the afternoon, I'll call you as soon as I'm ready for you.'

There seemed to be no objection to that, reflected Hayward. He had no wish to be twiddling his thumbs while these people went through their boring procedures. He also did not want to take the call at the Inside Page office. There were far too many keen ears in that place, and Hayward had no intention of being pre-empted on the story. No, he decided, home was safer.

'All right,' he agreed, 'I'll be at home from mid-afternoon. The number's on my card. Here.'

Carson took the printed card, staring at it gravely.

'Swindon,' he murmured. 'And you are quite certain?'

'You don't have to take my word for it,' Hayward pointed out. 'Our criminal friend will give you the proof tonight.'

'That's true. Till tomorrow then.'

When Hayward left, it was with a feeling of surging confidence. There was ten minutes of prime time in this story, even perhaps twelve, if he was lucky.

He would have been less ebullient if he had been able to look through the closed door of Carson's office. The moment he was gone, Carson picked up the telephone.

Inspector Gardener must be informed immediately.

14

Thursday 11.30 a.m.

Adam Spencer Holden let himself into the house, pushing back the two days of accumulated mail which lay on the mat. He felt and looked dreadful, which was scarcely to be wondered at, considering he'd drunk too much on the previous evening, and even that had not enabled him to get a proper night's rest. It had been a thoroughly miserable night, in a tourist hotel full of mirrors and black plastic. Sleep had been denied to him, and he had spent a good deal of the time sitting on the bed, alternating between making endless cups of coffee and raiding the refrigerated liquor cabinet for the miniature bottles of spirits. The glossy blow-ups of Sheila and Hayward were spread out all over the room, and he would prowl around, staring in confused disbelief, and planning his revenge. Finally, at dawn, he had fallen into a fitful doze, from which he had emerged to find himself too late for breakfast, and with a bill for sixty-two pounds.

It was at once an annoyance and a relief to find that he was the first one home. Annoyance, because he was anxious for his first glimpse of Sheila's face. There must be something to be read in her face, he felt, with images of her recent activities large in his mind. Relieved, on the other hand, because of his own poor physical condition, which put him at a disadvantage. In his own surroundings, he would be able to make the necessary effort to pull himself together, get some fresh clothes on, and get the booze out of his system. He was conscious of having wasted a lot of valuable time. Knowing what he knew, he had had twenty-four hours in which to organise his thinking, and instead he had lost that precious advantage by his own stupid actions. By now, he should have been in ice-cool control, dictating the course of events of which Sheila had no prior warning. Instead, he would now have to do everything in a hurry, knowing that she could arrive home at any moment.

Ignoring the scattered mail, he went straight to his study, out of habit, to open his briefcase and dispose of his papers. Placing the Plymouth and Swindon files on his desk he stared at them for long moments. His decision to cancel his visit had more far-reaching effects than the simple postponement of routine business matters. Effectively, that decision had also ended the career of Adam Spencer Holden, criminal. Throughout the years, he had never once departed from the ground rules. Any simple deviation from the norm, and an operation was automatically aborted. There had never been any last-minute adjustments to cope with unplanned developments. Either every condition in the plan was met, or there was no operation. He had intended that this week would mark his farewell performance, and it had not happened. Even one more week would be too late, because it was expected of him in his new role that he would have found ways by that time to delegate these regional trips. An important area of his life had been brought to an abrupt halt, and he winced at the realisation. He was going to have to seek other excitements, other outlets for that side of his nature which demanded action and an element of high risk.

Women?

Perhaps. There were probably plenty like his precious Sheila, if only he could be bothered to look. And, thinking of Sheila, he must bear in mind that she might appear at any minute. Without thinking, his hands checked that the desk drawers were locked before he rose. One was not, and he stared at it for a moment, uncomprehendingly. A swift try, and he pulled it open. The clippings were gone. Although he knew it was pointless, he carried out a thorough search, in order to satisfy himself that he had not misplaced them in a moment of aberration. There could be no question about it. The clippings had been taken, and that could only mean that Sheila had them. Why?

The scent of danger cleared his mind abruptly. A moment earlier, he had been thinking of his charming wife in the role only of adultress. Now, she was more, much more, as the missing clippings indicated, but he could not as yet assess her changed position. Had she taken them to the police, or what? No. He doubted that. She could scarcely, he thought bitterly, go to the authorities with something so important, and then proceed to explain that she would not be available for discussion during the next two days, owing to a prior commitment to fornication. It was untidy, and Sheila was not an untidy person. But this discovery certainly changed his own position. He was not now merely the wronged husband, waiting to exact retribution, although that still applied. He was also a very much wanted man, who could find himself at considerable risk if Sheila appreciated the import of those fading newspaper extracts. The initiative had been wrested from him, he realised, and he must wait to see what she intended. His brain now racing in top gear, he came to another realisation. Sheila had been careful to take the book in his absence. Was it not a reasonable assumption that she might wish to return it in the same way? To keep from him the fact that it had ever been removed? Certainly he must give her the opportunity, and that necessitated his immediate absence from the house. Sheila would be certain to ensure that she and the children were at home at the usual hour, and he must not make his appearance before then.

Holden was cool again now, detached. Tidying up all evidence of his return home, he left the house and made his way through the side roads back to the station.

Thursday 11.30 a.m.
Inspector Frank Gardener was a frustrated man.

The previous day had been full of promise and high hopes. It had been his first experience of organised police activity from the controller's point of view. Many a time in the past, he had participated in large-scale operations, but always at the sharp end. Seemingly pointless patrols, and long hours of unproductive surveillance, only to learn that all the action had taken place in another part of the city, if at all, had bred in him a degree of cynicism about such things. There was a vague question mark hovering around the originators of the plans. Did those people really know what they were doing? It was a perfectly natural reaction, and, in earlier generations, it had been defined by military tacticians as the 'footslogger mentality', but Gardener had no way of knowing that.

Swindon had been an eye-opener, and a valuable addition to his knowledge. He had learned at first-hand the problems faced by the planners. There were miles of streets to be covered, dozens of likely premises. Given unlimited reserves of manpower and transport, it would have been a comparatively easy exercise, but these resources were not available. The Mr. Gloves operation was an additional burden to the normal policing of the city, and had to be covered somehow by stretching and bending the existing resources. Inspector Gardener had been witness to the strategy of the men directing the operation, and learned many lessons in the process. The final arrangements had left him with nothing but admiration for the detached expertise of the planners. Although a lowly inspector, he was nevertheless the personal representative of the Assistant Commissioner of New Scotland Yard, and was treated more as a junior partner than a bystander.

'Done much of this sort of thing, Gardener?' queried one chief super, a bluff hearty figure of a man.

'Not from this vantage point, sir,' he admitted. 'I've been on the other end plenty of times, wondering what it was all about.'

'Know what you mean,' grunted his superior. 'Spent a few years out there myself. Bit different in here. I call it the loaves and fishes syndrome.'

'Sir?'

'There was a man once who managed to feed five thousand people with two loaves and five fishes. Always wondered how he did that. The first time I was faced with one of these jobs was when I finally found out.'

And, staring at the operations map,

with its red pins and inter-twining blue and yellow ribbons, Gardener understood what he meant. Mr. Gloves was going to need a great deal of luck to escape those intricate arrangements.

In the late afternoon, Gardener had learned from A.C. Donald Saunders of the advent of a television reporter, who had somehow stumbled across the story, and who had claimed to have inside knowledge that the next raid would take place at Swindon. Gardener had doubted the man's credentials. It was far more likely that he had somehow learned of the forecasting work which had been carried out by the insurers, and could see the outlines of a nice item for his company. 'Police incompetence exposed', or some such rubbish. Still, rubbish or no, the man would need some careful handling once Mr. Gloves was in the net. That was something outside Gardener's authority or competence, and he put it out of his mind. His first and only duty was the apprehension of Mr. Gloves.

But Mr. Gloves had failed to materialise. Now, waiting in George Carson's office at the Mutual Insurers Committee premises, Gardener re-lived those anxious hours in the operations room, as zero hour approached and, minute by minute, ticked remorselessly away. The atmosphere, thick with the smoke of innumerable cigarettes and pipes, as control lights flashed on the board, and on-the-spot radio reports crackled into the ears of grim-faced waiting men. Then, as the master clock moved inexorably past ten-thirty, ten-forty-five, and finally eleven o'clock, the gradual dissipation of tension at the realisation that the quarry had gone to ground, and the operation was in vain.

No-one had blamed Gardener, but he felt responsible all the same. He had seen the tremendous effort mounted by the local force, and to have it all fizzle to nothing in this frustrating way had borne in on him a great sense of personal shame. It was still burning inside him when he sat alone in the hotel dining room for a hurried early breakfast, in time to catch a fast train to London. His frustration mounted further on his arrival at New Scotland Yard, only to learn that the Assistant Commissioner had been summoned to an important meeting at the Home Office, which would probably keep him away most of the day. There was also a report from Blackburn, which had been the possible alternative strike-point for Mr. Gloves, confirming that they had had no case during the previous twenty-four hours which could possibly have met the modus operandi which had been notified to them by the A.C.

More disappointment.

The prospect of kicking his heels all day would not have been acceptable to Gardener at any time. In his present frame of mind, he had no intention of allowing it to happen. What he needed was action, and there had to be something he could do. A telephone call to Carson had brought a ready invitation to go across and see him, and here he was, waiting for Carson to finish with his present visitor.

'Ah there you are, inspector, do come in.'

George Carson stood at the open door

noting the grim expression on Gardener's face. Poor chap, he reflected, he's probably about ready to blow a gasket. It was clearly no time for sympathetic, clucking sounds.

'Have a seat,' he invited, when they were inside. 'Looks as though we gave you the wrong horse last night. Did the local people kick up very much?'

'Not to me,' returned Gardener. 'They were very good to me, considering all the trouble they went to. What they'll say privately to Mr. Saunders is anybody's guess.'

Carson grinned.

'Well, I shouldn't worry about it. He's taken plenty of stick in his time, and I don't suppose this'll be the last. The point is, where do we go from here? I should think your opinion of our expert forecasting is hovering round about zero minus.'

To his surprise, the policeman shook his head.

'Not necessarily, sir. I didn't get a lot of sleep last night, as you can probably imagine. I've been into every angle of this case a dozen times, and I don't see that any blame attaches to your people at all. I think the chances are very strong that Mr. Gloves was due there last night. The reason he didn't show up could be quite ordinary. A sudden bout of 'flu, an unforeseen family problem, anything like that. Or, it could have been something else, something much more in my line.'

'Oh?' Carson could detect a certain hesitancy in Gardener's manner, and prompted him to continue. 'Please go on.'

'Well, sir, this television chap of yours. I'm wondering about him. When I was first told about his visit here, I must admit I was a bit sceptical. I thought he'd probably caught a whisper from one of your computer firms, and I know his type. They don't need a lot to get them ferreting, and Mr. Gloves is on the public record, if someone knows how to use it.'

He paused, and Carson nodded encouragement.

'But you've changed your mind?'

'That's what I wanted to see you about, Mr. Carson. To get the details of your talk with him. Because, you see, if I was wrong in what I thought, then his suggestion of Swindon takes on a whole new dimension. Could you tell me about your talk with him, please.'

'Certainly. Let's see now — '

Carson closed his eyes and began to repeat his conversation with Bruce Hayward, so far as he could recall it. Gardener listened carefully, and with a growing conviction that he was at last beginning to get somewhere positive.

'Thank you very much,' he said gratefully, when Gardener had concluded his recital. 'From the sound of all that, there's very little doubt that my initial reaction was wrong, wouldn't you agree?'

'Well,' admitted Carson, 'I would have thought it a bit premature, but then, you didn't have all this detail, did you? Now that you've heard it, what do you think?'

'I think I want to talk to this gentleman, this Hayward. You see, you had only a forecast, and the forecast was Swindon. Hayward claims inside knowledge, and that produced Swindon as well. Therefore, unless Mr. Gloves has got the 'flu, and I don't exclude the possibility, there is a good chance that this Hayward somehow tipped his hand. Unintention-ally, no doubt, but it has cost the ratepayers a lot of money, and wasted a lot of police time.'

Carson pursed his lips doubtfully. He could understand that Gardener was looking for activity, but he had serious reservations about the wisdom of threat-ening television journalists. Men like Hayward could cause a lot of embarrass-ment all round.

'You could be right, of course,' he agreed. 'But I don't see there's a great deal one can do about it.'

'I don't agree, sir, with respect,' announced Gardener. 'Don't forget, I've had all night to think about this. I've come to the conclusion there's quite a lot we can do. But I mean 'we' quite literally. It would certainly involve your complete cooperation.'

He spoke with such earnestness and conviction that George Carson found himself intrigued.

'Anything within reason,' he concurred. 'What did you have in mind?'

'Well, sir — '

Thursday 3 p.m.

When Bruce Hayward had arrived home he was annoyed to find that Joy was well advanced in her day's drinking. She had greeted him with a glassy stare, and was still dressed in the same lumberjack shirt and jeans she had been wearing when he left her two days earlier. Surely she must have been to bed?

'How was Amsterdam?' she queried.

'The same as ever,' he replied coldly, pushing past her.

'No strikes or anything?'

It sounded like a trick question, and he thought swiftly over the scraps of news he had managed to absorb in odd moments.

'Nothing that affected me,' he evaded. 'Why?'

'Then where's my prezzy?' she demanded. 'Or did you drink it all on the plane?'

Damn. The duty-free liquor had slipped his mind, in all the excitement. He had never forgotten it before.

'I didn't bring any,' he replied shortly, seizing suddenly on the opportunity to turn his omission to advantage. 'I was standing in the duty-free shop this morning, and it occurred to me that I was only encouraging you by bringing the stuff home in quantities. Until you get yourself under some kind of control, you'll get no more free booze out of my overseas trips.'

Joy had been furious, and the news of this cutting off of a hitherto reliable supply source put from her thoughts the carefully rehearsed series of questions she had intended to put to him. Vague suspicions had been forming in her mind for some time, as to his activities away from home, and that business with the police had given her new grounds for anxiety. But, in the face of this sudden, and, to her, monstrous deprivation, everything else fled out of her consciousness.

'And just what the hell is that supposed to mean?'

The front door of the house was still open when the row began, and they moved gradually inside, where the smell of stale liquor, and the tell-tale display of empty bottles, spurred Hayward on to new heights. Finally, he grew tired of it.

Clearly, there was to be no inquisition about Amsterdam, no enquiries about the people over there whom Joy knew slightly, and he was too exhausted from his recent activities to prolong the discussion.

'We'll continue this later,' he announced coldly. 'I'm going up to have a bath. I suggest you have this place cleaned up a bit by the time I come down. It looks like a sergeants' mess on a Sunday morning.'

That had provoked a further guilty tirade from Joy, but most of it sailed over his head as he walked out, leaving her standing. He stayed in the bathroom for a long time. Owing to some peculiarity in the construction of the house, downstairs sounds carried very clearly up into the bathroom, and he listened for movements, but there were none that he could detect. She had probably fallen asleep in a chair or something, he decided, and wondered how he would deal with that development. Eventually, and with reluctance, he climbed out of the bath, and towelled himself dry. No use hiding up here indefinitely, he realised. He would have to face her again sooner or later, and he might as well press home his advantage while she was so clearly in the wrong. Besides there was the other matter, which could crop up at any minute. There was no clock in the bathroom, but it must be close to three o'clock, and the chap Carson, or one of his staff, could telephone at any time. It wouldn't be a good thing for them to hear Joy's slurred syllables on the line. Moving into the master bedroom, he peeked at the clock. Yes. Five minutes to three. He had better get dressed.

Detective Inspector Frank Gardener climbed out of his car, and walked up the curving driveway to the Hayward house. Must be some good money in the reporting business, he assessed, sizing up the exterior. The front door stood open, which offended his training. The square tin box over the porch announced that there was an expensive burglar alarm system in the house, but it wasn't going to be very effective if people left the door wide open.

He leaned on the bell, and waited. At first, there was no response, then a man's

352

voice shouted from somewhere upstairs. After this, there was movement inside, and a woman walked unsteadily down the hall, and towards him.

Not a bad-looking woman, he decided, if she gave herself half a chance, which was not the case at the moment. The fair hair was awry around bleary features, and her breath when she spoke told him the rest of the story.

'Yes?'

'Good afternoon madam,' he returned civilly. 'Is Mr. Hayward at home please?'

'Who're you?'

Gardener recognised the truculent tone, which he knew from experience could turn quickly to belligerence. He wanted his visit to be as quiet and unobtrusive as possible, and the last thing on his agenda was a doorstep altercation with a drunken woman. Producing his identity card, he held it for her to see.

'I am a police officer, madam. Will you please tell your husband that I'm here. This shouldn't take very long.'

The sight of the card, coupled with Gardener's grave formality, caused something to stir at the back of Joy's mind. The police had been on the telephone once already and Bruce had told her it was to do with Lionel McEwan's car.

'Ah yes,' she accepted. 'It's about Lionel's car. Come in, and I'll tell him you're here. You're lucky to catch him. He's only been back from Amsterdam about an hour.'

Gardener smiled politely, and went into the hall. Somebody must have had quite a party, by the smell of the place. And what was that about Amsterdam? Hayward had been in George Carson's office only the previous afternoon, so he must have made a lightning trip. As for Lionel's car, well, that was a total mystery. As far as he knew, Hayward had only one first name, and that was Bruce. The woman called up the stairs, and her husband came quickly down, ignoring her and staring at the visitor.

'A police officer?' he queried. 'Could I see your credentials?'

'Certainly, sir.'

Once again, Gardener held out his

card, and Hayward inspected it with narrowed eyes. Scotland Yard? Well, he decided, whatever this chap wanted, it wasn't for Joy's ears.

'You'd better come inside.' Hayward began to lead the way into the living room, then checked himself. He didn't want this policeman to see the chaos in there. 'Perhaps we'll be better in the dining room. Would you like some coffee, or tea?'

'No thank you, sir.'

Gardener seated himself at the heavy oak dining table.

'Shan't keep you a moment.'

Hayward left him there, and went away. The policeman could hear the furious undertones as Bruce Hayward spoke to his wife, but was unable to make out the words. After a few moments came the sounds of her making her way upstairs, and Hayward re-appeared in the dining room.

'Sorry about that,' he excused. 'My wife hasn't been sleeping well, so she's going to try and rest awhile. Now then, what can I do for you, Inspector?'

Gardener waited until Hayward was seated, facing him over the table. There was no politeness in his tone when he next spoke.

'Only one thing, Mr. Hayward. I want the name of the man behind all these robberies.'

Hayward had already concluded there would be some connection with his recent visit to George Carson, but he had not allowed for such a direct approach. This Inspector Gardener must think he was new to the game, or something. Well, he wasn't.

'Oh come now, inspector, I'm not a novice. I don't have to reveal my sources to you. If that's all you have to say — '

'Not quite,' replied the unmoved Gardener. 'This programme of yours, Inside Page, is only a registered trade-mark. The real owners are Apex United Holdings. Under the law, the action of any servant of the company is the responsibility of the owners.'

'So?'

'Again, under the law, the action of a servant, in pursuit of the interests of the company, may be deemed to be the responsibility of the direct superior of that servant. In your case, that is the producer of Inside Page, a Mr. Ronald Kaufman.'

'I am familiar with the law, thank you. I don't see that it takes us much further forward.'

The inspector had now unzipped the slim leather document holder he was carrying, and opened it flat on the table.

'At three-thirty yesterday afternoon,' he intoned, 'after having explained your position, you made certain proposals to Mr. George Carson of the Mutual Interests Committee, a City of London representative body, established to cover the common welfare of the leading insurance companies.'

Bruce Hayward was becoming slightly uneasy. This man from Scotland Yard was altogether too formal, too coldly confident.

'I had a chat with him, if that's what you mean.'

'My understanding is that it was considerably more than a chat. According to Mr. Carson, you described to him certain matters which until then had been known only to the police. You informed him that you were aware of the identity of the criminal behind these cases, and that you would reveal it to him today, following the perpetration of yet another crime in Swindon last night.'

'I'm not responsible for what Mr. Carson says,' snapped Hayward, by now alarmed.

'Nevertheless, that is what he is charging,' insisted Gardener.

'Charging?' echoed the reporter. 'Are you saying this man is laying charges against me? Well, to hell with him, and you too. It's only his word against mine.'

'That is not strictly the case,' Gardener contradicted, then changed the subject. 'Do you know what these are?'

He began to spread documents in front of him on the table.

'They look like charge sheets,' suggested Hayward. 'The man must have gone off his head. What am I supposed to have done?'

'Let me read you just the headings,'

replied the inspector. 'Number one, Incitement to Conspiracy. Number Two, Withholding of Information Vital to Police Enquiries. Number Two consists in fact of more than one hundred separate indictments. Number Three, Criminal Concealment. Number Four — '

'That's enough,' snapped Hayward. 'I don't have to listen to this nonsense in my own house. I suggest you take all that stuff away and burn it — '

'That is incitement of a police officer to destroy official documents,' interrupted Gardener, 'but I think we have enough for the present without that. Where was I? Ah yes, Number Four. Wilful Misleading of the Police in a Criminal Matter — '

' — there you go again,' Hayward cut in. 'I have never even spoken to a policeman about any of this.'

'That's not what the charge says,' he was told.

'Yes it is. You said 'wilful misleading of the police etc'. How can I do that without talking to them?'

'You have already admitted talking to

Mr. Carson. The gentleman is an officer of the Court, among other things. In that capacity it is his bounden duty to pass immediately to the appropriate authority any information he receives which is pertinent to a criminal matter. You are surely not even going to pretend that a person pursuing your calling is not well aware of such an officer's responsibility? It doesn't say much for your professional status, and no one would believe it for a moment.'

Carson an Officer of the Court. That was something Hayward had not known, and the confidence which had been gradually returning began to seep away again.

'Even if any of that is true, and I don't say it is, where does this 'misleading' business come into it? I simply told him about Swindon being the next town to suffer and — '

' — and as a result,' continued the remorseless man opposite, 'a special operation was mounted. Eighty seven police officers of all ranks were involved, and twelve vehicles. Total cost to the police authority — '

' — I don't believe you. There wasn't time enough.'

Gardener smiled thinly, and stared at him for several seconds.

'You underestimate us,' he said softly, 'but there is no need for you to take my word. I noticed a telephone in the hall. Why don't you call the local press over there? They are vastly intrigued by all the police activity, and will confirm what I tell you. Well?'

Hayward nibbled at his lower lip. Clearly, it would be a waste of time to make the call. This fellow Gardener was a tricky customer, but he would not attempt such a cheap bluff, which could be exposed so easily. With an attempt at bravado, he sneered,

'I'll take your word for it. Obviously you intend to go ahead with this charade, so there's no point in pursuing this conversation. Go ahead and charge me. Be damned to you.'

'Charge you, Mr. Hayward?' The inspector feigned astonishment. 'Whatever put such a thought into your head?'

Thoroughly confused now, Hayward

screwed up his brow in perplexity.

'Why, you did. Not five minutes ago.'

Gardener shook his head.

'I said no such thing. It surprises me that someone like yourself should be so careless on points of detail.'

'Yes, you did. You said — '

' — I said charges were laid. I did not say against whom. Perhaps if you looked at the headings.' Gardener now turned the documents so that they were facing the unhappy man on the other side of the table. 'As you see, there are two persons charged. Sir Francis Forbes-Meadowes, Chairman of Apex United Holdings, and Ronald Kaufman, producer of Inside Page. These are the people who carry the ultimate responsibility for your actions. Your own role is only that of a servant of the company. I think it unlikely, and indeed I shall recommend to the contrary, that you will be charged with anything at all. You will appear simply as a witness for the prosecution, and I felt it was important you should be aware of this.'

Forbes-Meadowes and Kaufman. Any remaining vestiges of resistance drained away from the shattered Hayward. There would never be any proceedings, of course. The whole thing would be tidied up by counsel for both sides, long before any such stage was even contemplated. That wasn't the point. No one at Inside Page knew anything about the Mr. Gloves case, and they could prove it without much difficulty. Which left only Hayward. He it was who had represented himself as speaking for the programme. That was quite usual procedure, in the early stage of an item, and would not cause raised eyebrows in the ordinary way. But it was never expected that any action by him would have the kind of result now being contemplated. They would disclaim him, all of them. He would lose his job, automatically, but that wouldn't be the end of it. He would be black-listed throughout the industry, and no information service would ever hire him again. Sir Francis Forbes-Meadowes would see to that.

'You bastard.'

He uttered the words softly, from behind clenched teeth, but Detective

Inspector Gardener was not to be drawn.

'As I said, I felt it was only just that you should be made aware of the position. Not very good, is it? I mean, from your personal point of view. So unnecessary, too. Still, you know your own business best. I'd be the last to dissuade you. That's what democracy's all about, isn't it? A man being able to do what he feels to be right. Well, I mustn't take up any more of your time.'

Gardener rose to his feet, and began to replace his papers.

'Wait.'

Hayward stared up at him, his face working in impotent fury.

'If I tell you what you want to know, what guarantee do I have that you'll drop all this?'

The inspector looked faintly surprised.

'Drop it? Guarantee? Very flattering of you, but you over-estimate my authority. I am a humble detective-inspector. Decisions of this kind are taken at a much higher level. All I could do would be to inform my superiors of any developments. After that, it's out of my hands.

Mind you, I like to flatter myself that due regard will be had to my comments.'

And, he added mentally, if you don't stop twisting that right ear around in that fashion, there's a very good chance it'll come off in your hand.

'Look, sit down. I'm trying to think,' urged Hayward.

Gardener hesitated, as if considering whether or not to remain, but it was no more than a ploy. He had every intention of staying. All the conversation up to that point had been directed towards precisely this objective, and he wasn't going to lose it now. Looking doubtful, he sat down stiffly.

'I gather from what you said,' began Hayward, 'that the business at Swindon was a bust. Don't like that. Could mean that I'm wrong.'

'It could indeed,' returned the inspector smoothly. 'In which case, it's rather important for your man to be eliminated from our enquiries. The name, please.'

'Could cause a lot of unnecessary trouble.'

'You should have considered that before. The name.'

Gardener's tone now carried a decided edge. Hayward nodded, swallowed, and blurted it out.

'Holden. Adam Holden.'

The listener was glad of those years of training which now enabled him to write down the vital information without a tremor of the hand.'

'Address.'

He ought to have realised that it would be someone not far away, he reflected, writing carefully. Carson had told him that the informant claimed to have inspected a book of newspaper clippings kept by Mr. Gloves. That implied some access to his most private papers, and where else would they be but at home. This wasn't a typical underworld situation, but one which suggested that the two men involved knew one another on some personal level. Golf club, or children at the same school, that kind of thing. That was the next piece of information he required.

'Now then, you told Mr. Carson you had seen some kind of scrapbook kept by this man Holden. How did that come about?'

'Doesn't really matter, does it?'

'I disagree. If I find that you broke into his house for the purpose, and he certainly lives close enough, then I might have some difficulty in persuading my superiors to treat you lightly.'

Blackmailing swine, thought Hayward bitterly.

'Oh, you needn't worry about that, inspector. It was all perfectly above board.'

'I'll be the judge of that,' decided Gardener.

'If you must know, his wife showed it to me.'

That intelligence produced raised eyebrows from the listening man.

'His wife? Are you suggesting that she's involved in this?'

'God, no. Quite the reverse. She only brought it to me because she couldn't understand it. She thought, because of my job, that I might be able to make some sense of it. Believe me, she hasn't the faintest idea of what's going on.'

'I see. You say she brought it to you. Do you mean she brought it here, to the house?'

Hayward's features became very tight.

'No. I'm not prepared to discuss that any further. It has no relevance whatever to the main story.'

And I'll be the judge of that too, reflected Gardener. But not at this moment.

'Did you keep it? The scrapbook?'

The reporter shook his head vehemently.

'No, certainly not. She was anxious to get it back into his room before he found out it was missing. Look inspector, you can forget about his wife. She really doesn't feature in this at all.'

No point in pushing, decided the policeman. He had quite enough to keep him busy for the present.

'Very well, if you've nothing more to tell me, I'll be off.'

For the second time, he got to his feet, and this time he meant it. Hayward, too, rose and stood facing him.

'What're you going to do?' he queried.

Gardener stared at him, unblinking.

'Will you be at the Inside Page offices tomorrow?'

'Yes, I should think so.'

'No sudden trips abroad? I know they must crop up in your business. Be a pity if you were missing, and I wanted to talk to you.'

Hayward didn't like the sound of that, but he was now anxious to co-operate.

'I'm not expecting anything like that at the moment. There's been nothing to take me out of the country for weeks past.'

And that took care of Amsterdam, much to Gardener's satisfaction.

'That's good. I'll know where to find you. I'll bid you good-day.'

'But the charges,' protested his nervous listener. 'How will I know what's going on?'

'You'll know,' was the assurance. 'I shall personally see to it that you have advance warning of any action we may take.'

With that he went out, leaving the thoroughly cowed Hayward to his own lively imagination.

Thursday 4 p.m.
Adam Holden timed his arrival home for four p.m. Sheila ought by then to have the

children back in the house, which would thus provide the normal background of domestic chaos for his homecoming. Sheila would be well launched into her role of housewife and mother, and would have had ample opportunity to shed her other self, the one reserved for Bruce Hayward, and now recorded for posterity on the glossy photographs in his brief-case. He wondered whether there might be any tell-tale little signs, but why should there, he reflected? There never had been before, and there must have been befores. Quite a lot of befores, for all he knew. There might even, he admitted grimly, have been lots of Bruce Haywards over the years. There was nothing of this on his face, as he let himself in.

'Ah there you are,' she called from the kitchen. 'Daddy's home, children.'

The children made their usual muted sounds, annoyed at the interruption to their television programme. He wondered where they had been in his absence, but there would be some carefully-prepared story about last-minute pressing invita-tions from school-friends.

Going into the kitchen, he gave Sheila a quick peck on the cheek as she busied herself at the cooker.

'Found a marvellous leg of lamb going cheap today,' she explained, 'so I'm doing that Provencale recipe that you're so fond of. How was the trip? Same old routine?'

'Dullish to boring,' he confirmed. 'Smells good. I'll just go and sort out my papers, and then we can have a glass of sherry to celebrate.'

'At this hour? What are we celebrating?'

'Oh, I don't know,' he admitted. 'We'll think of something. Down in a minute.'

Everything was exactly as it should be, he admitted as he made his way upstairs. Well, what had he expected? Sheila in silk pyjamas, with a rose in her teeth? Of course it was all normal. It had to be, if he wasn't to suspect. Upstairs, he closed the door carefully behind him, and went straight to the desk. The drawer was locked now, and he turned the key softly, sliding it open, to reveal the book of clippings, back in its place. It was fortunate that he had made the decision to leave the house earlier. The additional hours had given him time to cool down, to take a more balanced view of this new situation he had to meet. To have acted precipitately would have been understandable, and perfectly natural, but it could also have resulted in the initiative slipping from his grasp. As things now stood, he would be in total control. Nothing would be said until after the children were safely tucked up for the night, and even then it would be a calm and measured tread, so far as he was concerned. That was the great advantage of being the one in possession of all the facts. The other party had to dance to the tune provided, totally uncertain as to when the tempo might change. Despite his more rational thinking while away from her, he had still been conscious, on seeing her face to face, of his own strong impulse to have it out there and then. The presence of the children had provided a fortunate barrier, and stiffened his necessary resolve to remain cool. What he must do was to plan each move, leading every conversation into pre-ordained channels, while the unsuspecting Sheila wove the threads of his net ever tighter around herself, by unwitting revelations. Oh yes, he was looking forward to nine o'clock.

Then he recalled that he had promised Sheila a glass of sherry, and made his way downstairs. A quarrel had developed between the children as to which television channel should be watched next, and Sheila had been called in as mediator. Holden knew from experience that his own presence would only complicate matters, because the children had an uncanny knack of splitting their parents over issues of this kind, whereas one alone could normally resolve matters without too much difficulty.

He withdrew to the dining room, and was thus the obvious choice to answer the door when the mellow tones of the chimer announced a visitor.

Frank Gardener had not driven directly to the confrontation with Mr. Gloves. Instead, he had pulled in at the side of some public playing fields to mull over the situation after his talk with Bruce Hayward. A pick-up football match was in progress, all enthusiastic kick-and-rush, a far cry from the polished tactics of the professional sides he enjoyed watching. More satisfying though, so far as the participants were concerned. Within five minutes he saw three goals scored, and there were several arguments about rule infringements, none of which would have happened if there had been a referee. It was all rather analogous to his own position, in a way, except that, in his case, the disagreements were all taking place in his own mind.

There was little doubt about his correct course. He ought to get back to the Yard, and get to work on the background of Adam Spencer Holden, so that he could place a detailed dossier on the whole affair in front of the Assistant Commissioner the following morning. It would then be for the A.C. to decide as to what action should be taken. It could even be decided, he admitted to himself, that his part in the business was now over, and that a higher-ranking officer should take charge. Despite the pettiness of the individual crimes, Mr. Gloves had

374

assumed an importance out of proportion to his proper status. The top insurance companies were alive to the case, a television reporter had stumbled across it, and, on the policing side, no less a personage than an Assistant Commissioner was involved. All the ingredients were present for a first class disaster if things were mishandled at this stage. There would be precious little sympathy, in any quarter, for a humble and temporary detective inspector who made a mistake. By far his safest course was to have all the facts ready for his chief.

On the other hand, there was the unpredictable position of Mr. Gloves himself. Holden, as he must now think of him. He hadn't been predictable at Swindon, had he? Why not? Why should he abandon that particular project on the very day when his wife had taken his clippings to Bruce Hayward? Perhaps he had found out about it, and was even now on his way to Terminal Three at Heathrow, the departure point for the furthest reaches of the globe. What would Gardener's position be, in that event? He would be the man who knew about Mr. Gloves, but allowed him to escape, because he had lacked initiative. Until now, Gardener had rather relished his unusual position, that of reporting direct to the Assistant Commissioner, with no intervening chain of command. It had afforded him a rare freedom of action, and a refreshing change from the normal routine of completing endless reports, copies here and there. What he needed at that moment was someone to whom he could report, but it was not to be. The A.C. was not available, and that left only himself.

Another excited roar from the pack caused him to look out of the window. There was the ball, unarguably stuck at the back of the net, and yet another goal had been scored. That was what the game was all about, when you trimmed off all the surplus. Never mind the rules, never mind the referee, or any other consideration. The result of the game depended ultimately on the goals scored.

Reaching over, Gardener switched on the engine. He might achieve some kind of fame in the next hour, he reflected. It was possible he might become the shortest lived detective inspector in the history of the Yard. Was there an entry about that in the Guinness Book of Records?

Ten minutes later he drew to a halt outside his quarry's home. He probably wouldn't be there at this early hour, but he ought to be able to get some idea of what time he was expected. It was therefore with some surprise that he found the doorbell answered by a man.

'Yes?' queried Holden. It had to be Holden.

'Are you Mr. Adam Holden?'

Holden didn't like the look of his visitor. Well dressed, altogether presentable, but carrying with him an aura of some kind, which was somehow familiar. Officialdom?

'I'm Holden. What can I do for you?'

'I wonder if you can spare me a few moments,' replied Gardener, glad of the experience which had taught him to contain his natural excitement. 'I am a police officer — my identity card — and I think you may be able to assist with my enquiries.'

Sheila. She had taken the bloody scrapbook to the police after all. Busy little cow, what with that, and thrashing around with Hayward for the past two days. Why should she suddenly do all this to him, and still carry on as though nothing had happened? What did she hope —

'Are you all right, sir,' was the solicitous enquiry.

'Eh, oh yes, quite all right. Just listening to the children arguing. What was that you said? Yes, of course, glad to help if I can. What can I do for you?'

'Not here, sir, if you don't mind. Is there somewhere we could talk? I realise it's a bit difficult, with the family home, but it is rather important.'

Important is it? To whom, wondered Holden. The inspector's stilted formality was odd, and possibly a reflection of his position. After all, he was unaccompanied, for one thing. He hadn't produced any kind of warrant, and he had not asked Holden to accompany him to the station.

378

The one thing he must not do was to reveal his concern. He must play the role of a puzzled householder, willing to co-operate with the authorities, but unable to see how he could be of any service etc. If the visitor was unsure of his ground, all might not be lost. It all depended on his own calmness.

'Very well, come in,' he invited. 'The only peace and quiet in this house is up in my study.'

He led the way upstairs, closing the living room door as he passed, where Sheila was still acting in her dual capacity as judge and jury. There was no visitor's chair in the room he called his study, and he collected one from a bedroom, ushering Inspector Gardener ahead of him.

Gardener sat on the bedroom chair, which looked decidedly out of place in the bare masculine surroundings. Holden had evidently recovered from his momentary loss of composure, and now sat facing him across the wooden surface of the desk.

'This is all very mysterious, inspector,'

he began, pleasantly. 'We don't have too many visitors from Scotland Yard. How can I help you?'

Gardener looked embarrassed.

'Matter of fact, Mr. Holden, I'm not sure you can help me at all. That's why I'm here. I thought a little informal chat might help to clarify a few points.'

Holden cocked his head to one side enquiringly, but made no reply.

'The fact of the matter is, sir, we have had a case on our hands for many months now, and some new information has just been received. This case concerns a man, let's call him Mr. G., whom we have been chasing for a long time. I don't want to bore you with too much detail, but I ought just to sketch in the background. It goes back more than four years.'

He described the kind of operation carried out by Mr. Gloves, and, without enumerating every case, gave an indication of the wide areas of the country which had been covered in the course of his movements.

Holden listened carefully, permitting no emotion to show on his face. There was no doubt that this policeman knew just about everything there was to know about his activities. Whether he would be able to prove it was another question. Gardener finished speaking, and waited for a reaction.

'That's quite a history,' acknowledged Holden. 'And it's been going on for four years, you say. Bit of a master criminal, your Mr. G.'

Gardener shook his head slowly.

'He'd like to think so, no doubt. In fact, he's a shoddy little back street villain, frightening elderly shopkeepers and emptying the till. He's no better than some young tearaway on a motor cycle. He probably sees himself in some inflated capacity, but that's all he really is. We've built up a reasonably good image of him. He's a fairly crude person, probably normally engaged in some labouring capacity, and his job takes him all over the place. Luckily for us, the computer whizz kids have been able to produce a predictability forecast on his pattern, and we shall have him in the next few weeks.'

Holden found himself relaxing

inwardly. This chap was clutching at straws. Him and his 'labouring capacity' indeed. Nevertheless, he had turned up at Holden's house. Why?

'A fascinating story, inspector, and I'm sure you'll catch him soon, as you say. It doesn't tell me why you're here.'

Gardener shifted uncomfortably, like a man who was uncertain how to proceed.

'Well, Mr. Holden, the fact is, and I know it's nonsense, but it has been suggested to us that you might be the man we want.'

'Me?'

Holden blinked, and looked aghast. Gardener hastened to continue.

'That's why I've made this informal call. It puts us in a very difficult position, you see. We can't ignore what we've been told, but at the same time we don't want to be made to look fools. Rights of Entry Warrants, and all those procedures, are expensive and time-consuming. Before we are compelled to resort to those extremes, I thought a preliminary chat would probably clear things up. It could be a simple matter of malice on the part of our informant, although I don't see what he hopes to gain by it.'

'He?' Holden's mind was racing. It was possible he'd been mistaken, then. Perhaps Sheila had not taken the scrapbook to the police, after all. But she'd certainly taken it somewhere, and the only man he could think of was Bruce Hayward.

The inspector was watching Holden's face, and knew there had been no mistake. The seriousness of the charge would have produced a more positive reaction in a genuinely innocent man. Anger, outrage, bewilderment. Something. The poker features opposite belonged to a man retaining iron self-control, and there would have been no need of it if he were innocent.

He was clear of any lingering doubts. He was talking to Mr. Gloves.

'Yes sir, it is a man. I am not at liberty to divulge his name, naturally. Can you think of anyone who would wish you harm? Someone who would be liable to concoct such a story about you?'

Very slowly, Holden clenched his fists,

a movement not lost on the vigilant Gardener.

'Oh yes,' he breathed, and there was now the beginning of controlled fury in his tone. 'Malice, did you say? Oh yes, I can think of such a man, indeed I can. Since you said this is an informal talk, do I take it that whatever I tell you is in confidence?'

Gardener looked doubtful.

'I don't know about that,' he hedged. 'It would be my duty to record anything relevant.'

' — that's just the point,' cut in the other. 'It isn't relevant to your ridiculous Mr. G. But it's very relevant to a certain bastard who might want to cause trouble for me.'

'Oh, I see. Well, that might be different. If it's something of that kind, a family row, or neighbour problems, it might not need to go any further. Might be quite helpful, in fact. Clearing the air, if you know what I mean.'

He seemed to be playing into Holden's hands. At one stroke, he could discredit Hayward, for he was now convinced it must be Hayward, and at the same time satisfy this Scotland Yard man's suspicions.

'There is a man,' he said slowly, 'who is after my wife. Calls himself a television journalist, but in fact he's no more than a muck-raker. It would just about fit his style to dream up a yarn like this — '

' — to what point?' Gardener interrupted. 'What would he hope to gain?'

Holden shrugged.

'To cause me embarrassment, I suppose. Anything. The man's insanely jealous of me, and people like that don't always think very clearly. They'll say anything.'

The man from the Yard seemed to ponder on that before he spoke again.

'I have no knowledge about your private life, Mr. Holden, and I doubt whether it's relevant. Our man claims to have seen proof. According to him he has seen a scrapbook of newspaper items, an entire history of the jobs carried out by our Mr. G., all cut from the local newspapers concerned. That is an odd thing for him to invent, wouldn't you say?'

Adam Holden had now calmed down again. The scrapbook rested in the drawer close by his right hand, and talk was only talk.

'It sounds very elaborate,' he concurred. 'What did your people make of it? Did it look genuine?'

But Gardener was not to be drawn. Instead, he changed direction.

'Tell me about Swindon.'

'Swindon?' echoed Holden, startled at the switch, and playing for time to adjust. 'I don't understand you.'

'Weren't you supposed to be in Swindon yesterday?'

'I had thought about going, yes. Something cropped up, which was more important, and I cancelled the trip. I don't see what you're driving at, inspector.'

'Then I'll tell you,' and Gardener's tone was now menacing. 'Mr. G. was expected in Swindon last night. We were waiting for him, on the strength of our own predictions. This informant of ours confirmed that you planned to be there, quite independently of our own forecasting. That's what I'm driving at.'

This produced a somewhat nervous laugh of dismissal.

'You're going to be pretty busy if you start questioning everyone who went to Swindon yesterday. It's a large place.'

'It is. But I'm not interested in everyone. Just you.'

Holden spread his hands wide, in a gesture of resignation.

'And I wasn't there,' he pointed out. 'So that's the end of that.'

'I've heard enough.' Without preamble, the police inspector rose to his feet. 'When I came here, I had expected to clear this matter up. I was wrong. I find your attitude evasive and unco-operative, your answers unsatisfactory. It's too late now to get things moving today. Tomorrow, I shall recommend to my superiors that we obtain a warrant to search the premises.'

Tomorrow? The word rang sweetly in Holden's ears. He felt like a condemned man whose execution had been cancelled by the last-minute intervention of the

Home Secretary. He would have ample time to destroy all traces of his crimes.

'You may do whatever the hell you like.' He too, stood up, looking affronted. 'You'll find nothing here, and we'll see what my solicitor has to say about this whole affair.'

Gardener actually grinned at him.

'Don't expect to find anything,' he stated cheerfully. 'Make a rare old mess though won't it? The neighbours will be curious to know what the nice policemen are doing. To say nothing of your wife. Wonder what her reaction will be.'

Holden did not intend to join in any speculation about that. He would deal with Sheila. And Hayward. But the visitor's admission that he didn't expect to find anything was puzzling.

'You said you don't expect to find anything. I don't understand.'

'Not here, no,' confirmed Gardener, standing now at the door. 'You'll have plenty of time to destroy the evidence, I know that. But you can't get at your company records, particularly the accounts. The warrant will cover that side as well. Your expenses claims will confirm all the dates and places. All we have to do then is to consult the hotel registers. Not a complicated business, once we get started. Don't bother to see me out. You'll have plenty to think about.'

Holden stood quite still, his face ashen, as he listened to the departing man descend the stairs. Expense accounts, hotel registers. Yes, there was no doubt about it, the police could build up a history of his movements, and tie them in with their Mr. G. Why G? He wondered, then dismissed it as unimportant. Well, supposing they did, what did they have at the end of it all? A list of dates and places. Circumstantial evidence, nothing more. They couldn't produce one witness who could identify him, not one finger-print that placed him at the scene of a crime.

All this raced through his mind in seconds. The only real and substantial links between himself and Mr. G., were in this house. The scrapbook, the clothes. That clever inspector had over-reached himself, shown too much of his hand.

Without tangible evidence, he had nothing he could take into a courtroom. All that Holden had to do was to dispose of the incriminating connections, and he had been given ample time to do that. So much for the brilliant minds of Scotland Yard. It would take a better man than Gardener to recover from that mistake.

A strange sound assailed his ears, and he crossed to the window, staring down at the striding figure of the inspector, as he walked towards his car.

The bloody man was whistling.

15

Friday 10 a.m.

Assistant Commissioner Donald Saunders rubbed a weary hand across his face. He had come away from his meeting at the Home Office with a whole series of new and urgent instructions, and it had been almost two in the morning before he got into bed. At seven-thirty he had been back at his desk, shouting for coffee and subordinates and more coffee. Now, for the first time in almost twenty-four hours, he was able to give some attention to the growing pile of routine matters which lay on his desk.

After all the high pressures of the past day, what he needed was a little light relief, he decided. Not many of the waiting files and papers were able to offer much in that direction. In the nature of things, trivial cases did not find their way onto his desk, and there would be a fine old row if they did. No, most of this stuff was quite weighty, and — ah. That chap Gardener wanted to see him, and was somewhere in the building. He'd also been looking for him the previous day, apparently. Yes, that might fit the bill. Bit of a change from Parliamentary Questions, and still more representations from foreign diplomats and so forth. A nice little bit of back-street thuggery would be an acceptable change of direction at that moment. Saunders pressed down a switch.

'Detective Inspector Gardener is somewhere around,' he said crisply. 'Whistle him up here, please, and coffee for two when he arrives.'

He broke the connection without waiting for an acknowledgment, picked up the nearest file, and began to study the report which was clipped to the top. Five minutes later there was a tap at the door, and, in response to the bellowed invitation, Frank Gardener came in and stood respectfully before him.

'Ah, there you are. Sit down, man. You wanted to see me. Not much luck with your mystery man, I gather, either at

Swindon or Blackburn. Can't win 'em all, eh? What do you suggest we do now?'

Gardener swallowed. The decision to proceed alone, in the absence of the Assistant Commissioner, was one thing. Having to account for it, in the formidable presence of the man himself, was quite another.

'I tried to report yesterday, sir, but you were engaged elsewhere.'

'Yes, yes,' snapped Saunders. 'So we've lost a day. Never mind, we must make it up now.'

'Well,' Gardener was evidently having difficulty in getting started, 'the fact is, sir, that I didn't think I ought to be twiddling my thumbs. I have taken certain steps, and made some progress. Indeed, subject to your decision now, the case could well be over.'

He paused then, awaiting his superior's reaction.

'I see,' Saunders stared at him long and hard. 'Over, you say? I think you had better take me through this. Ah, coffee.'

Gardener sat, unmoving, until the door closed behind the attractive blonde wpc.

'To start with sir, I went and had a chat with Mr. George Carson — '

He went on to recount his activities of the previous day. Assistant Commissioner Saunders was too practised a hand to reveal any emotion, but it was noticeable that the coffee grew cool in front of him as he paid careful attention to what was being said. The story took several minutes to relate, and when it was ended the A.C. finally leaned forward, stirring absently at his cup.

'It's rather a lot to take in at one go,' he decided. 'I'm going to need a few more answers. To start with, how on earth did you persuade Carson to join in this lunatic idea of preferring charges against Sir Francis Forbes-Meadowes and the chap — er — '

' — Kaufman, sir. Ronald Kaufman. There are no charges, sir. All I did was to ask Mr. Carson to agree to my using his name, in the course of my conversation with Hayward. Outside of that, he would deny it, and so would I.'

The only sign of his inward relief at this news was a slight twitching at the corner of the A.C.'s mouth. His first thought had been that the new recruit had gone power-mad in his absence. This might not be too bad, after all. Not bad at all, in fact.

'Tell me about Holden,' he invited. 'Did you really feel you had the right man?'

'Convinced of it, sir. There's a world of difference between the attitude of an innocent man, and that of a man who's determined to be found 'not guilty'. I knew I had him, and he knew it, too.'

'And yet,' Saunders pointed out, in deceptively silken tones, 'you gave him twenty-four hours in which to destroy the proof. All that nonsense about expense accounts and hotel registers doesn't give us one piece of tangible proof. It almost looks as if you wanted the chap to get away with it.'

Gardener cleared his throat. He was getting to the crunch now, and the next few minutes were vital to his career.

'Let me put it to you as I see it, sir, starting with the TV man, Hayward. His guns have been spiked. Yesterday, he could have caused a lot of embarrassment all round. Today, he has nothing. Less than that, in fact. Today he is a man waiting for Nemesis to call.'

'He could go to his bosses, if he got desperate enough,' objected the Assistant Commissioner. 'He could tell them there was a vicious attempt by the authorities to blackmail them all. A big whitewash operation, he could claim. Very emotive word, whitewash, and those fellas love it.'

The inspector nodded.

'He could sir, but he would only sink himself. No charges have been laid against anyone, and you have no knowledge of what they're talking about. If you find that some detective inspector has said something he shouldn't, they may rest assured that you will know how to deal with him. However, after thorough investigation, it will transpire that it's only hearsay. A private conversation between their man Hayward, and your inspector. One man's word against another's. Your man's position is unassailable. Their man's is not.'

'Why?'

'The case concerns one Adam Spencer Holden. Hayward claims the man is a common thief, an odd sort of a charge to be making against a man of Holden's background. Perhaps Hayward has some other motive for wanting to discredit Holden. Hayward's wife thought he'd been away in Amsterdam, but we know otherwise. We also know that Mrs. Holden is sufficiently close to Hayward to have shown him her husband's scrapbook in his absence. Holden himself claims that Hayward is after his wife. I think the chances are quite strong that Hayward has already caught her. He was very evasive about the lady, and particularly about where they were when she showed him the clippings.'

'Um,' Saunders sipped at the now-cold coffee. Blast. 'So what have we got? One man, Hayward, making unsubstantiated allegations about another man, Holden, whose wife he just happens to be screwing at the time. The foundations for these allegations is a book of newspaper clippings which no longer exists. We hope.'

'Devoutly, sir. Holden is nobody's fool. He's proved that in his Mr. Gloves career. That scrapbook is now ashes, I'd take a heavy wager. Hayward is not only a spent force, but he could be something else to us.'

'Such as?'

'Well, sir, always subject to your authority, I thought another little chat with the gentleman might help. Give him a few days to sweat. If I were to tell him that the charges were on ice, but could be laid at any time, he might be amenable to keeping us in the picture as to what's going on in his world. It would be helpful to know, in advance, if they were cooking up some yarn about police brutality or corruption or whatever.'

Donald Saunders was beginning to rather enjoy himself. He'd wanted some light relief, and his new chap was certainly providing it.

'Suppose, for a moment, that I agree with you about Hayward. That still leaves Holden, doesn't it? Your Mr. Gloves. How do we proceed against him, without the evidence?'

Frank Gardener sensed he was making good ground, so far. His next proposal might ruin everything.

'I rather felt it would be in the best interests of all concerned, if we just forgot about him. As you pointed out, we haven't anything nearly strong enough to take into a courtroom. Even those clippings wouldn't have helped us much. Holden could claim that he was an amateur criminologist, and had been following the career of Mr. Gloves. We haven't one tittle of evidence that places him at the scene of any particular incident, not one witness who could identify him. We have no case, sir.'

Much as he disliked having to listen to it, the A.C. recognised the truth of Gardener's argument.

'So he gets off scot free?' he enquired coldly.

'Far from it, sir. He's aware that we know all about him. I left him in no doubt about that. That means he'll never put another foot wrong, for one thing. For another, he'll always be living on his nerves, wondering when our people might turn up at his office, asking to see the firm's records. Lastly, he knows, or suspects, that his wife is playing around with Hayward. That won't do much to help his peace of mind. Given the choice between a few months in a nice quiet cell, and the kind of future Mr. Holden will be facing, I know which I'd go for.'

The Assistant Commissioner had the natural unfavourable reaction to this reasoning that could be expected from any police officer. But, with his additional years of experience as a top level administrator, he could also recognise the value of a 'best compromise' solution when it was offered.

'Don't know that I like to see the bugger get away with it,' he grumbled, 'but I know what you mean. That leaves only our friends the insurers then. They are the main injured parties in all this. Do you imagine they're going to thank us for producing a nil result?'

Gardener coughed lightly, raising a hand to his mouth.

'Matter of fact, sir, I did take the opportunity of having a few words with

Mr. Carson about the implications of trial proceedings. I pointed out to him that Mr. Gloves had been able to get away with what he was doing, as a result of the companies' failure to bring him to public attention. Perfectly understandable, to those in the know, and I made that clear. Unfortunately, once these things became public knowledge, the newspapers would have a field day. On top of which, the investors would start asking questions and, worst of all, we might all find ourselves saddled with a whole crop of copy-cat Mr. Gloves springing up in all directions. Could be very nasty all round. Sir.'

Saunders grinned openly then.

'So, at the end of it all, what have we got? One tame mole, inside the television industry. One unmasked Mr. Gloves, living in who knows what kind of private hell, and our friends the insurers, only too glad to pull over the veil, eh? Is that it?'

'Well, sir, I wondered whether you might feel that a 'Case Solved' note be sent out, covering the hundred odd cases outstanding.'

Yes, decided Saunders. Definitely, yes. He was thinking of some advice given to him years earlier by a very prominent officer of the time. 'You'll find a lot of able men here, Donald. Efficient men, brilliant, some of 'em. But every now and then you'll come across a man who's lucky, and that is the magic ingredient. Give me a lucky copper, every time.' It would seem that he had such a man in Detective Inspector Frank Gardener.

'Well, now, there'll be some tidying up to do, of course, but when that's done, this case is closed. Want to go back to Midshire?'

Gardener made a face.

'Not very much, sir. I'll be looking out for something a bit more active, after this.'

'H'm.'

Saunders lifted a thick grey file from the heap and slid it across the table.

'That's a new report by the Anti-Terrorist Committee. Several thousand words of recommendations in there. Take it away and study it. Let me have your thoughts on it. Not more than two foolscap sheets, Monday morning, first thing.'

'Sir.'

Frank Gardener gathered up the file and left the room. It looked as though his series of gambles had paid off.

The hunting of Mr. Gloves was at an end.

THE END

TURN DOWN AN EMPTY GLASS

Basil Copper

L.A. private detective Mike Faraday is plunged into a bizarre web of Haitian voodoo and murder when the beautiful singer Jenny Lundquist comes to him in fear for her life. Staked out at the lonely Obelisk Point, Mike sees the sinister Legba, the voodoo god of the crossroads, with his cane and straw sack. But Mike discovers that beneath the superstition and an apparently motiveless series of appalling crimes is an ingenious plot — with a multi-million dollar prize.

DEATH IN RETREAT

George Douglas

On a day of retreat for clergy at Overdale House, a resident guest, Martin Pender, is foully murdered. The primary task of the Regional Homicide Squad is to track down the bogus parson who joined the retreat. Subsequent events show that serious political motives lie behind the killing, but the basic lead to it all is missing. Then, three young tearaways corner the killer in the woods, and a chess problem, set out on a board, yields vital evidence.

THE CALIGARI COMPLEX

Basil Copper

Mike Faraday, the laconic L.A. private investigator, is called in when macabre happenings threaten the Martin-Hannaway Corporation. Fires, accidents and sudden death are involved; one of the partners, James Hannaway, inexplicably fell off a monster crane. Mike is soon entangled in a web of murder, treachery and deceit and through it all a sinister figure flits; something out of a nightmare. Who is hiding beneath the mask of Cesare, the somnambulist? Mike has a tough time finding out.

MIX ME A MURDER

Leo Grex

A drugged girl, a crook with a secret, a doctor with a dubious past, and murder during a shooting affray — described as a 'duel' by the Press — become part of a developing mystery in which a concealed denouement is unravelled only when the last danger threatens. Even then, the drama becomes a race against time and death when Detective Chief Superintendent Gary Bull insists on playing his key role of hostage to danger.

DEAD END IN MAYFAIR

Leonard Gribble

In another Yard case for Commander
Anthony Slade, there is blackmail at
London's latest night spot. Ruth
Graham, a journalist, and Stephen
Blaine, a blackmail victim, pit their
wits against unusual odds when
sudden violence erupts. Then Slade
has to direct the 'Met' in a gruelling
bout of police work, which involves a
drugs gang and a titled mastermind
who has developed blackmail into a
lucrative practice. The climax to the
case is both startling and brutal.

HIRE ME A HEARSE

Piers Marlowe

Whenever Wilma Haven decided to be wayward, she insisted that she was seen to be wayward. So perhaps she was merely being consistent when she hired a hearse before committing suicide, then proceeded to take her time over the act in a very public place. However, Wilma died not from her own act, but by the murderous intent of an unsuspected killer, and Superintendent Frank Drury of Scotland Yard becomes embroiled in his most challenging case ever.